Ci

Dead

Stories from the Zombie Apocalypse

William Young

DEDICATION

These stories are dedicated to you, the reader. If you've ever been through your own nightmare, your own apocalypse, then you'll understand these stories. Sometimes, events in your life just happen, and all you can do is deal with them. You think life is over and will never get better, and then one day, things are different and   life   is   better.

CONTENTS

ACKNOWLEDGMENTS

I wasn't going to write zombie stories. Not on purpose as zombie stories, anyway. But I wrote four zombie stories as part of a different project - a sequel to The Divine World - and my wife read the zombie stories and told me to write a book of zombie short stories because she liked the four I had written. The Muse had spoken.

DEATH TAKES A HOLIDAY

Los Angeles, California – Day 1

Dr. Lucinda Bright was escorted through the off-stage corridors of the airport, her mind buzzing at her sudden importance in the scheme of things. As the on-call medical liaison specializing in bloodborne pathogens for the Southern California District Anti-Terror Task Force - a title that was supposed to be little more than a resume enhancer - she'd been called away from in the middle of the night to provide her expert opinion on what to do with a handful of Eastern European tourists who'd been exposed to a passenger's blood on the way to Los Angeles.

She had never really expected to be called by the authorities as a result of volunteering for the task force several years earlier – and she didn't consider herself among the authorities simply because she had a laminated plastic badge hanging around her neck – but here she was, being escorted by Transportation Security Agency officers to examine a tourist on his way to Disneyland for the Christmas and New Year's holidays.

Tourist, not terrorist, she thought to herself, but protocols were protocols and she had volunteered all those years ago to do this job if need be.

The group turned a corner and then banged through a door into a hallway and passed conference rooms, exam areas and interrogation cells into which only the unluckiest of travelers were ever escorted. The fluorescent lighting, worn low pile carpeting and dull off-white walls lent a bureaucratic dreariness to the areas which only enhanced their sense of foreboding. It was a décor perhaps intentionally designed to maximize a person's sense of irresolvable frustration and unrealizable anger: you are helpless, submit.

"Dr. Bright?" said a man in a suit, detaching himself from a small cloud of uniformed government types from a variety of emergency services branches.

Bright nodded and smiled, "Cinda, please."

The man hesitated a second as he shook her hand, "Cinda, I'm Special Agent Charles Hoffman with the FBI," he said, dropping her hand and quickly flapping a wallet open with a badge inside before slipping it into his jacket. "Come with me, please."

"I understand we have some sort of issue with a passenger vomiting blood on a plane from Europe," Bright said as she followed a half-step behind Hoffman, his stride quick and purposeful.

"Oh, yeah, something like that," Hoffman said over his shoulder.

They passed through the group of paramedics, firefighters and airport police officers and stepped down the hall toward a wall with a long window. Bright felt the presence of the first responders behind her as they trailed silently along, waiting for an expert opinion on what to do next. Bright stopped and stared through the two-way window at a collection of men, women and children.

Bright looked through the window at the group and saw a bunch of faces staring back at her. They all seemed bored.

"Why are we holding these people?" Bright said, turning to look at Hoffman. "I was told we had a patient who had been vomiting blood on the plane."

Hoffman nodded. "Yeah, he was taken to County General a couple of hours ago when the first responders were trying to figure out what to do with him. Apparently the TSA agents told them he would have to be classified a potential terror risk because of the vomiting, but since he was unconscious they let the medics take him out. These guys, though, are another matter. Our subject vomited a spray of blood over them."

Bright looked at Hoffman. "You allowed them to shower and change?"

Hoffman nodded.

"Do we know if he bled on anybody not in there?"

Hoffman shook his head. "Just them. Family members and friends. And an unrelated couple from Italy. The flight crew reacted pretty quickly and moved him to a galley area after he started coughing up blood, but he obviously got a lot of people covered beforehand. According to them, this guy apparently stood up to go to the bathroom and just barfed over two rows of passengers."

"Was he sick when he got on the plane or was it something he ate?"

"According to is wife, he was coming down with something when they boarded the plane in Sofia, but she said it didn't seem like anything to worry about. She said she thought it might be the airline food he ate," Hoffman said. "And he didn't barf on these folks until they were only about half-an-hour out from LA."

Bright frowned and checked her watch. It was 2 a.m., and these people had been in the room for nearly six hours. She sighed.

"Well, we're going to need to keep everyone in the conference room in quarantine until we figure out what this guy is sick from," Bright said. "If he hadn't vomited blood on them, we could let them go, but they could be infected so they'll just have to wait until we know."

By the time Bright made it to County General later in the morning, Hristo Gruev, 37, was dead. His body had burned through with fever and now sat in the air-conditioned morgue in the basement. The blood samples taken from him were currently going through lab analysis, leaving nothing for Bright to actually do other than wait for the results. She sipped on a cup of stale cafeteria coffee while sitting in the pathologist's office waiting area – an end table and two plastic chairs – when her phone trilled its text message tone. It was her supervisor:

"Patient died? Others still in quarantine? Tell staff autopsy is highest priority from highest authority. Probably nothing. Keep me informed of any changes"

The door opened and a fiftyish man with thinning hair and a white Van Dyke beard entered, the embroidery on his lab coat read "Yul Ze'ev, MD." He was carrying a paper cup of Starbucks coffee, the aroma of which quickly permeated the room and dwarfed the tiny coffee-like scent her cup had been offering. Bright suddenly lusted for his coffee. She stood up and unconsciously motioned toward him with her deficient cup of java.

"Dr. Ze'ev?" she asked.

"Yes, and you're Lucinda Bright from the anti-terrorism task force, no doubt?" Ze'ev said, nodding his head amiably and smiling. "I guess we've got something interesting to figure out in short order, which is more than I can normally say."

"You don't get a lot of business here?"

"Oh, sure, but it's all cops wanting me to hurry something or reporters trying to find something out, never an actual mystery that needs to be solved."

"A mystery? You haven't seen the body?"

"Had my assistant email the file to my phone, read it over breakfast. First guess is Ebola, though it doesn't exactly fit all the symptoms," Ze'ev said, motioning for Bright to follow him as he pulled open the door to the examining room. "Plenty of other diseases to consider, to be sure, but not many that have someone bleed out so quickly. It's going to be a while, though, before any of the blood tests come out with anything. Holidays and what. But if there's anything obvious, we should know in a couple of hours."

"Ebola?"

"Probably not. We should know something in a day or two."

"I've got more than a dozen people in quarantine at the airport in a conference room. A day or two? Really?"

Ze'ev shrugged. "You can move them somewhere, right?"

Bright let out a bitter laugh. "Yeah, according to protocol, the county jail, but that's already over capacity, so, no."

Ze'ev sipped his coffee and then laughed. "Yeah, that's the government for you, it makes all sorts of plans on how to deal with things, but doesn't do anything to actually prepare for the things it might have to deal with. You have to wonder why FEMA and the rest are surprised and off-guard every time a hurricane hits. I mean, there it is on the weather channel, building up in the ocean, moving slowly toward land, turning and turning and getting closer every day, and then when it makes landfall, everyone in government acts totally surprised at the damage it causes. Idiots."

Bright had no idea what Ze'ev was talking about and she motioned to the wall of refrigerated storage compartments. "The body's in one of those?"

Ze'ev nodded, sipped his coffee. "Yup. Lemme see," he ran his finger down a roster on a computer print-out lying on a desk. "Seventeen."

He pulled the door open and slid out the table. Ze'ev checked the identification tag on the body and looked up at Bright, "Hristo Gruev?" Bright nodded and Ze'ev walked over to a phone on the wall, tapped in a few digits and spoke into it. He turned to Bright, "It'll be a little while until they move the body onto the examining table. Come, let's see if we can't find anything on the preliminary intake report."

They left the room and went into Ze'ev's office, a cluttered space with an obsolete desktop PC, a reasonably modern laptop, and manila folders strewn about the flat surfaces of the room. The walls had dozens of photographs in black and white of what Bright assumed were Ze'ev's trophies from autopsies: an X-ray shot of a steak knife in a skull, a photograph of a keychain in a stomach, an 8x10 of a male with a gag ball in his mouth and a cell phone in his rectum. Bright rolled her eyes.

"Let's see," Ze'ev said, tapping on a tablet PC he had pulled from under a stack of papers. "Admitted about thirteen hours ago, dead for nearly ten. One-oh six point three temp, severe dehydration, skin lesions and blood loss from the mouth, nose, ears, penis and rectum – well, that's all the holes. He was unconscious and pupils unresponsive. Breathing was slow, heavy perspiration. They gave him an IV solution and pushed him into a room to wait for you and your team to arrive."

"He showed the first symptoms about twenty-four hours ago. It's a fast-acting bug, whatever it is," Bright said.

"That it is; nothing I'm familiar with off the top off my head," Ze'ev said. "Seems to go at the body's fluids, from the looks of this, almost as if it's trying to squeeze everything liquid out, almost as if it's trying to turn the victim into an instant mummy."

There was a clatter from somewhere outside the room, muffled by distance and walls but still discernible as metal banging into metal. Ze'ev rolled his eyes. The banging continued for a few more seconds and then stopped. Ze'ev looked at his watch.

"I'll give them a few minutes to pick everything up before we head down and start the autopsy, this way we can all pretend nothing weird just happened," Ze'ev said.

Bright followed Ze'ev down the hall and into the autopsy room and stopped in her tracks. The drawer with Hristo Gruev's body in it was pulled open and an empty gurney lay on its side nearby, the body of a medical intern lying next to it, pooling blood onto the floor. Ze'ev rushed through the room to the fallen man, but all Bright could do was stare.

"Jason! Jason, are you okay? Can you hear me?" Ze'ev bent over the intern's body and checked for a pulse. "He's alive."

Bright regained her composure and walked the rest of the way into the room. "He's bleeding from the arm," she said as she came alongside Ze'ev and kneeled down.

Ze'ev scrunched up the intern's shirt sleeve and both looked in consternation at what appeared to be a bite wound on the intern's forearm, a deep, lacerating cut which had removed a chunk of flesh.

"Is that a bite wound?" Bright asked.

Ze'ev half-nodded. "Yeah, but not a normal one: this is a bite for eating, not to inflict pain."

"Get bandages, I'll apply pressure," Bright said, motioning for Ze'ev to move aside. "Is he hurt anywhere else?"

"Banged his head pretty good hitting the floor," Ze'ev said, standing up and hurrying to the other side of the room. He picked up the phone, "I need a first responder unit to the morgue stat, we've got an injured staff that needs immediate emergency treatment."

Ze'ev returned and placed a bandage on the wound.

"What would have bitten him?"

Ze'ev half-stood and banged his head into the open tray door.

"Jesus!" he said, his eyes rimming with tears as he shoved the tray back into the wall. He paused for a moment and focused on the intense point of pain on the crown of his head, willing it to fade away. He took a long, deep breath and opened his eyes.

Ze'ev turned to Bright and shrugged. "Who, you mean, and why?"

"What do you mean?"

"No 'what' bit him. That's a human mouth bite on his arm. Believe me, I've seen hundreds of them, maybe thousands. Usually they're just bruises with indentations, maybe once in a while you'll get a body in here with punctures from somebody's mouth, but that's rare. This wound, this bite, you never get that from a person. Dogs, yeah, sometimes. People, never," Ze'ev said. "Which means you have to ask, 'who bit him?'"

"And why?"

"Exactly," Ze'ev said, turning to the intern and patting through his clothing for any obvious signs of other trauma.

Bright looked around the room and immediately noticed a puddle of blood on the floor near the equipment table, and a small rotary saw lying on the floor. She walked over to it and saw a spray of blood across the counter and onto the wall. The various tools were in disarray, a smear of blood across them as if someone had been desperately snatching for them.

"He doesn't have any cut wounds on him, does he?" Bright asked.

"No, why?" Ze'ev said.

"There's a rotary saw and some autopsy tools here that have blood on them." Bright noticed a bloody palm smear on the table.

Ze'ev gave her a curious look. "Those tools should all be clean and ready for the autopsy."

He got up and walked across the room and looked down at the equipment. Ze'ev gave Bright a look of mild bewilderment and almost shrugged. "Let me see if I can't get a hold of Marcus. He should have been here helping Jason. Maybe he knows what's going on."

Ze'ev picked the phone off the hook on the wall, punched in a code, and spoke. Overhead, the speakers let out the muffled, softened sound of Ze'ev's voice calling for Marcus Glass to come to the morgue examining room. Behind them there was a slight groan and the gentle sound of a pair of double-doors swinging to a close. Ze'ev turned.

"What the fu—yee-oww!" Ze'ev said, his voice changing from deep confusion to clear pain.

Bright spun around and stared for a moment at the sight of Hristo Gruev biting deeply into Ze'ev's neck, Gruev's hands clasped tightly around Ze'ev's right arm and shoulder, blood coursing down Ze'ev shirt and gurgling up across Gruev's bared teeth and lips. Ze'ev smacked Gruev with his left palm several times, his hand making dull slaps on Gruev's forehead but doing nothing to phase Gruev. Bright took a pair of steps sideways and tried to make sense of what she was looking at: Gruev should be dead.

Yul Ze'ev let out a second yell now. It was an animalistic plea for help from the heavens, a sound uttered by uncountable numbers of prey as they realized the bite they were suffering would be fatal, the grasp of the claws un-releasable; that life was rapidly coming to a close should some divine intervention not materialize. Bright recognized the sound on some primal level, and she moved forward quickly and grabbed Gruev's right arm at the biceps and elbow, trying to bend it up and away from its grip on Ze'ev.

But Gruev did not budge. Beneath her fingertips she could feel the thick deadness of Gruev's arm, as if she were grabbing modeling clay. His body temperature should have been that of the morgue's storage tray's refrigeration, but instead he was burning hot, a warmth that should not have been inside of a dead body. She could hear him breathing as he resisted her attempt to move his arm, a slow, almost-silent in-and-out of air that would've been lost in the sound of the room's ventilation were she not so close to him. She flicked her eyes to Gruev's face and watched as he slowly moved his head from side to side, trying to bite off a piece of Ze'ev neck. Gruev's eyes were slits, his brows furrowed with intense concentration.

The air was filled with sudden noise and commotion, and a half-second later she was pulled away from Gruev and Ze'ev while a pair of paramedics wrenched Gruev off of Ze'ev, each medical technician taking one of Gruev's arms at the shoulder and breaking him off of the pathologist. Ze'ev collapsed, his arms around his neck, blood seeping through his fingers.

Bright turned and watched the paramedics as they struggled with Gruev, a lump of Ze'ev's neck in his mouth. Gruev wriggled to break free of the paramedics while he continued chewing, his naked body streaked with rivulets of blood. Although he was supposed to be dead, Gruev was winning the wrestling match with the two paramedics, slowly breaking their grips on him.

"Call security," the paramedic on the left said to her, his voice tinged with annoyance more than fear.

Bright rushed over the phone on the wall, picked up the handset and scanned it for a listing of punch codes, found it and entered the numbers.

"Security."

"Hello, I'm Dr. Lucinda Bright from-," she paused a moment, composed herself. "I need security to the morgue operating room as quickly as possible. We have a patient who's attacked two staff members and is currently engaging two emergency medical technicians. Please hurry as both staff have suffered serious wounds and are in need of emergency medical treatment."

Taking Gruev down had required the use of two Tasers, and even then Gruev had only been stunned long enough for the security guards to fix a pair of handcuffs on him before he had started to try to get up off the floor. Unable to rise, Gruev had spun slowly on the floor, his legs pushing him lazily, aimlessly, relentlessly.

Ze'ev and the intern had both been taken to the emergency department for treatment and each was unconscious. Marcus Glass was dead, his body had been found down the hallway from the morgue, his throat torn out and right thumb bitten off. Hristo Gruev, pronounced dead only eleven hours earlier, was now strapped to a bed in a room with a two-way mirror, a pair of armed sheriff's officers outside the door to the room, an Internet camera focused on him and monitors of every sort imaginable plugged into his should-be lifeless body.

But there he was on the other side of the glass wall, moaning incoherently and straining against the bed's leather straps, a fact that totally baffled Bright and Special Agent Hoffman. He turned away from the glass and shook his head slightly, perturbed.

"We're sure he was 100 percent dead?" Hoffman asked.

"Well, I wasn't the attending, but according to his chart, he died," Bright said. "There was no heart rate on the cardiac monitor. No active breaths. They did an apnea test and the CO_2 was greater than 120 without any breaths. The only thing confusing throughout all of this is that Gruev's body temp never got below 104 despite the environmental cold and lack of any other vitality in the vital signs. His brain was cooked. He was dead."

"All the way dead?" Hoffman asked "I mean, there's no chance he was kind of almost dead, and putting him in the refrigerated drawer in the morgue might have put him in hibernation or something?"

Bright wanted to roll her eyes in disbelief, but, clearly, something had gone wrong and Hristo Gruev hadn't died. She shrugged. "I don't know. I've never heard of something like this happening, but there's a first time for everything."

Hoffman stepped up to the glass and leaned close to it, staring through it at the man strapped to the bed, blood trickling out of the corners of his mouth, his fingers clawing at the sheets.

"What does he have? Rabies?" Hoffman asked. "Would that make him attack people like that?"

"I don't think so," Bright said. "Some of the symptoms are similar: fever, twitching, the strange breathing pattern. But I don't know that I've ever heard of blood loss like this."

"Couldn't that maybe be the foaming at the mouth you hear about?"

Bright shook her head. "No, but I'm going to test for it, anyway. Something's wrong with him."

"So, what do we do with the rest of the people who've come in contact with him?" Hoffman asked. "I've got a dozen people who've been waiting in an airport conference room since yesterday and I don't think I'm going to be able to hold them there much longer."

"We're going to hold them another twenty-four hours. If they don't exhibit any symptoms, they should be okay," Bright said. "We'll want to notify this guy's wife we've got him here and bring her in so we can get the required authorizations for treatment, but the rest can go to Disneyland if nobody gets sick."

"What about the people he came in contact with here?"

Bright poured a cup of coffee from the pot in the observation room, added some Coffee Mate to it and swirled it into a tan color. She sipped and thought.

"We've got the two injured men in separate rooms, under observation with guards outside their rooms to prevent accidental exposures to unauthorized people, so we should be okay on that account," Bright said, walking up to the wall alongside Hoffman. "The other man, Marcus Glass, died from his wounds. His body was transferred to a funeral home about an hour ago. I met his parents and explained what happened, as best I could, but they couldn't believe we thought Gruev was dead."

Bright took a sip of coffee and considered the situation, turned her head to Hoffman and sniffed out a tiny laugh, "I'm sure someone will get sued because of this."

DAYS GO BY

Bridgeport, Pennsylvania - Day 132

For rotting corpses, zombies don't exactly smell bad. Rotting corpses are supposed to smell bad. You watch a crime show about a coroner or CSI unit, and they smear that white stuff under their noses sometimes when they're going to investigate a body. Bodies are supposed to decay, melt into goo and turn into bones. Not zombies. Zombies are kinda like the Energizer bunny: they just keep going and going.

Until you put a big hole in one's head. Or chop its head off. Or burn it. Or spray it with enough acid. Or flatten it with a steamroller. Otherwise, they're sorta like that black knight in that Monty Python movie, you can keep hacking parts off, but they just keep on living, trying to get you. Run, walk, crawl, slither.

Why they want to eat you is a big mystery to me. They're supposed to be dead. Or, undead. I'm not exactly clear on that one. Before Kyle got eaten by a pack of zombies on Fourth Street two weeks ago he had been researching zombie history and come to the conclusion that zombies were re-animated corpses, brought back to life by black magic. He thought Holy Water in a Super Soaker might be a way to kill them, so he loaded up a tank at St. Augustine's and headed down Fourth Street to the Wawa convenience store, which is where a lot of the zombies kind of hang out when there's nobody to try to eat.

Almost just like before there were zombies, only back then the people would stand in front of the store with cups of coffee and smoke cigarettes. Now, they groan and shuffle back and forth.

Anyway, Kyle rode his bike into the parking lot, started squirting at the zombies, and before he could start pedaling away the borough secretary came up on him from behind and grabbed his hair. She must've been about sixty before she was turned into a zombie, but one thing about zombies is they're freaking strong, and all hundred pounds of the lady – Mrs. Scotoline – dragged Kyle to the ground and bit him on the shoulder. A couple of seconds later and Kyle stopped screaming as a dozen or so zombies had him and tore him apart. What's left of him is still lying in the parking lot.

Kyle never said how Holy Water would stop black magic, but I thought it was a dumb idea at the time. These are zombies, not vampires.

But you know what does smell after a while? People. Living people. I'd like to say you get used to it, but you head outside for a while in the fresh air and when you get back home, all you smell is sour stink. Almost makes you want to risk a dash down to the Schuylkill with a bar of soap, but the last person that did that was Marsha something-or-other, and now she's a one-armed zombie that mostly hangs out around Christine's hair salon down the other end of Fourth Street. You don't realize how much that daily shower really does for you even when you don't think you're dirty.

So, life kinda sucked before the zombies. My mom and dad made me do homework first thing every day after school: before dinner, before video games, before anything. Homework. And my dad kept signing me up for baseball and football. Baseball is boring and football practice sucks. I don't know why I just couldn't play video games or watch YouTube or whatever, but I couldn't. Some of my friends had parents like mine, but most of my friends had their own televisions and computers in their bedrooms. Not me. Life sucked. Kinda, like I said.

And then the zombies came. My friends had told me about them, sort of, at lunch. Weird stories they heard about from their parents about Los Angeles and New York and Europe. Or Russia. Russia's in Europe, I think. Close, probably. Anyway, all I knew about zombies I knew from the movies. So, not much, really. Fast zombies. Slow zombies. All of them want to eat you.

All that is true.

The only rule of zombies is there is no rule for zombies.

Or does that count as a rule?

Whatever. So, I've been mostly living in the second floor of Salvi's & Friends Pub with eight other people. Used to be eleven of us, but you know about Kyle and Marsha, so now there are just nine of us. Been in here for about five weeks, now, and all the food and beer is gone. The toilets don't work and there's no running water, no electricity, no anything like before. I mean, not that I'd been in here before the zombies, I hadn't, I'm only fifteen and not allowed in bars.

Kyle and I got in here the day the zombies came over from Norristown. They were mostly illegal Mexicans, the shorter, darker brown kind that you sometimes see hanging out in the parking lot of The Home Depot or Lowe's early in the morning, or like the guys who did most of the construction on the townhouses on Union

Avenue last summer. You'd walk by there and all you heard was table saws, hammers and Spanish. Only in America, right?

So, it was about one o'clock in the afternoon and Kyle and I were at the park on top of the hill behind the grade school when we started hearing the shots. Lots of shots. And then the siren from the Swedesburg fire company went off and Old Man Joe Morris told us to get the hell home because the town was done for. Then he and Don Fox took their rifles and headed toward the school on the other side of the park. Haven't seen Old Man Morris since, but Don Fox is a zombie that mostly hangs out around the Rib House, only he's missing both arms and looks like someone set his head on fire.

I didn't make it home. Of course, I wasn't supposed to be outside of home, either. Dad took Mom, Kelly, Molly and Craig up to Pop Pop's house out in the country with our dog, Rocket, thinking maybe it'd be safer up there away from so many people, since zombies seem to be drawn to people. I was supposed to stay and guard the house, only Dad took the HK .45 and the Mossberg shotgun and left me with Mom's little five-shot .380, which is good for shooting muggers and carjackers, but not so much for zombies. Not that it matters, since I forgot it on coffee table in the living room right next to the keys to the house.

All because of Kyle, of course, who came by that afternoon to tell me he heard Old Man Morris and Don Fox were going to snipe zombies from the top of the hill and did I want to come watch? He had two pairs of binoculars, so I said sure, and then – you guessed it – click!, the front door locked behind me. And since the windows on the first floor were all boarded up inside and out, well, there was no way back in if you weren't Spider-Man.

I'm not Spider-Man, I'm Ralph McGuire. That's "Rafe" like the actor, but I get "Rahlf" all the time.

So, I ended up in Salvi's. Just barely. Like I said, some zombies are fast, and there were some fast little illegal Mexican zombies that came across us as we were walking down Grove Street talking about how bad my Dad would kill me if I had to pry off some plywood from a window, break the glass, and kick my way into the house. I knew there was canned food, water, and all my clothes in there. Plus, that's where my Dad was coming back to after he dropped off my Mom and sisters and brother.

And then the zombies were just there, kinda running up the alley at us in some sort of stutter-step half-skip run, if you can imagine that. I think they must have played a lot of soccer when they were alive to have been able to run like that.

So, Kyle and I had to start running down the street looking for someplace to hide, and – of course – every house in town is locked and most of them are boarded up, more or less. So we ran a couple of blocks with those zombie Mexicans on our tails and Kyle sees a bunch of people prying open the door to the pub while a lady with a shotgun is blowing holes in a handful of zombies – the normal American kind – and we ran over to them. Almost got shot, too, but at the last second the lady – Valerie – realized we weren't fast zombies and didn't shoot us.

Plunked a couple of the Mexican zombies, though.

After we got inside, everyone started pushing things against the door. The first floor windows already had some metal screens on the outside, although most of them were high enough on the walls than nobody – well, no zombie, anyway – would be able to climb up and in through them. After that, nobody really knew what to do, and all the adults started kind of arguing about who should be in charge, almost like we were on that television show Survivor.

I guess maybe we kind of actually were. Only nobody gets voted off, they get eaten off.

Valerie was the only one with a gun, and even though she only had seven shells left everyone sort of let her be in charge. I mean sort of in charge, because Steve "I'm a trial attorney" Douchenozzle was always horning in with his opinion on what should be done and how. Not that there was really anything to be in charge of: there were just eleven of us in a bar, it's not like we needed to write a Constitution or something.

That first night was the only real excitement. About an hour after sunset, there was a huge commotion a couple of blocks over toward Swedesburg. A lot of gunfire and shouting moving down Prospect Street. A couple of us managed to get up on the roof, but you really couldn't see anything except a sliver of Fourth Street near the industrial park building. Looked like twenty or thirty people fighting off a horde of zombies while cutting through the chain link fence somebody put up the week before. It wasn't a real good fence, just one of those temporary kinds they put up around construction sites to keep kids and homeless people from getting hurt or stealing tools. And so Steve can't sue them for negligence.

That's when a security guard came running out of the self-storage locker building and began waving for the people to go away. There was no way to hear anything from the roof of Salvi's, but you could tell the guard was trying to get them to stop and go away, and he didn't care about the zombies making their way down the street toward the group of people on the outside of his fence. But they ignored him and managed to cut the chain locking the gate and the entire group rushed in, pushing him off to the side. Then a couple of mini-vans and some dirt bikes drove through the gate before everyone pushed them closed and shot some of the zombies on the outside of the fence. Since then, nothing. But you hear the dirt bikes riding up and down the railroad tracks every so often.

In fact, there are a lot of people still in town. You see them up on the rooftops during the day, acting like guards. And everyone has the same idea, too: scavenge. But that's almost as dangerous as the zombies, because if you try to get into a house that's got people in it, you can get yourself shot.

I was out with Carla working up the alley between Grove and Bush streets when we saw two older guys trying to pry open the back door to a house when someone from inside just shot a guy with the pry bar through the door. The guy stumbled around the backyard for a minute while his buddy shouted at the people in the house about murdering his friend instead of just telling them to go away because the house was occupied. But nobody inside said anything, and the shot guy collapsed in the back yard while the other guy cut through the space between some houses and disappeared onto Grove Street.

Carla and I had to start hustling because if there's one thing that will bring zombies, it's the sound of something loud like a gun. Del said he thinks any manmade sound will bring them, because if you watch the zombies on Fourth Street, they can tell the dirt bikes are running and will start walking down to the tracks. Sure enough, before we made it to Rambo Street on the way back to Salvi's there were a dozen zombies coming up around the corner from Ford Street, shuffling right at us. Slow pokes, so Carla and I were able to cut through some back yards and up a couple of streets until we came to Desimone's Café.

That's where Mom and Dad would go sometimes on something they called "Date Night." It had a restaurant in the back that served Italian food, and a bar in the front that still lets people smoke cigarettes, and my parents both smoke, so they like to go there. Valerie, Marsha, Del and Lester all smoked cigarettes, too, until about two days after we got into Salvi's and they all ran out. Now, the only cigarettes left in town are in the Wawa, and nobody's stupid enough to try and get into it.

Desimone's was burnt-out when we walked by, and there were maybe ten zombie bodies on the sidewalk outside, a couple of them pretty burned up. We peeked inside the building, but there was nobody in there, just charred furniture and broken glass. The place was fine just a couple of days earlier, when I went by it with Carla on my way to check and see if my Dad had come back, yet. He hadn't - the house was still locked - and we had to run like hell from some fast zombies that had been standing behind some trees in the lawn of Our Mother of Sorrows Church.

There ought to be a way to figure out the fast zombies from the slow ones, but so far nobody can do it. They all just stand there moaning or shuffle slowly around until they have a reason to go somewhere. These ones were pretty fast, though. If they hadn't been running across the street, we wouldn't have heard their shoes slapping on the ground and they might have gotten us. Instead, since it's so quiet anymore, you could hear them coming across the road, and Carla turned around on the porch while I was standing on a metal garbage can looking through the transom – the only window on the first floor Dad hadn't boarded over on both sides – to see if he was in there.

Carla just said, "Shit, runners."

I turned around and looked, and sure enough, there were five of them coming across the street pretty fast in a lurching skip-hop kind of run. Anyway, you can't really fight five fast zombies if there's just two of you, and all we had were a baseball bat and a cheap-o "industrial" chef's knife from the bar's kitchen. My Dad's kitchen knives are way better than the pieces of crap whoever cooked at Salvi's had to use, but that's probably because Dad calls himself a "gourmet cook." Mom says he just likes expensive kitchen gadgets.

So, we had to haul off down Coates Street pretty fast, and then started cutting through some of the back yards. One thing I never really knew about Bridgeport before the zombies came was how many back yards had fences around them. It's like all of them, practically. So, you have to do a lot of climbing, which is a good thing because the zombies aren't so good at it. Unless you're not very good, either, in which case you'll end up like the barber from Nick's. He tried to get in the industrial center building the day after the group broke in, but there was nobody at the gate, and when he started to climb the fence a bunch of zombies got to him and pulled him off and tore him to pieces.

We were cutting through one yard when all of the sudden the back door to the house opens and an old guy leans out and starts waving one of those old-style revolver pistols in the air.

"Over here, quick," he said.

Carla and I both stopped in our tracks, because nobody did this anymore. Not that anybody ever did, I guess. But, now? That's when he pointed the gun past us into the yard behind his at the dozen or so slowpokers shuffling straight at us. And then we were inside his house and he bolted the back door with a metal rod that slid behind the door.

He lived like my grandparents. All of his stuff was old tech, like he'd just chosen a year to quit updating his life. He had a tube TV with a VCR; a stereo system that played records, cassettes and CDs; a couch covered with handmade Afghan blankets; and an old style tan computer that sat on a small table in the corner of the dining room.

We had been inside for about two minutes when the zombies started pawing at the back door we'd come through, trying to find something to grab on to and pull off, which is why everybody boards up the windows: they'll just break right through if the glass ain't strong.

They can be relentless when they know there are living people inside somewhere. I saw one with a screwdriver one day but couldn't figure out what it would do with it. Maybe something inside its old life told it the tool could be useful? They bang and scratch and pull at stuff until something gives way, and then they just pry their way in. That's probably what happened to Desimone's.

The old man said his name was Paul and that he hadn't talked to anybody since the zombie's took over the town. His wife had been out getting some last-minute groceries and had never come back. Since then, he'd been stuck in his house, watching out the windows from the top floor at what little he could see on Hurst Street. Which was nothing, except maybe the occasional group of zombies shuffling down the street toward the sound of dirt bikes or gunfire, which are the only sounds anybody hears with regularity anymore. Every once-in-while he said he'd see someone coming or going from a house, although mostly he saw the random group of two or three people trying to break in across the street.

The most activity he'd seen was a couple of days after the zombies came across the bridge when the apartment building on the corner of Fraley Street burned down. Zombies and people everywhere for a while, and then just zombies and the bodies of the people they'd eaten. Other than that, he didn't know anything about what was going on. Nobody did, really: there was no TV or radio or Internet anymore. Nobody knew if cell phones still worked because nobody had one with a charge, and the walkie-talkies I had were locked in my house with everything else.

We told Paul he could come stay with us down at Salvi's and that we had been trying to find a way to get in touch with the people in the industrial center, but he didn't want to go anywhere in case his wife – Michelle – came back. I wanted to tell him nobody comes back anymore. I mean, if my Dad hadn't come back, then nobody comes back: my Dad wouldn't have left me here, not on purpose. Pop-Pop only lives an hour away up near the Amish country in Berks County. Dad should've only been gone for three or four hours to just drop everyone else off, but now he'd been gone for weeks.

And, anyway, Paul had tons of canned food and bottled water in his basement, enough to last a couple of months, I'd guess, if he didn't have to share. He gave us a couple of cans of Dinty Moore Beef Stew and some canned peaches to take back to the rest, and when the zombies in the back moved on to wherever it was they go when they get tired, Carla and I slipped back out and made our way back to the pub.

"Hey, food," Steve Douchenozzle said after we got back in and put the cans on a table.

Kyle used to say this was the Zombie Apocalypse. I don't know. Zombies, sure. Apocalypse? I don't know what that means, not really, anyway. End of the world kind of stuff, but the world's not exactly ending. Sun comes up every day, just like it always did. Out there are other people just like me, just like my group, hiding in some building waiting for someone to figure out just what happened and make it better. That's probably what my Dad is doing; probably why he didn't come back like he said: he's out there trying to fix this. He's good at fixing things and he was in the Army before he met Mom, so he knows a thing or two about fighting.

I just hope he's not mad at me for locking myself out of the house.

KILLING COUNTRY MUSIC

Nashville, Tennessee - Day 117

Chase Montgomery had come to Nashville with his discount-store acoustic guitar, broke-down pleather cowboy boots and Levi's jean jacket when he was nineteen years-old, intent on becoming the next country music star. In the fifteen years since then, he'd written thirty-nine songs, cut two self-released albums, played uncountable honky-tonk gigs, and killed four of the biggest country music stars. Three of them with head shots from over fifty yards.

For the first time in his life, Chase felt like he was doing what he had always been meant to do. That it was killing zombies didn't phase him. In fact, it never occurred to him that the one thing in the universe he was apparently cut out to do was to rid the world of the undead. Had you asked him several months earlier, he'd have told you he was still destined to be a country music great, but he might have also snorted out a laugh and added, "The greatest undiscovered country music writer, ever."

Chase had ended up like 99.9% of the star-seeking wannabes, working in the service economy at a job that was flexible enough to allow him a part-time music career. But the job washing and prepping new cars for delivery had turned into a sales job, and that had turned into a manager's position, and before he realized what had happened to his career has a country musician, he was a married man living in the suburbs with a wife and two little girls. He also had an American Vintage Reissue of a 1957 Fender Stratocaster with a maple fret board, a 1959 Les Paul designed Gibson, and the Washburn acoustic-electric he'd bought a few months after moving to Nashville, his first name brand guitar. He also had two banjos, a mandolin and a collection of amps and other equipment that he played in his sound-proofed garage on Saturday nights with friends with similarly de-railed country music careers: the Suburbs Garage Band.

That had all changed in January, after Los Angeles had been quarantined. Nobody in, nobody out. The California Army National Guard had been deployed in a perimeter around the city and the Air Force flew combat air patrols over it twenty-four/seven. Some sort of plague, said the papers.

But then it hit New York City, Philadelphia, Detroit, Oklahoma City, Dallas, and dozens of other cities in February. While there were still newspapers to read and cable news networks to watch, the word was that the world was quickly succumbing to a fast-moving strain of highly-contagious influenza. Moscow had been surrounded by the Russian Army. Paris was burning. China had closed its borders. The plague spread rapidly and cities across America imposed martial law, interstate travel stopped and by mid-March downtown Nashville was empty.

Chase's neighborhood in the suburbs had closed to outsiders before the electricity failed, but only just barely, with everyone linking together fences hastily bought at home supply stores and placed in desperation. Since then, they'd had packs of zombies come shuffling up the streets trying to get in, but they were dispatched fairly easily. Everyone had a gun, and everyone knew how to shoot. After a couple of weeks of pooling food resources, Chase's group of friends had decided to form foraging parties, and they had made every-other-day raids on some shopping center or such, somewhere, shooting up hordes of zombies and making off with whatever non-perishables they could before the sounds of gunfire attracted too many of the undead.

It was on one such raid that Chase had killed Treat Hemingway, a legendary Nashville session guitarist and songwriter. He'd penned nineteen number one singles and co-written fourteen others, and had played guitar in studio or on tour for just about every country music star of note.

"Wow, that's Treat Hemingway," Chase said as he stared through a pair of binoculars down Hillsboro Pike. "He's a freaking zombie."

Chase adjusted the focus on the binoculars. Treat was standing with a horde other zombies, all of them with blood spatter on their chest and arms, mucus drool foaming out of their mouths. The skin on some of them was peeling off, exposing cheek or finger bones. A few had the deformed mouths of what Chase termed "super-biters." The gang of undead shifted and shuffled in an asymmetrical pattern in the parking lot outside the Bluebird Café, a vision that was more unreal than undead seen through the glass lenses. Chase pulled them from his eyes.

"Who's Treat Hemingway?" Randy Mills asked, shifting his Remington rifle in his hands and raising it up to look through the scope.

"Dude in the purple-and-white plaid short-sleeve button-down shirt, with all the leather cords around his left wrist," Chase said. "He's mine."

Chase unslung his Winchester Model 70 and sighted down through the scope at the cluster of walking dead.

"But who is he?" Randy asked.

"Just one of the more successful songwriters in the history of country music. Guy's written like twenty number one songs for everyone from Garth Brooks to George Strait to Sara Evans. The guy's like the golden goose, fart's out hit singles while reading the paper during his morning dump."

"You know him?"

"Not really. Met him in the Bluebird six or seven years back for a songwriter's night; gave him a song," Chase said, placing the crosshairs on Treat's forehead. "Never heard from him."

"Which song?"

"Tears in My Whiskey."

"Damn, that song should've gone number one ten times over," Randy said, placing his crosshairs smack-dab in the middle of Treat's chest.

Right then the mezzo alto whine of ATV engines began forming in the distance, rising to a crescendo a few moments later as the four- and three-wheelers rolled down the side road and turned onto the main pike artery. They stopped and grumbled in the middle of the street, the sound of mechanical panthers purring in syncopated four-four time. Chase took his head away from the scope and glanced over at the group.

Gottlieb waved at him to join up while Percy pointed back toward the area of the Whole Foods market that had been the object of the raid, and to the large crowd of zombies moving toward the small motorcade.

"Let's go, gentlemen!" Gottlieb yelled, turning and also pointing to the approaching gaggle of undead.

Chase nodded once and looked back through the scope at Treat Hemingway, for a moment almost feeling sorry for the ... thing. Chase pulled the trigger and felt the stock snug sharply into his shoulder, watched Treat's head explode in a spray of gray matter and pink mist. A half-second later, Randy's Remington sounded off and the zombie just to the left of Treat's collapsing body jerked violently around as the side of its skull was blown off. Both men lowered their rifles and regarded each other.

"How is it you always get the famous ones?"

Chase shrugged. "You didn't know who he was."

"True. But I'll bet Gott and Percy do," Randy said. "You've got talent or luck or something."

"Let's blow this popsicle stand," Chase said, striding quickly toward the waiting ATVs.

That night, Chase couldn't get the thought of killing Treat Hemingway out of his mind. Chase had killed dozens of zombies, but Treat was the first one he'd killed that he had known as a person. Not known, personally, as a person, but known as a person he had actually met. Famous in Nashville in the behind-the-scenes way certain rich-and-powerful people in any industry are: Treat Hemingway could make-or-break your career if he cared to. It wasn't until after Chase had killed Treat that Chase realized how much Treat had lived a life Chase would have loved to live: wrote when he wanted, recorded when he wanted, toured when he wanted, and wasn't in any way, shape or form in the public eye, forced to give interviews or photo ops or make appearances to assure his success.

People would die for that kind of artistic freedom.

A couple of days later, Chase was riding shotgun on the back of a four-wheeler, his Winchester laying idle on his lap, his eyes roving the scenery for undead. The sound of engines brought the zombies out in the way a hit song could fill a dance floor, and neither Chase nor any of his friends could figure out why. Somehow, they knew the sound of machines and knew that meant living humans. Dogs barking, birds chirping, the wind rustling the branches of a tree, none of that attracted notice.

"There's a ton of 'em up here just milling around in the parking lot," Gottlieb said over the walkie, after the convoy had come to a halt and the vehicles had been hidden. "Must be two-hundred of 'em."

Chase looked around at the others in the group. "Shit, do we even have two-hundred rounds of ammo with us?"

Chase had ten rounds for his Winchester; a clip in his Sig Sauer P226. And, he had a Gurkha knife he hated to use because of the blood spatter: zombie blood stank with a smell not unlike that of skunk spray. After a second, the others in the party each gave an indication that the size of the zombie grouping was more than they could handle. Killing a zombie with a gun required a head-shot, and nobody could make a head-shot easily. The chances worsened dramatically if either the shooter or zombie were moving, and all bets were off if both were.

Chase pressed the walkie button, "Forget it, Gott, that's more than we can deal with today. We'll have to find something to raid on the way back."

"Okay, we're coming back," Gottlieb said.

But he and Randy Mills didn't come back. The group overstayed its agreed-upon wait time by ten minutes, certain that the two would make it back. After half-an-hour, most in the group were bordering on the fear that the zombies had somehow tracked them to where they waited. Chase looked around at the group, felt the nervous uncertainty of fear spreading through them. The world was quiet. Zombies were quiet.

"Well, I'm going to go see if I can find out what happened to them," Chase said.

Barney Stilton sagged with disbelief. He was the fifty-four-year old regional manager for a shoppers club store chain, and it had been his idea to try to infiltrate the regional distribution center that was the target of the day's operation. His idea meant he should go with Chase.

"I'm with you," Barney said, stepping off the ATV and walking over to Chase. "If they somehow got in the building, they might need my help getting out."

There was a long pause among the remaining men, each of them searching for a reason to step forward, for a reason not to. Nobody liked leaving the safety of the larger group and its envelope of firepower. Travis Cheadle nodded and stood up off the seat of his Arctic Cat TRV 700 and nodded at Cal Bosworth to move up to the driver's position. Travis tapped the magazine of his FN P-90 machine gun.

"We might need something with a little volume if we're going to get them out of there," Travis said.

Chase shrugged at the rest of the group. "Alright, move off down the road to the next intersection, if it's safe. We'll be on the walkie, but listen for the calls, too."

The three men moved away from the little caravan, picking their way cautiously through the trees and undergrowth of the woods between Old Hickory Road and the distribution center. For whatever reason, zombies tended to stay near areas with buildings, avoiding wilderness. Not that the stretch of woods Chase, Travis and Barney were stepping through was wilderness; it was merely undeveloped land in suburban Nashville, waiting for someone to turn it into a housing development, shopping center or nature preserve. Half-way through they heard the low growling of the ATV engines as the rest of their party rode off to the next rally point.

Barney gave Chase a quick glance, and Chase put his right pointer finger across his lips: stay quiet. They came to a stop on the edge of the woods and each man took a knee, weapon at the ready. Across an acre of asphalt behind a ten-foot high chain-link fence sat the regional distribution center. Milling around the loading dock were zombies, scores of them, some of them wearing the uniform of the chain store.

"Didn't you guys close down operations before the plague struck here?" Chase asked, scanning the landscape through his binoculars.

"Yeah, why?" Barney asked.

"There's ten or twenty people down there wearing your store's uniform," Chase said, pausing his scan on a woman who had likely been in her twenties before turning undead, her long brown hair caked with grime, her red shirt torn and stained, her face ashen, the skin taut. She might have been pretty, once.

"It was all volunteers at the end," Barney said, "people who didn't want to leave town or hide in their home were allowed to continue unloading trucks here. Corporate was pre-positioning items it thought would be useful once the plague lifted. But the plague moved quicker than anyone thought, so we never got to shut it down."

"Hey! Over there," Travis said, pointing over the barrel of his machine gun down the line of trees toward a corner of the parking lot where a gaggle of zombies were gathered. "Up that tree."

Chase looked through the binoculars and saw Gottlieb tangled in the branches of a tree, a couple of feet above the outstretched arms of the undead. Chase scanned for Randy but couldn't find him. Chase felt around his waist for his duck call, lifted it to his lips and let out a series of quacks while watching through the glasses. He could see Gottlieb perk up in the tree, his head turning, looking for the source of the duck call. The zombies noticed nothing. And then Chase dropped the duck call from his lips and opened his mouth in amazement.

"Holy crap," Chase said. "Tim McGraw is a zombie."

"What? Really?" Travis said, lifting his head and searching through the crowd of zombies at the foot of Gottlieb's tree. At a hundred yards off, it was too far away to make out anyone distinct.

"Oh, yeah, that's him for sure," Chase said, "He looks fresh, too. Must've only been turned recently."

"Probably was doing what we're doing right now," Barney said, "trying to get in the building for supplies."

Chase handed the binoculars to Barney and lifted his rifle to his shoulder, looking down through the scope and bringing the cross-hairs on to the head of the country music star. McGraw was dressed in blue jeans and a sweatshirt, a camouflage Army jacket overtop. He had an empty holster on his right hip and his left arm dangled limply at his side, soaked through with blood at the shoulder.

"Oh, yeah, that's him alright," Barney said.

"Well, I'm going to blow his head off," Chase said. "You two move through the tree line and get closer to them. I'll fire a few rounds from here then move when they start coming for me. Then you two take the rest down, get Gottlieb and run like hell for Old Hickory Boulevard. Give me blow on the duck call when you're in place."

While Barney and Travis moved through the woods, Chase kept his crosshairs sweeping through the crowd at the foot of the tree, counting seventeen walking dead. He also kept frequently checking everywhere else, making sure none of the zombies on the other side of the fence had made his position, and that there weren't any soloists straggling through the woods near him. There was no fast-and-true rule to zombies: they could be anywhere and everywhere, and usually were. He heard the sound of a duck call and sighted back through his rifle, first acquiring Gottlieb in the tree, who had now seemed to gather in what amounted to a ready-crouch for jumping down. Chase blew his response through his duck call and saw relief flood through Gottlieb's face as he finally allowed that the sounds were from rescuers and not fowl.

Chase put his rifle's sight on Tim McGraw's head and squeezed the trigger, the country singer's head opening up in a burst of brain matter and atomized blood. Chase chambered another round and took aim at the next zombie, putting a round right through its left eye and splintering the former man's skull. The rest of the zombies at the foot of the tree now all turned en masse and faced where Chase knelt in the underbrush. They began an exaggerated shuffle-stagger toward him, a gait that should've made people giggle at the drunkenness of the walkers, but instead instilled fear. Chase let loose with another round and frowned when he saw it hit the zombie's shoulder, only just causing it to stutter-step in response. He quickly realized he had to conserve his small amount of ammunition and began picking his way backward along the tree line.

He stumbled over something and fell to the ground hard, rolled onto his side and stared at the mutilated body of Randy Mills. Without even a conscious thought, Chase raised the rifle above him as a self-defense move at whatever might be near when a woman in her 50s, a zombie, loomed over him. Blood spittle dripped down her broken chin. Her fingernails were chipped and worn to the quick, her gray skin worn to tatters and peeling from her face, exposing gums and teeth. She reached down for him and coincidentally tangled the rifle between her arms, twisting this way and that as if her hands were in a stockade. Blood dripped onto Chase's shirt. The smell of her breath was foul.

Chase jerked the rifle to the side and rolled quickly away from the undead woman. She lost her lost balance and fell to the ground on her hands and knees above his rifle. With a fluid movement Chase was up in a hunched over squat, pulling his curved Gurkha knife from its sheath. He brought the blade up, changed his handhold on it and brought it down in an arc through the zombie's neck, slicing it off. There was an eruption of blood from the exposed artery and the body collapsed to the ground. Chase turned quickly in place, scanning the area for more zombies creeping through the underbrush. Nothing. He wiped the knife on the back of the woman's dress, sheathed it and picked his rifle up just as he heard the pounding footsteps of Barney, Travis and Gottlieb.

Travis stopped, turned, and let out a staccato of fire from his P-90, a couple of micro-seconds of noise mixed with interjections of silence as Travis pressed and released the trigger in even, short bursts.

"Nice move, Chase," Gottlieb said. "Almost thought you were a goner."

Chase looked past them at the two zombies left of the little pack that had treed Gottlieb, sighted them through his rifle and took each down in quick succession.

"Damn, Gott, I'm not gonna let some lame old lady walker take me out. I'd never live it down."

They all paused for a brief second to regard the body of Randy Mills, a friend who would become a zombie in the not-too-distant future. Barney holed Randy's head with a shot from his pistol and then looked over his shoulder at the distribution center.

"The ones by the loading dock are moving this way."

The raids and zombie killing became the measure of the days for Chase, pieced together in his mind's eye as clearly as he saw the notes on the fret board of a guitar. It made sense, somehow, though he could not quite explain how he had managed to figure out which undead were runners, which were walkers. He just knew when he saw them, knew in the same way he knew how to make any of the chords on his guitar without looking at his fingers or the strings. Indeed, it was something he could tell more readily than which people on the car lot were sellable and which were not.

Life had become something unintelligibly different in the months since the zombie plague had wiped out most of the human population, but it had not made it less worth living. At least, not to Chase, who had never really hated his job as an automobile salesman, but had always known it wasn't his destiny, even though he had long ago come to the conclusion that it would be his unintended, but lucrative, career path through life. Anyway, he saw more of his wife and daughters in this new life, and that made him happier on a deeper, more elemental level. That every time he saw them might be his last now occurred to him, which made it all that more meaningful to him: dying in a car crash on his commute was something that he never really factored into his life, although it was, statistically, the biggest risk he had taken with his life each day.

He poured himself three fingers of Elijah Craig bourbon and sat down on a stool in his garage. He wondered for a moment about Tim McGraw and the life that man had lived, reaching the epitome of success and fame, having it all in a world in which anything could be had, where there were no boundaries, no limits on what you could have. McGraw and Treat Hemingway could do whatever they wanted, could have anything they desired in the world in which Chase had wanted to live, but they had become just ordinary zombies in the world in which Chase now lived.

The old world was over, and nothing in it counted any longer. Chase sipped deeply on the bourbon and let the sweetness linger on his tongue before swallowing. For the first time in his life, he was finally gaining a reputation for something he was good at: killing country music.

WAITING FOR THE GREAT LEAP
FORWARD

Liepvre, France - Day 159

They were just three, now, down from eleven a week earlier. Remy hated life now more than ever before. As the only man in the group, Syrah and Yvette expected him to be able to protect them. And create fire. And find food. And figure out directions to wherever it was they were going. Scratch fire – that was what had gotten so many of them killed the week earlier: apparently, smoke and the smell of cooking food attracted zombies, and before anybody had had a chance to eat, dozens of the undead were trampling through the parking lot the group was in.

And then they had become dinner. Well, Nicolas, Martin, Valerie, Marie and Gerard had become dinner. Everyone else had run full-steam out of the lot and down the railroad tracks. The six left had holed up in an abandoned train station the next few nights, making no noise and attempting to sleep in shifts, but someone had fallen asleep on shift one night and they had all awoken to the shrill screams of Bernadette being bitten on the arm by a zombie, and Remy had had just a split-second to grab his shoulder bag before sprinting out the emergency doors with Syrah and Yvette, Luc and Pierre right on their heels.

But they had gotten stuck in a traffic jam on a clogged road outside Nancy, picking their way quietly through the parked cars. Some of the cars still had the real dead in them, collections of bones and moldering clothing, but some had the undead in them, laying motionless, waiting for something living to walk by. Pierre had been taken almost immediately by a faded-gray, skeletal goth queen in her early twenties, a girl any of the three men would've found attractive in her pre-undead state, her dark hair streaked with purple, her lower lip pierced, the hint of a tattoo on her shoulder. She must have known it, too, some leftover memory from her alive life, because Remy had watched as Pierre paused to regard the undead girl and consider her before-death beauty, preserved in pseudo-death and only slightly altered by her skin's discoloration and the amount of blood drool on her chest.

Remy had meant to shout a warning to Pierre to move, but Remy, too, had been transfixed at the left-over female attractiveness of the zombie girl. That moment had only lasted a few seconds, the zombie girl almost-but-not-quite smiling at Pierre before she lunged at him and bit a chunk of flesh from his neck. Pierre's startled yelp of pain had roused a score of other somnolent zombies from their hidey-holes among the automobiles, and it was all Remy, Syrah, Yvette and Luc could do to escape with their lives, the pleas for help from Pierre ignored and drowned out by the pounding of their footsteps.

Luc had been their group leader during the two weeks they'd been on the run after leaving the university dormitory in Rheims. At twenty-four, Luc was slightly older than Remy and was the only person Remy had ever met who had actually served in the military, spending two years in the Army as an infantryman. Plus, Luc had a machete, the closest thing to an actual weapon anybody had. So everyone had agreed, tacitly at least, that Luc should be the leader of their group. Remy would've voted against it had they actually voted on it - he distrusted the military and the kinds of warmongers who joined - but he had grudgingly admitted to himself since then that Luc was the only one among them who knew how to read a map, hotwire a car or cut the heads off the undead. And, in the end, it had been his prohibition on fires of any sort that had kept them alive the first week.

But that had all ended two days ago when Luc lost his balance while climbing up a utility pole to get a vantage point on the road ahead. He had fallen thirty feet from the top rung of the pole and cracked his skull on the asphalt, his body twitching as the life ran out of him. At least he got to die all the way, Remy thought as the girls begged him to do something to save Luc. But Remy knew nothing about first aid or medicine, and Luc didn't last long enough for Remy to have been convinced to try. Luc's eyes glazed over while he stared up into the blue sky and cumulus clouds, and Remy had turned to look up at them, curious what Luc's last visual input had been. Given the final visage Pierre had seen, Remy figured Luc had gotten off lucky.

They had covered Luc's body under a make-shift grave of branches and small rocks before moving on down the road to Liepvre, only knowing that's what lay ahead of them because of the signs along the road. The girls tried to get Remy to agree to stay off the road and walk through the woods, as Luc had done with the group when he had been in charge, but Remy had only shrugged his shoulders and noted that that technique had only gotten them so far, and he wasn't up for twisting his ankles on buried stumps and the tiny tunnels to animal warrens.

He also didn't know how Luc had managed to navigate cross-country and didn't want to get lost in the woods.

"What the fuck do zombies know about roads?" he had asked, finally, in sheer exasperation when Yvette had questioned him for the thousandth time about walking down the middle of the road. "They're fucking zombies, not enemy soldiers. They don't have a plan, they aren't doing patrols, they're just fucking mindless reanimated corpses roaming the landscape."

And then he had laughed, hysterically, collapsing to the ground and gathering his knees to his chest as he giggled thinking about the new reality. Reality: mindless reanimated corpses roaming the landscape. He had never been a zombie movie fan because it had never interested him: what could possibly be so scary about zombies? For him, the question had always been even simpler than that: what would cause a zombie, much less a zombie plague? Not, he knew, some American germ warfare experiment gone wrong. That would kill everyone, but the Americans would go first, if the world were lucky, for having fucked around with genetic shit in the first place. Fucking Americans. Remy hated them and their corn-fed beef, sport-utility vehicles, television sitcoms and Nicholas Cage movies.

Why, dear God, Remy wanted to know, did Nicholas Cage star in so many movies, so many of which clearly sucked because Nicholas Cage was in them? This was the problem with America writ large: no matter how bad or incompetent or arrogant something from America was, there was no shortage of assholes willing to buy it.

But, of course, now there was no shortage of zombies and no explanation for them and, titfucker of all, the Americans hadn't been heard from since they had shut down their borders and started shooting airliners bound for North America out of the sky. Some help those motherfuckers had turned out to be. And then his cell phone had died and he'd lost the Internet and nobody had a battery-powered radio and they had all just holed up in the university dorm room and wondered who was in charge and what would happen next. Remy had argued for staying in the dorm. Inside, they were safe from the zombies and the elements. The authorities would come for them as soon as they could; they wouldn't forget to check a university for students.

Which is when Yvette had heard that Luc and Pierre were planning on getting out of the dorm and looking for help. Yvette convinced Syrah to join her with them. And since Remy and Syrah had been having sex for the previous six weeks, well, it hadn't been too difficult to talk him into the need to find a better place somewhere outside the dorm even though he had pointed out there was more than enough food and water for another couple of months if they ate sparingly and just waited for help. The government, he argued, would be looking for them here in the dorm, not out on the streets. And besides, the zombies were outside on the streets, even if the neighborhood around the university had seemed deserted of them lately.

But everyone believed Luc's explanation that the government wasn't coming because it no longer existed, and those who had been in it were most likely doing whatever they could to save themselves.

Once they were all out on the road as a group, Syrah had stopped having sex with him because of the nature of group living and Remy had finally gotten pissed off enough that he wanted hot food instead of another can of cold ham and pea soup, at which point the zombies had found them and eaten half the group.

The threesome walked down the middle of Rue Maurice Burrus toward Liepvre, heading for Yvette's father's house in a suburb of Strasbourg: a destination of last resort now that Luc wasn't in charge. Remy had no idea what to do or where to go, so when Yvette said that her father would know, Remy figured the few days walk was worth the risk. He wished they had never left the dormitory, but he didn't want to have to go through Nancy again.

Remy stared absently at the landscape as they made their way down the road, the three of them silent, each of them paying some amount of attention to the possibility of zombies, but all of them lost in their heads wondering about the new meaning of life. If this was the future, what, then? Endless zombie wars? A return to what? – the pre-Industrial age? Remy shook his head at the thought of that: no media, no nightclubs, no cocktails, no online pornography, no office job doing whatever it was he had been going to college for five years to figure do for the rest of his life. Would the return of 1820 have any need of a computer savvy graphics designer?

Just then he felt his right forearm get squeezed. He turned and looked down into Syrah's dark brown eyes. She looked bemused.

"What are you thinking about?" she asked, a small smile.

"You," he said. "Us."

"What do you mean?"

"I was thinking that I need to make love to you again, soon, to reconnect to some sort of reality that I can understand and make sense of, and not have to constantly be aware of this new incomprehensible world we live in," Remy said, "but mostly because I miss the tenderness of your kisses, the touch of your fingers on my back, the sound of your soft voice in my ear."

Syrah's face had barely had the moment to change from curiosity to bewilderment for Remy's response when the sound of running suddenly filled the silence. They all turned their heads looking for the source of the footfalls when a crack rang out. And then, a half-second later, several blasts reverberated from the mountains around them, and Remy finally located the sound of the runners, a group of five "sprinter zombies" now all falling to the ground amid an aerosolization of blood straight out of an American war-porn movie.

Before the first of the zombie bodies had fallen to the ground, Syrah had started a shriek of fear and panic and dug her fingernails into Remy's arm. A micro-second later, Yvette joined Syrah in her death yell, but two seconds later, both young women had been stunned into silence at the motionlessness of the now truly-dead zombies on the pavement meters from them. Remy looked around and saw two men and a woman approaching them, each with a rifle of some sort more-or-less pointed at him and the two girls.

"Just the three of you?" a man with a rifle asked, his hair pulled back in a ponytail, several weeks of beard growth rimming his cheeks.

Remy was a bit stunned, still. Firstly, by the closeness of the now authentically dead undead, but also by the sight of three authentically alive humans with guns. He had never seen a gun before in real life, and stared at the weapon in the man's hands as if it were some forbidden implement from a mythical time period. And then he realized Yvette and Syrah were staring at him, wondering what he was going to do. Fuck! ... He was in charge.

"Uhh, yeah, just the three of us," Remy said, motioning with his hands and then shrugging, hoping the movements would convince the gun wielders of their non-offensive status.

The other man and the woman split, each of them moving off to either side of Remy and his two companions. The man scanned the intersecting road while the woman kept her eyes on the threesome. The bearded man approached them directly, his rifle held at waist-height in both hands.

"Walking down the middle of the road without any weapons of any kind?" the man said, pausing and scanning the woods lining the north side of the road before turning his attention to the fields on the other, in-between Rue Maurice Burrus and the N59 highway. He raised his left hand in the air and waved it back and forth. "Are you three trying to get eaten or do you want to find out what life as a zombie is like?"

Remy was filled with a sudden twinge of anger at the half-joke. There were no rules about the current zombie apocalypse, no government regulations about how to act or what to do. Hell, he had wanted to stay in the dormitory and wait for help, how was he supposed to know what the proper course of action was outside?

"We're trying to get to Strasbourg," Remy said after a moment, turning his head to the fields off the side of the road and noticing several other armed people moving off to the west.

The man tilted his head slightly and furrowed his eyes. "Strasbourg? What the hell for? There's only zombies there, and tens of thousands of them at that. You wouldn't make it within ten kilometers of the place though, seeing as you're not armed and on foot."

Remy glanced at Syrah and Yvette. Yvette sagged slightly at the news, enough to let on that she had only ever thought there was an outside chance of hope. The world really was dead. Undead.

"Well, you three can stay with us until you decide what you're going to do," the man said. "I'm Thierry. It'll be dark soon, come with us. You'll be safe."

An hour later they passed through a make-shift barricade of felled trees and sandbags. On the side of the road, in what used to be a football pitch, a series of what Remy took to be burial trenches were dug into the field, the first two already topped with dirt, filled to capacity. A makeshift gate was pulled open just as a half-dozen other armed people materialized from the sides of the road and from behind houses and joined them. Inside, Remy stared in awe at the amount of people near the barricade who were armed with rifles and pistols.

"Wow, you guys sure have a lot of guns," Remy said as he watched a pair of women push the woven-branches gate back into place. "Are they all legal?"

Thierry sniffed out a laugh. "Legal? Are zombies legal? Come on, follow me."

They walked into the center of town down Rue Clemenceau, passing by houses and closed-up shops, and turned onto Rue de la Gare, walking up it a short way until they heard the sound of children at play. And smelled meat cooking on a fire.

"You've got fresh meat?" Remy asked, his mouth watering as his nose filled with the savory smell of grilled game. "What is it?"

Thierry sniffed, shrugged. "What I wouldn't give for beef."

"You have children here?" Syrah said.

"Oh, yeah, lots of them," Thierry said, motioning them off the street and through a parking lot that led into a paved playground area behind a school.

"I haven't seen children in months," Syrah said as she turned around the corner of the boys school and saw almost two dozen kids at play on an asphalt court buffered from the roads by several buildings.

She started to cry at the sight of the them, their ages from three to eleven, as they kicked footballs, played escargot or drew on the pavement with chalk. Several parents, each of them armed with a weapon of some sort, stood close watch nearby, their attention focused not on the children and whether any would get bruised from a tumble to the earth, but outward, looking for sudden infiltration by the walking dead.

"I never thought I'd see children again," Syrah said as she paused to watch them a moment longer.

This was a concern that had never even occurred to Remy. Children? The only reaction he had to the word was a cautionary one, a reminder to constantly ensure that the women he slept with were on the pill or, if they weren't, that he wear a condom. But, mostly, to make sure the woman was on the pill. Aside from guarding against the accidental creation of a child, children were something that Remy never thought about or noticed. That Syrah was moved to tears by the sight of a group of children at play rankled Remy on some level, redefined her in some way, turned her from a sexual being into a breeder to be wary of. Anyway, who wanted to have children in the pre-zombie world, when the living was fun and children would only ruin things? Now that there were zombies, who in their right mind would want to bring a child into the world?

Suddenly Thierry stirred to life and tilted his head in the air, sniffing on the breeze. Remy stared at him, wondering if these small-town mountain hunting types had figured a way to smell zombies on the wind. Remy hated hunting, though he had never done it, nor even fished. He considered it déclassé, something nobody should have to do and fewer should want to do. Humans hadn't climbed from the muck of millennia and created skyscrapers and smart phones just so some small percentage of the population could indulge their natural urge to kill wild animals. Wild animals were a part of nature, they served a purpose, and that purpose did not involve hunting and killing them for pleasure.

"Boar!" Thierry said ecstatically, slapping Remy on the back. "Tonight, my new friends, we shall have boar!"

After a dinner of boar, roasted carrots and parsnips with dill, and a salad of wild flowers and lettuces in a balsamic dressing – a meal so good Remy realized he had forgotten what cooked fresh food tasted like – Thierry and the rest of the townsfolk took their empty plates and left the threesome alone with a bottle of Riesling. Remy had done everything he could not to roll his eyes when presented the bottle of German wine, but he was glad for it: it had been weeks since he'd even seen a bottle of alcohol, let alone wine. It was sweet and cool going down, and after a while of passing the bottle between them, Remy could feel the relief ease into his body as the wine diffused throughout it.

Remy leaned back against the trunk of a tree in a buffer scrim between parking areas, the asphalt unyielding beneath his legs but his mind drifting peacefully through the twilight sky. It was good to be alive, again, and he felt the rush of desire for Syrah as he watched her sip from the bottle. His eyes flitted briefly to Yvette and he wondered about her, too, and if the girls would mind if he took turns sleeping with them so long as the three of them were a unit.

And then he felt tired, energy seeping from him as the wine worked its magic on his body and soul. His mind relaxed and his body let down its guard. Every cell inside of him wanted nothing more than to turn off all the alarms and physical requirements of a life in constant fear and submit to sleep. The last time he had gotten any real sleep was when he had fallen asleep in the train station a week earlier, convinced they were safe because they were inside a building.

"I wonder where we can sleep," Remy said.

"Thierry said there's a hotel just up the road a hundred or so meters," Yvette said. "The Two Keys Inn."

"He also said there are sticks with white strips of fabric tied to them in front of empty houses and apartment buildings with unoccupied units. He said the owners are either dead or undead and won't mind if we move in," Syrah said.

Remy and the girls got up and began walking down Rue de Saint Antoine, looking for an open house. None were available. Inside many, the flicker of candlelight could be seen, reminding Remy that once not too long ago, that flicker would have been the blue of a television screen, numbing the occupants with mindless programming and blinding them to the realities of life.

Now, finally, people were forced to live life in a genuine manner and in some harmony with nature.

They turned left onto Rue du Chalmont when Remy realized that if they didn't find a place soon, they'd be walking around in complete darkness. This unnerved him, but not so much because of the possibility of a stray zombie coming across them but rather because of the large amount of people wandering around with firearms. He wondered who had trained any of them to use them?

"Hey, here's one with a flag in front of it," Yvette said.

They had been walking in silence since leaving the courtyard behind the boys school, and the sudden sound of Yvette's voice had startled Remy. He had been lost in thoughts about the new order of things to come, how the property of the world would be re-distributed among the living after the undead had been dealt with. Now that there were fewer people, there was more than enough for everyone. Finally, there was a way to make the world fair. They were suddenly doused in a powerful white light, the beam playing across each of their faces as each reflexively lifted an arm to block the ray.

"You're the living?" a voice asked, gruff and tinged with anger.

"Are we alive?" Remy asked, "is that what you're asking? Yes, yes, we are very much the living."

The beam dipped down to their kneecaps, but the damage to Remy's night vision had been done, and he could make nothing out in the crepuscular gray of twilight.

"Walking around in the dark without any weapons isn't exactly the smartest thing to do these days," the voice said, the tone pained obviousness, a bored elementary teacher lecturing a child.

"We're looking for a house with a white flag in front of it," Syrah said. "This one has such a tag."

The beam swerved across the ground and bobbed around the front yard of the house before settling on a small stake with a length of torn white sheet attached to it. The beam lingered a moment, played across the façade of the house, then meandered down and across the ground to a spot in the street between Remy's group and the speaker.

"Well, you should get inside," the man's voice said. "Lock up and take shifts through the night on guard. It's pretty safe around here, but we still get the occasional zombie that makes it through the perimeter."

The beam switched off and the sounds of several pairs of boots crunching on gravel receded into the darkness. Remy turned and looked at the girls, who were waiting for him to decide something.

"Works for me. Let's get inside," Remy said.

The pounding on the front door at dawn was so sudden and furious that Remy startled awake on the couch in the front room of the house, sliding off it and onto the floor as he sat up and twisted to orient himself on the origin of the banging. Yvette was sitting on a rocking chair on the opposite side of the room, reading a book she must have chosen from the bookshelf in the room, and laughed briefly at the sight of Remy on the floor. The noise had caused her to drop her book in shock, too, but Remy hated being laughed at and scowled for a half-moment before gathering his wits.

Remy pulled the door open and beheld Thierry, smiling broadly and armed with a shotgun held idly at his side. Three other men and a woman – all of them armed in some manner – stood in the background by the edge of the road, chatting amongst themselves.

"Good morning, my new friends, I trust you slept well and safely last night," Thierry said, "but the day is young and there is much to be done."

"Done?" Remy said.

"Oh, yes," Thierry said. "Meals to be made, children to be cared for, fences to be made stronger. Come over to the courtyard behind the boys school in twenty minutes for breakfast and assignment to a work detail. Lots to be done before sunset."

Thierry turned and walked off with his group down the road, not looking back. Remy stood in the door and watched them until they turned a corner, then slowly turned on his heels and regarded Yvette and Syrah, who were both standing in the middle of the room, watching him.

"Jesus. They want us to start working for a living already," Remy said, trying to figure out what alternatives there might be. Continue on the road to Strasbourg and risk the zombies? They had no weapons and had probably been incredibly lucky not to have been killed or infected since leaving the dormitory.

Yvette motioned to the kitchen behind her, through an arch from the living room. "Well, there's no food in there or the basement pantry. My guess is everything was collected from all the houses and stored somewhere else. There's nothing for mice to nibble."

After a breakfast of pancakes and home-made berry-syrup, Remy had been assigned to a group heading to the farms around Saint-Hippolyte, a small town about eleven kilometers to the southeast. It would take a little more than two hours to get there on foot, pulling wagons. Remy had protested, not wanting to walk through the wooded hills.

"Why can't we just drive there?" Remy had asked.

"You brought gasoline with you, did you?" Thierry asked and laughed. "We haven't had any gasoline for weeks, now. Maybe we can siphon some from an automobile while we're down there, should we get lucky that way."

Syrah and Yvette had both been assigned to the kitchen in the boys school, and Remy waved slightly to them as he trooped out of the town with Thierry and seven others – three men, four women. Everyone except Remy was armed, although two of the women carried large knives instead of firearms. The day was spent scavenging through fields and abandoned houses for anything that could be eaten. They saw nobody, neither alive nor dead, which Remy thought both odd and comforting.

At twilight, back in the house, Yvette opened a bottle from a local winery while Syrah lit a candle and set it on the coffee table in the living room. Remy had nothing to show for his day, having turned over his collection of turnips and onions to the boys school before dinner. He did, however, possess a small pike he found in a work shed on one of the farms, which gave him some sense of comfort that he could now, at least, try to defend himself should he need to.

"Another Riesling," Remy said. "Not bad."

"It's from somewhere outside Selestat," Yvette said. "They've got hundreds of bottles of wines stored in the basement of the school."

"And who-knows-how-much canned food and bulk flour and whatnot larded away in the classrooms," Syrah added. "After the town closed itself off when the quarantines began, everyone pooled everything together so it wouldn't be left to spoil in individual homes. Then they divided into teams to spread the workload around. We spent all day washing the morning dishes and then making the beans for dinner."

Remy gave the girls a look of compassion, indicating that he felt their pain, and took another small swallow of the wine.

"It beats sitting around in the dorm all day playing cards," Yvette said.

Remy thought about that for a moment, already knowing he'd be doing more scavenging the next morning as his group continued to work through the farmland for food, fuel and other useful items from before the zombies. Fucking zombies. Nobody had any idea where they had come from, how they were made, or why they existed. One day, life had been complex and filled with a million struggles, a constant sense of trying to find dignity and justice in the modern world of nameless, faceless men and the vast machinery of Western life and its total indifference to the individual. Now, most of those people were walking dead, and those that were alive were struggling to figure out what the new rules were.

On the walk back from Saint-Hippolyte, Remy had figured the new rules should be obvious to those that remained alive: kill the undead, redistribute the property equally, limit the amount of new children brought into the world, and ensure everyone understood their part in a harmonious and cooperative society. Only nobody wanted to talk about how to restructure society on the walk back home from the farms, although everyone had agreed that killing the undead should be a top priority.

Remy took another sip of the wine and stared at Yvette for a moment: she had said she was glad for the labor, the security of the town, the opportunity to live rather than survive. So was he, he realized. And, yet, he missed his cell phone, reading blogs on the Internet, picking up girls at the discos for one night stands, sitting at a table on a sidewalk and sipping coffee, listening to his iPod, and all of the other things that had been his life just a few months ago.

Modern life suddenly didn't seem as oppressive as the new version of life did. There had been so many things to do that deciding among them had been the defining aspect of difficulty, he realized, as he took another sip of wine – the only wine available – and regarded the girls in the candlelight. Now, there were only two girls to choose from – one, really, if that were still a going concern. Maybe there had been too much choice for the average person in the world before the zombies. Maybe that's what had made it so confounding to the average person: how could anyone know what to choose?

But now, with almost nothing to choose from, it was easy to figure out what made you content: a woman, a bottle of wine, the flicker of a candle. Dinner wasn't what you had to choose amongst, it was what was offered. Remy smiled to himself as if he had made some sudden great insight into the nature of life: choices were a trap, you only need a few options to make you happy, not infinite ones. He smiled. He had a blonde and a brunette in his room; he only had to choose.

ALL HELL BREAKS LOOSE

Los Angeles, California - Day 21

Brooke Tammerlin felt Joshua Sparks' fingers lace through hers as they stepped onto the sidewalk outside the bar and for a second she could feel her wedding ring get pressed into her finger. For a millisecond she remembered that she was married, that her husband had just texted her from work on the other side of town wishing her a good time out with her girlfriends, and then she forgot about the ring and her marriage and felt the warmth of Josh's palm, the light pressure of his fingertips on the back of her hand.

She had known Josh twenty years earlier in high school and had never thought about him since. Rather, she had known Josh was in her high school twenty years earlier and never thought about him then, either. But she had run into him one night in a bar on the last girls night out and began idle chit chat with him while her two friends reviewed the karaoke song menu. He was a nice guy, almost bland conversationally, but he had an easy laugh and knew when to flatter a girl. He was a normal guy with a blue collar job, a soon-to-be ex-wife, two little girls and a shiny pick-up truck that was immaculate on the inside.

He had mentioned right away that he was going through a divorce when she noticed the wedding ring on his hand. He had told Brooke that until the divorce was final, he was still officially married, and so he was going to wear the ring right up until the end. That sense of commitment had made Brooke feel something for Josh that she no longer felt with her own husband. Hours later, they had drunkenly made out in the parking lot alongside his pick-up truck, exchanged cell numbers, and begun the intoxicating initial stages of an affair that had led to this night: dinner, cocktails and then sex in his apartment. Which is what both of them were anticipating as they walked down the sidewalk away from the bar, she eager for a charge of romance in her life and he just looking to get laid.

Brooke had been listening to Josh talk about a soccer trip he was planning to take his two girls on in a few weeks time but she had been imagining the scene to come in his apartment. How would it transpire, she wondered? Part of her just wanted to strip naked immediately and fuck, replace the boring routine of marital sex with a new paradigm, and part of her wanted him to find some way to seduce her, to make the moment something she would never forget, the beginning of the next phase of her life.

Which is when a blood-spattered Latino man ran past them on the sidewalk, his eyes wide with terror.

"Jesus, what the hell happened to that guy?" Josh said, absent-mindedly releasing Brooke's hand as he turned to watch the man run away from them into the night. He turned to Brooke, "Did you see that guy? He had blood all over him."

She hadn't seen. She'd been inside her head, fantasizing about what was about to happen just a few minutes from then, if he would notice the brand-new pink underwear set she had bought specifically for the night.

"What?" Brooke said, turning and looking. "Was he shot or something?"

Josh shrugged. "I don't know. He's gone, now. He went that way. Blood all over him, though."

"I thought this was a safe neighborhood."

Josh smiled, a smile she had grown to love the two other times she'd been with him in person, on nights she'd told her husband she had to work late but had met Josh for beers and flirting. His smile was wide and genuine, his teeth white.

"Oh, it's safe," Josh said. "Probably some dude trying to break into a car and got beat up by the owner or something."

"You get a lot of that around here?" Brooke asked.

"Yeah. It's a nice neighborhood for cars, so this is where the thieves come to steal them," Josh said. "Caught an asshole trying to break into my truck last summer, but he ran off before I could get to him. I probably shouldn't have shouted at him when I saw him trying to slim-jim the door, but at the time I was more worried about him getting in the truck and driving off than I was about beating the shit out of him."

Brooke smiled at the notion: Josh didn't seem like the kind of man who could beat the anything out of someone, even if he looked lean and trim in his button-down plaid shirt and blue jeans, his receding hairline close-cropped and conveying the impression of speed. They got to an intersection and paused for traffic; she felt Josh lace his fingers back through hers. A thrill ran up her spine at his touch: this is what it felt like to fall in love, the heady dose of infatuation, the draw of pure lust, the overwhelming sense of excitement that good things were going to happen to you. He pulled her to him, wrapped his free hand around her waist and kissed her, the press of his lips firm and slightly wet. She felt light, as if she would float, and watched him longingly as he pulled his head away from hers and smiled. She hadn't felt this way in a long time.

They turned a corner and saw a group of people near a cemetery, some of them with their cell phones out, pointing them at something. On their side of the street another knot of people stood watching the people with the cell phones. Josh and Brooke closed in on the group and then paused alongside them to see what they were looking at. Inside the cemetery were a pair of young men with small handheld digital cameras pointed at a group of a dozen people in soiled clothing, shambling about as if they were extras in a zombie film.

"What're they doing?" Brooke asked.

"You get film students out here from time-to-time filming short movies for college," Josh said. "The cemetery is famous for some reason I always forget and the college kids like to use it for that reason."

Josh turned his attention to the group nearby. "What're you guys doing?"

A guy turned and looked at Josh, glanced at Brooke approvingly, and then motioned across the street. "Watching them film the dudes filming inside the cemetery. I think they must be doing some sort of movie or something. The guys in the cemetery keep running circles around the actors while these guys across the street are just taking video on their cells and talking about what they're seeing."

A girl with her hair in a ponytail nodded and turned to Josh. "Yeah, I think it's some sort of cinema verite thing. Cool shit if you do it right."

Brooke looked across the street at the group with cell phones and noticed one of them had moved inside the cemetery through a nearby gate and was recording from inside. She'd never seen a movie being made, and hadn't realized it might look like this.

"That's kind of cool to film a movie this way," Brooke said to Josh.

Josh shrugged. "I guess. You want to get closer? We can stand beside those guys if you want."

First dates had never been this cool before, Brooke thought, as she nodded at the idea and followed him across the street. Her husband had taken her to dinner at a TexMex place and a Whiskeytown show in a small club. She had thought her husband was cutting edge at the time. Now, he was just some guy she knew who complained they weren't having sex enough. Josh led her across the street and they watched as the zombie actors lurched and stumbled at the two cameramen inside the cemetery.

And then one of the cameramen stumbled and fell down, his camera bouncing on the grass. Brooke watched and felt the warmth of Josh's palm against hers, and for the first seconds of what she saw next, she was totally unperturbed. One of the zombie actresses closed on the fallen cameraman, bent over him and wrenched his head sideways so violently she heard the crack of his neck as it broke. And then the zombie actress knelt down and began squeezing the cameraman's skull between his hands. She was almost certain the actress had grunted out something that sounded like "brains."

"That's so cool," a young man with a Texas Longhorns ball cap said, changing his attention from the screen on his phone to the real life rendition a few dozen yards inside the cemetery. "I wonder how they're doing the special effects. That looks so-"

At which point the other camera operator inside the cemetery noticed his fallen friend being torn apart by the zombie actress and paused, startled, "What the fuck? Gary?"

Gary's body was completely limp in the zombie actress' grasp, and the zombie was continuing to squeeze Gary's skull, resulting in streams of blood from the nose and eyes. Brooke turned her head slowly to Josh and gave the barest squeeze to his hand. "That's pretty gross."

Josh nodded. "And kinda cool. I wonder how they're doing it."

Just then there was a crack almost like the sound of a baseball being struck by a bat, a loud snap that spat through the air. The other zombie actors reacted to the sound and turned their attention on the female zombie pulling Gary's skull apart, a light steam rising off the brain matter into the cool California night air.

"Gary!" the other man said, sprinting to his fallen friend as the other zombie actors shuffle-hobbled to the spot of the now available brains. "What the fuck? What the fuck? Gary!"

The other man skidded to a stop and dropped to his knees just as three of the other zombie actors got to the spot, bent over him, and began breaking his arms and neck, simultaneously biting into him. Blood spurt everywhere, but the man screamed only for an instant until his neck was broken and his head hung limply on his chest, blood soaking his shirt.

"Oh, my God, that is so cool," the Longhorns ball cap guy said to his buddies, who were nodding along and watching as the dozen zombie actors feasted on the two cameramen.

Brooke felt sick in the pit of her stomach. She had never seen anything so gruesome in her life, and the fact it was college filmmakers at work was only kind of comforting. She had always assumed that what she saw on the movie screen looked fake in real life: her husband was a wanna-be screenwriter who occasionally got work as a production assistant on films and would tell her how phony the props and costumes looked on set. But what she was watching inside the cemetery looked real from her vantage point on a sidewalk fifty feet away. She felt Josh give a little squeeze to her palm and glanced up at him, batting her eyes only slightly for effect.

"We should get moving. I'm sure they'll yell 'cut' at any moment," Josh said. "Then it's thirty or forty minutes of setting everything back up again for another take. Totally boring."

Josh turned away from the fence, took a half-step and stopped dead in his tracks. His fingers went slack in Brooke's hand and she somehow noticed the cool band of metal around her ring finger, a blip of reality that confused her senses and momentarily distracted her from what her eyes saw on the street.

"What the– " Josh said, his voice trailing quickly from astonishment to silence.

Shuffling down the street in a wide herd formation were more than twenty zombie actors. But that observation existed only for a moment, as the group across the street stood watching the oncoming batch of new zombies, several people of the group smiling in amazement at their luck at seeing such a weird show. Until one of the zombies grabbed the woman wearing her hair in a pony tail, yanked the it hard and bit the woman on her throat. An eruption of blood doused the zombie actress, dying girl and the young man standing next to her watching the horrifying spectacle.

At which point he grabbed the girl's arm and yanked her to him, accomplishing nothing.

"Hey, let her go!" he shouted.

But in those few seconds, the approaching zombie actors had engulfed the little group on the opposite side of the street, and within moments there were shrieks of terror, shouts of surprise and last gasps for life. Blood ran on the street at the feet of the zombie actors as they held the bodies of those in the group between them and took bites from their flesh.

Brooke froze in place at the sight. "I don't think this is a movie."

Josh watched the carnage across the street and stood stock still, his eyes flitting among the various zombie actors on the other side of the street. He looked into her eyes and smiled. "It has to be, Brooke. There must be hidden cameras somewhere. Or maybe these guys with the phones are in on it."

The Longhorns baseball cap guy next to them had been recording the scene with his phone and turned to them. "I don't know what this is, but it's super-realistic."

"I think this is real," Brooke said softly. "I think those people just got killed by those ... people."

As they watched, a man from the group of onlookers across the street stumbled out of the crowd of zombies, his left arm dangling by a tendon at the shoulder, blood coursing down the side of his body, his face deeply grooved with scratches. He took a few steps and looked around in a daze, saw Brooke and Josh and made an uncertain step toward them.

"Help me," he said, his voice weak and barely audible.

He took another step and collapsed to the asphalt.

"I think we need to get out of here," Brooke said, common sense suddenly flooding her body, romantic notions dissolving as the primordial fight-or-flight responses kicked in deep in her brain. "Josh, we need to get the hell out of here."

Josh turned to her and nodded several short, quick jerks. "Yeah, let's go this way."

He grabbed her arm by the wrist and pulled her alongside him, away from the group of onlookers. Brooke looked over her shoulder at them. Even they were backing down the road away from the zombie horde, but still recording everything with their phones. She wondered if maybe she was overreacting, if maybe this wasn't some elaborate movie set, and then a pair of zombies – two ashen-faced black teenage boys wearing lots of gold necklaces, baggy jeans and over-sized nylon jackets – stepped out of the shadows from a narrow alley on Josh's side and grabbed him by the arm. For an instant, Brooke noticed the one on the right had a deformed mouth, wider and filled with larger teeth than normal.

One of the boys yanked Josh away from her, ripping his hand from hers and causing her to stumble in her heels. She regained her balance just in time to see Josh take a swing at him. His hand connected with the zombie's shoulder, but to no effect. Before he could say anything, the other zombie with the large mouth pulled Josh's other arm to its mouth and bit deeply into it, blood pooling around the zombie's lips as it shook its head to sever flesh from the limb. Josh shrieked in pain, twisting around the bitten arm to try to land a punch on this other zombie, but the first zombie grabbed Josh's head in its palms and bent it down, biting Josh on the back of the neck and crunching into backbone. Josh vibrated violently for a second and his body went slack in the clutches of the two zombies.

Brooke began to run, unaware she had just urinated in her favorite designer jeans, the pair her husband loved on her and said brought out the best curvature of her ass. She had been hoping Josh would notice that, too. She hadn't made it too far down the street before the guy in the baseball cap and his two companions passed her, none of them even glancing at her as they sped by. Brooke turned her head over her shoulder and saw even more ... zombies? ... moving onto the main street. This could not be, she thought. There can't be zombies. Not zombies.

And then she bounced into something and tumbled to the ground, banging her skull against the curb and bringing tears to her eyes. She rolled on the ground for a moment clutching her head at the point where the pain felt like a spike through her skull. She opened her eyes and realized it hadn't been a something she had run into, but a mottled-gray, mucus-and-blood covered balding man in his pajamas. And he was about to grab her by the head when she rolled over to her side several times, pushed herself up from the ground, kicked her heels off and sprinted down the street.

Flight mode was quickly turning into panic. Brooke didn't know the neighborhood she was in and her car was parked in front of Josh's apartment building, which was in the opposite direction. Very soon, she was going to be a shoeless, urine-stained thirty-nine-year old woman lost in Los Angeles, with a would've-been-soon-to-be-estranged husband on the other side of town at work, and a should've-been-new-lover dead on the street, neither of which was in a position to help her out.

She didn't realize she was crying until she had to stop to catch her breath. Hot tears were streaming down her face and she was gasping for air amid the weeps. Everything had gone wrong. Josh had just been murdered. Her future life had just vanished into thin air. For a while, during dinner with Josh, she had actually imagined what it would be like to be single again, dating Josh, with every-other week off from her own three children: free from the crushing burden of being a mom and a wife. She had felt like freedom – happiness – was almost in her grasp. She had been falling in love, an emotion that had been lost to her for more than a decade, and it had been taken away from her on the night it was supposed to have been given to her. It was so unfair.

She opened her purse and fished out her cell phone, doing the only thing she knew she could do for help: call her husband.

"Hey, honey, what's up?" Charles asked.

She gasped and tried to catch her breath, looking around the neighborhood, wondering what to say. She couldn't tell him she had skipped out on girls night out after a beer with her friends while she checked her make-up and changed her outfit for her date, and she wasn't sure what to tell him about the attack that wouldn't involve telling Charles about her date. She just hadn't had any time to think about it.

"Are you crying?" Charles asked a moment later.

Brooke nodded and rubbed her hand beneath her nose, "Yes."

"What's wrong? Are you okay?"

"I don't know, everything just went wrong," she said after a pause, subconsciously editing Josh out of her story and inserting her girlfriends on the fly. "We just left the bar and were walking to the car when we were attacked by ... oh god, it's going to sound stupid ... but we were attacked by a group of people dressed up like zombies."

There was an awkward pause on the other end of the line. Then, softly, any incredulity hidden, "Zombies?"

"I know, I know, it doesn't make any sense, but I think they killed several people on the street right in front of me," Brooke said, the words coming out of her mouth in small bursts. "It doesn't make any sense. I saw them breaking people's arms and biting them on the neck."

She broke down into spasms of tears as she thought about the carnage, the blood, the sudden onset of mayhem. It had been such a beautiful night, and then horror. A police cruiser with its lights twirling turned the corner in front of her and sped up the road toward where she had been.

"Biting them on the neck? That's vampires, babe," Charles said on the other end, his voice light, trying to find a way to disarm the situation, to calm her down.

"Oh, god, not vampires, Charles, zombies," Brooke said.

"Did you call the police?"

"No, but they're already on the way," Brooke said. "Can you come get me and take me home?"

There was a pause on Charles' end. He was at work and his shift wouldn't end until midnight.

"What about your car?"

"I don't want to go back that way," Brooke said, turning her head to look up the street at where she had just been. "I'll get it tomorrow. Besides, I peed my pants getting away from them, so I don't really want to walk around in public."

She was sure she could hear the sigh on the other end of the phone, although she knew from fourteen years of marriage that Charles was good at masking his emotions and playing the person you needed him to be. He had come to LA years ago to be a screen writer, but she always thought he should've been an actor. Either way, he'd still be working retail, trying to break in. But that was all she had, now, and she felt an intense sadness knowing that it would be all she would ever get: just a normal life with a 9-5 job, an ordinary nobody for a husband, three demanding kids, and a DIY fixer-upper house in the suburbs. Dinner, laundry, daycare drop-offs and pick-ups, housework, and grocery shopping all suddenly re-materialized as weekly negotiations to be continued with her husband. Life had just been about to get exciting.

She hung her head in her lap. "Please, just hurry."

THE LAZARUS QUESTION

Atlanta, Georgia - Day 11

Geoffrey Haversill stared at the monitors showing Hristo Gruev and wondered what the hell was keeping the man alive. He had had nothing to eat or drink since being brought to the Centers for Disease Control's headquarters a week ago, and the man had not died. Hristo Gruev wasn't alive, either, not in any sense of the word that Haversill was familiar. But there Gruev was, on camera, swaying from side to side as if he were a blind man passing time listening to the rhythm of the world. Haversill paused as he thought that line, wondering what the musician's name was ... Steve? Stephen? Stevie? Not Stevie Ray Vaughan, though, that was the dude from Springsteen's band.

Or was that Van Zandt?

Haversill drummed his fingers and stared at the man on the monitor, the dead man walking. There was no way for him to be alive. But, still, there he was, alive and kicking.

Haversill riffled through the paperwork on the desk, hoping something unusual or obvious would suddenly jump off a page, signaling to him what it was he was looking for. They had tried to subdue Gruev and get samples from him, but Gruev had fought them the entire time, injuring one of the medical technicians: Gruev was significantly stronger than a normal man given Gruev's slim build and had nearly overwhelmed the team. The few samples they had managed to obtain had so far had yielded nothing.

So they had just locked Gruev in the room until someone higher up the chain defined the procedures to be used to examine him.

Haversill had been watching Gruev now for six days, and nothing about Gruev indicated the man was alive other than the fact he was alive. Confined in the small containment cell on the other end of the CCTV deep in the bowels of the building, Gruev never complained. Never asked for anything. Made only the most superficial efforts to try to get out. Gruev only reacted to stimuli when one of the technician's would change his meal tray, but Gruev didn't eat. He didn't drink. He didn't sleep. He just was.

"Got anything?" Sarah Purcell said as she entered the room.

"Nope."

"The guy's wife has gone to the Bulgarian embassy for help," Purcell said, sitting down and tapping through menus on a laptop computer. "It's only a matter of time until we have to release him."

Haversill frowned. "I don't know about that. He killed that morgue technician so he'll go to jail in California before he goes back to Bulgaria."

That jarred a memory awake. "The other tech and the coroner from the LA incident have both disappeared."

"They disappeared?" Sarah asked.

"Yeah, it's in today's morning update," Haversill said, motioning to a tablet computer on the desk. "The tech and coroner were both discharged later the day of the incident and the dead tech's body had already been transferred to a funeral home. None of them have been seen since that day. They just vanished. And the dead morgue tech's body was lost at the funeral home somehow. The LA people aren't telling anyone this, yet, because they also can't find any of the people Mr. Gruev barfed on while he was on the airplane."

Purcell had an astonished look on her face. "So, everyone this guy's come in contact with in the last, what, eleven days has disappeared?"

Haversill smiled. "Well, you and I are still here."

A dull moan came over the speakers attached to the laptop, a plaintive, primitive call that caused Haversill and Purcell to look at each other.

"I swear it sounds like he's saying 'brains,'" Purcell said.

Haversill rolled his eyes. The entire facility was abuzz with the notion they had a zombie in custody. "Bowersox says that, too."

The door behind them opened and in walked Carl Bowersox, the team leader for the group studying Hristo Gruev. He was holding a clipboard and flipping through a series of papers and photographs on it. He paused and let the door shut behind him, waiting for the sound of the latch to click before he looked up from the paperwork.

"Well, we still don't know what he has, if he has anything," Bowersox made a head move to indicate to the others that they all knew Gruev had something, it was just nobody knew what, "but one of the nuclear med guys ran a skin sample through a spectral analysis and found that the mitochondria in them all glow yellow."

Haversill let out the smallest laugh while Purcell just furrowed her brows.

"Glow?" Haversill asked. "I don't remember anything about them glowing, unless you put a laser on one."

Bowersox pulled the pages from his clipboard and set them down on the table. He fanned the pictures out for the other two to see.

"Well, they don't glow, Geoff, which is the strange thing about it," Bowersox said. "Or should I say, the most recent strange thing about Gruev. But I'm willing to bet that whatever's causing the glow is what's causing our problems here with Gruev."

Bowersox looked up at the two as Haversill and Purcell quickly exchanged a WTF? glance between them. Bowersox smiled.

"I've been here eleven years, Carl, and never once have I had to figure out why something was glowing," Purcell said, tucking her hair behind her ears. "Not only that, nobody has ever had to figure out why something was glowing, and I'm pretty sure we have nothing – no equipment, no tests, no procedures, nada – that could be used to even start figuring out why Gruev's mitochondria are glowing, much less come up with a reason for why they're glowing yellow."

Carl shrugged. "Yeah, I know, but I'm going to ask you to find a way to figure it out anyway. And we need to work fast. Everyone who's come in contact with this guy in California has gone missing, and the locals are starting to panic big time. We should have something on this by now, but we've got nothing."

Haversill tabbed through a series of folders on the laptop, scanned them, and looked up at Bowersox.

"He doesn't eat. He doesn't sleep. And he's unresponsive to most stimuli. He tests positive for nothing, and now you're telling us his mitochondria glow yellow," Haversill said, running the back of his right hand across his brow. "But the big problem is going to be actually running tests on him. We barely got anything the last time we tried, and nobody wants to go in and try again. Have you seen the guy's teeth?"

Bowersox nodded and shrugged. "Well, then we need to think outside the box and maybe venture into the realm of science fiction."

Haversill shook his head. "Horror, you mean."

"No, Geoff, I mean science fiction. Hristo Gruev is a real person suffering from something real that science can figure out. It might seem like horror, and let's hope it doesn't get to that, but right now we have science. And in this building we have some of the best scientists the U.S. government has. We need to figure this out."

"So, we're going to actually go down this road and figure out if he's a zombie?" Haversill asked. "I mean, okay, so we put out that joke position paper on the Internet letting everyone know we'd know what we would be doing in the event of a zombie outbreak, but I thought that was just because we wanted the CDC to seem hip and cool while telling the public to have emergency kits in their houses and plans to deal with real-life possibilities. But zombies?"

Purcell tented her fingers. "Well, there's no shortage of historical similarities to what Gruev is suffering from. It's in just about every cultural history there is. In Europe they had what they called revenants, which were undead that walked and attacked the living. The Arabs had ghouls, often appearing as women who lived in the desert and seduced men into the dunes with their siren-like calls, and when the man would show up, they'd change form and devour them. Even the Chinese had a version of this, which established the death rite culture of binding the dead with ropes before burying them. It's why we have locks on caskets.

"Pretty much almost any culture with a written history has a version of an undead person in it. A lot of it is just rooted in burial practices and a fear of the supernatural, that a dead person might come back to life for some reason if not interred properly, but there might be something more to it. It might make sense that there's a contagion of some sort we aren't familiar with that mimics death but which we haven't seen in a long time because of," Purcell said and paused, her eyes flitted through the corners of the room as she thought, "... I don't know, better diets or hygiene or who-knows-what. But there is a historical record to it."

Haversill looked at her and tilted his head. "Really? And there's a historical record of Minotaurs and Bigfoot and dragons - hell, every culture, especially the Chinese, have stories about dragons - and yet, no Minotaurs, no Bigfoot and no dragons. This is nonsense. If there were any real agent that both killed and reanimated a human body, we'd know about it."

Bowersox chuckled. "Geoff, we've only had 'modern medicine' for about half-a-century, and the more we learn about it, the more we realize there is to learn. Don't confuse the fact we have computers and diagnostic equipment that can peer into the human body in real-time, or our capability to create complex compounds to treat diseases, or the fact we can transplant organs from the recently dead into the living with the assumption that we know everything. We still can't even cure the common cold.

"And, we have a man in containment in the sub-basement that has been documented to have died, but is now alive. There are only two other people in human history that can make that claim."

"Two?" Haversill said, scratching his chin. "Jesus, okay, that's one. Who's the other?"

"Lazarus."

Haversill made a "Duh, I shoulda known that" roll of his eyes.

"And I have no doubt that if we spent some time looking into it, we'd find similar stories in other cultures. So, it is entirely credible that there is at least a slim possibility that there is something out there capable of reanimating a dead body, and we need to figure out what that something is."

Haversill looked at the monitor at the swaying figure of Gruev. His skin was gray. His eyes were blank. He looked almost angry. Haversill started in his chair.

"Shit, Carl, Gruev bit one of our guys that first day we were trying to get him pacified for samples. Do we know what happened to him?"

Bowersox shrugged. "If I recall, he was treated and released. It was a rather minor bite wound."

"We need to find him. He's the only guy we know of for sure who's been potentially exposed to whatever Gruev has. If this is zombie-plague-whatever, then we need to test him. If he's okay, then we're on to something else."

Bowersox sat in his office staring out the window at the Centers for Disease Control campus, pondering the complexity of the modern world. Various forms of plague had spread the globe in the past, and there had never been anything mankind could do about it. Infected fleas traveling on rats in the holds of ships or the backs of beasts of burden moving along the ancient trade routes had spread The Black Death across the planet, killing scores of millions. It was impossible to know, but estimates ranged from thirty to sixty percent of the world's population had died as a result. In modern times, somewhere close to 100 million people died during the Spanish Flu outbreak in the early 20th Century, almost five percent of the world's population, and roughly a half-a-billion people had been infected at one point or another – a quarter of the planet's population.

He and his compatriots in the field of disease control knew more now about pathogens and their spread, but he was nowhere near confident that the knowledge was useful in containing the world's bugs. Mankind had grown much more mobile since then, and there was still no way to detect or stop the unspeakable horrors gestating the in the gut of a flea, or the nasal mucus of a traveling salesman. Who could know the devastation of a biological agent spread through the malfeasance of even a few determined actors? For all he or anybody knew, Gruev's trip from Bulgaria to America had been a deliberate way to infect a certain segment of the modern world with whatever it was Gruev had.

And now, Bowersox had a real problem on top of that. Morgan Stanhope had been bitten by Gruev the day they tried to restrain him for medical testing, and Stanhope was now off the grid. An emergency response team had gone to his house just hours ago and discovered blood and bodily fluids on his bed, indications of something traumatic, but it would be a while before the samples yielded anything. The data all pointed one way: pandemic.

The authorities in Los Angeles had been warned to expect an outbreak and prepare for containment once it was identified, but everyone in-the-know was certain that any action would come too late, and that a horde of Patient Ones were likely already out in the world.

The only good thing was that the disease didn't actually seem to kill the subject, or at least not for long, so there was the possibility that whatever the agent did to a person could be undone. But where to begin to figure that out? It had taken six men in special protective clothing to restrain Gruev long enough to get a bite shield over his mouth. None of the tranquilizing agents they had shot into him through the slot in the door had had any effect, and Tazering him worked only so long as the charge was active. Studying him was going to be difficult, at best, if he were going to be kept alive. Or, rather, undead.

Not that anybody had argued for killing Gruev, since he was clearly a victim of something. They were there to figure out what he had, find a way to keep it from spreading to the general public, and then come up with either a cure or a quarantine plan to deal with the infected. But if they couldn't do what they needed before then with a living undead version of Gruev, it would only be a matter of time before someone advocated killing him and dissecting him. The ethical implications of this possibility boggled Bowersox's mind.

Bowersox thought about what they knew so far of the situation. They had a contagion that could kill a person and revive them inside a twenty-four to ninety-six hour window. Gruev had been feeling slightly ill for several days before he got on the plane, but once he had, the symptoms had overcome him, and in the flights from Bulgaria to America he had become delirious an died. About twelve hours after that, he had risen from the dead. Now, he was undead.

Bowersox thought of Lazarus, of what it must have been like to be dead, his body lying still in its tomb, and then to have had life placed back inside of him. What is life if it can be taken from the body and then returned to it? What is 'life' as a zombie? Haversill said Gruev seemed angry, and Bowersox had remembered a conversation he'd had with his daughter a decade earlier while they had been watching an episode of Buffy the Vampire Slayer in which Buffy had been resurrected. Maybe the dead didn't want to come back to life. Buffy hadn't. Maybe whatever came after this existence was worth the wait of going through it, no matter how long or short the stay on Planet Earth had been.

Maybe coming back from the dead would make you angry; you might just want to eat the living, make them pay. Jesus Christ had called Lazarus back to life from the grave, and Bowersox realized he had no idea what Lazarus had done after his grave clothes had been removed; it was all supposed to be evidence of the promise of life after death. It had never occurred to him that Lazarus would have had to return to all the hardships and drudgeries of life. Bowersox had always assumed it was allegory, not reality. He was going to have to look into his Bible and maybe call Pastor Tom after he got off work: why would Jesus call back to life on Earth a man who had died and was living in Heaven?

He drummed his fingers on his desk and gazed out on the city through his windows, acutely aware of the many errors of the past week-and-a-half. "We're going to have to figure out what yellow means."

GOLD GUNS GIRLS

Moscow, Russia - Day 269

Fyodor Volkov had everything in the world he had ever wanted, and it meant absolutely nothing. It was worth nothing, too. Mostly, anyway. He had spent twenty years climbing to the top of his ... field ... and now that success was rendered moot. He was busy surviving from day to day just like everyone else, foraging for food and water, avoiding military patrols and killing zombies.

He opened his eyes and stared at the ceiling in the darkness of the bedroom. Fyodor had no idea what time it was. The clocks on the various pieces of electronics had stopped working when the electricity had died months ago and he had never been one to wear a watch. He moved his hand and felt Natalie's bare ass beneath the sheets. He glanced over and saw the river of blonde hair cascading over her naked shoulders and across the sheets pulled up over the small of her back. She was the most beautiful woman he had ever made love to.

Scratch that. She was the most beautiful blonde he had ever had sex with. Fyodor Volkov had never known love, not romantic love, anyway, and had learned over the years to stuff the desire for such a connection into a small recess in his mind near the spot where his skull met his spine. Sex was easy for him, made almost simple by the fact he had become rich in his twenties, was good-looking and had figured out how to talk women into bed before he had money or status. He had game, and he knew it.

He squeezed Natalie's ass between his fingers and thumb, a quick pulse that might have made it through to her deep-sleep sub-consciousness as a sign of affection, slipped out of bed and walked into the living room. He pulled up a bottle of Stoli from an end table and tilted it into his mouth, letting the vodka slip in over his tongue and fill his cheeks.

And now here he was: thirty-eight years old, two bastard children – probably dead, along with their mothers, but whom he loved (the children, not the mothers) – apartments in Paris, Rio de Janeiro and Dallas, a custom-built Ferrari, a Sports Illustrated swim-suit model from Texas sleeping in his bed and everything he wanted whenever he wanted, and it might as well have been nothing.

He tapped a cigarette out of a pack and flamed it to life with a gold-plated lighter Natalie had given him last Christmas. He inhaled deeply and held the smoke in his lungs, noting the sensation of fullness that was only slightly different from a lungful of air, and then blew the smoke out in a stream. He stared at the cloud of smoke as it twirled in the currents of the room, thinning out and fracturing as it dissipated.

"Hey, Vasily, wake up," Fyodor said, kicking his drunk friend lightly on the bottom of a foot protruding from a blanket where Vasily lay on the couch.

"What?" Vasily asked. He hadn't been asleep, either.

"Do you think zombies can die of lung cancer?"

Vasily opened his eyes at this. "What?"

"Lung cancer," Fyodor made a demonstration move with his cigarette, lifting it in the air for Vasily to observe, then took a drag from it. "If you had lung cancer before you turned into a zombie, would the cancer keep eating away at you after you were a zombie?"

Vasily laughed. "I would bet it would make them stronger and more able to kill us. Wouldn't that be poetic justice, my friend? The undead gaining strength for the vices that would have killed them in their living lives. Only God would be so ironic."

"You don't believe in God."

"I also don't believe in zombies. And, yet, ... zombies."

Outside, there was a staccato of fire from an AK-47 machine gun, a sound familiar to both of them not so much because one heard it all the time anymore, but because they had used them themselves on many occasions before the world had gone to the dead. The sound made almost no dent on the reality of either man, and Fyodor took another swig of vodka before handing the bottle to Vasily.

"What idiot goes out in the dark of night anymore?" Fyodor asked of nobody.

Vasily suppressed a burp. "And with an AK? Only a fool goes out there anymore with anything less than a Saiga shotgun of some sort."

Fyodor motioned with his head and Vasily followed him out of the living room with the bottle of vodka. They went up the steps to the second floor and entered a common room appointed with leather furniture. A large LED TV and a surround-sound speaker system were mounted to the walls. A leggy brunette wearing nothing but her underwear was sprawled against the arm of a couch in a stupor, her eyes glazed over and fixed on nothing. She turned her dark eyes up at the two men as they paused in the room.

"We're out of coke," Mariya said, her voice hollow, the words matter-of-fact, plaintive almost, but not desperate.

Fyodor and Vasily exchanged a look.

"Have some champagne, honey, there's plenty in the wine cellar," Fyodor said, taking the bottle from Vasily and tipping a sip of vodka into his mouth. He turned to Vasily and said, "I've never seen a person go through so much coke in so short a time. Does she eat?"

Vasily shrugged. They walked out onto a balcony and took a helical staircase up to an observation deck atop the house. Broken clouds moved across the night sky, obscuring the stars, but both men ignored the beauty of the heavens and fixed their eyes on the horizon, which was aglow.

"I can't believe they burned the fucking city down," Vasily said, watching the distant smoke columns merge with the clouds.

"Of course they did. We're Russians. Nobody but Russians get to live in Moscow," Fyodor said. "Napoleon and Hitler both learned the hard way. Now, my friend, the undead learn."

A series of thunderous booms undulated through the night followed by the sound of distant whistling. The two men turned their heads in a direction and waited a few seconds for the same number of explosions to echo from the horizon. Fyodor took another swig of vodka and set the bottle down on a hand railing.

"Still fighting the last war, our glorious army at work killing zombies with howitzers," Fyodor said, patting through his pockets for his pack of cigarettes and bringing one alight. "I don't know when it became the custom of every Russian army to destroy everything in sight as a means of waging war. If we're losing, we burn it all down so the enemy can't have it, and if we're winning, we blow it all up so the enemy can't have it."

Vasily laughed.

"Vasily, we're all or nothing as a people, and soon we will be nothing. For our entire history, nobody has been able to conquer us, not really, not fully, but now, at the apex of human achievement, when life is easy, when you can watch porn on your pocket phone, get any drug you desire, eat anything you want, have any girl you choose, we finally found a way to kill us all off."

"Only, we didn't kill us all off, we just found a way to make all of the stuff we made to make life easy completely useless to us," Vasily said. "Now, all we want is to wander the earth undead, trying to eat the brains of our fellow man."

There was some rustling on a chaise longue and the two men quickly turned their heads to the noise. Fyodor was instantly relieved to see Nikita push her chestnut hair off her face and tuck some locks behind each ear. Her eyeliner streaked down her cheeks from having cried, but Fyodor had no idea what she might have been crying about.

"This used to be such a nice dacha to come to for a weekend trip, Fyodorovitch, but now it's just a fucking prison," Nikita said, her voice soft. "A gilded cage. I want to go home."

"You can't go home, Nikita, the army is burning it down as we speak," Vasily said.

Nikita let out the barest trace of a whimper, but she had already cried all of the sadness out of her, leaving nothing but a hollow spot inside her where she should have felt sorrow or despair. She felt nothing but the heaviness of helplessness.

"Are you going looting tomorrow?" Nikita asked.

"Foraging, Nikita, not looting," Fyodor said, taking the bottle from the railing and handing it to her.

"Whatever. I want to go this time; I want to see some of the world out there on the other side of the fence," Nikita said.

The two men looked at each other and Fyodor gave a slight nod. "Sure, Nikita, we'll get you up after dawn."

Fyodor motioned with his head and he and Vasily went back down into the house. Fyodor picked up a

Desert Eagle .50 caliber pistol off the kitchen counter and snugged it into his waist band while Vasily grabbed a shotgun from its resting place in a corner of the room. They stepped outside onto the patio and paused, listening for the sound of an undead walker that might have made it through the fence. None ever had, but there was no reason to be lax. All it took was one bite.

"We're going to need to pick up a new woman as well," Vasily said. "These ones are all burnt out."

"That's going to be tougher than getting coke or vodka. Nobody trusts anyone anymore, and promising girls drugs and food and security hasn't worked well the last few times. The girls that are left already know how to survive or have men," Fyodor said. "And we need to find something better than canned dog food, too."

Vasily laughed. "Yeah, Mariya was good for fucking after we gave her coke, but when she found out she had to eat dog chow, our luster wore off pretty damn quick. Here we are, millionaires with sports cars, apartments and access to everything the city had to offer, and now we're lucky if we can get some farm girl like Mariya. There was a time when Mariya would have been sidewalk trash to us, just some chick to ignore on the way to somewhere, and now she's the crazy fuck."

Fyodor paused for a moment and thought about the time they had rescued Mariya from the farmhouse she had been holed up in. A small group of undead had found a weakness in some plywood covering the front windows of her house and had begun pulling it down when her father, an over-weight middle-aged man wielding a .22 caliber rifle had stepped from a window on the second floor onto the roof over the front porch and begun plunking zombies. He lost his balance and slid off the roof and had been quickly torn to pieces.

Fyodor and Vasily had been watching from a copse of trees across the street, initially amused that the farmer had thought his little varmint killer would do much to the undead, and then saddened at his fate – who can predict a loss of balance on a pitched roof? It's like slipping in the bathtub: it happens, but not so much. Mariya had climbed out onto the roof moments later and begun wailing at the sight of her father being destroyed by zombies and Vasily had broken from the cover of the trees with his shotgun in hand, blasting holes in the pack of undead. In less than a minute the zombies were all dead, and Fyodor had walked across the street, scanning the distance for itinerant zombies drawn by the noise.

"Vasily, that was stupid," Fyodor had said. "You might have just drawn a hundred more to our location with all the shooting."

Vasily had ignored him and looked up at the girl on the roof of the porch. "Come with us if you want to live."

Mariya had been Vasily's sex slave for the first few weeks, but the gratitude of having been saved and the grief of the loss of her father finally having morphed into the realization she was still trapped, and then she had succumbed to the alcohol and drugs as a way out of her new predicament. Or, perhaps, a way to avoid the fact that they often had to eat food meant for dogs and cats.

The next morning, Fyodor gave Nikita a 20-gauge shotgun with shells filled with birdshot. He wanted her to be armed, to feel safe, but he didn't want her with a weapon that could be used to kill either him or Vasily should she have come to the conclusion that her only way out was to kill her velvet jailers.

Fyodor had always told the girls they brought back that they could leave at anytime, and he meant it. It was Vasily who would take them aside and reaffirm that commitment, and then point out the decaying skeleton of Irina just the other side of the fence, her bones picked clean by zombies and scavengers, killed by runner-zombies just ninety seconds after saying her tearful good-byes to them, Fyodor locking the gate behind her and wishing her good-luck.

There were no remains of Tanya to show anyone, and the digital cameras on which images of her were stored had long ceased to power up. That was back when they thought taking pictures would give them something to look back on in the future, when the zombies were gone. Back when they all thought the plague was a reason for a party.

The trio made their way down the street cautiously, Fyodor in the lead with Nikita in the middle. They were almost three kilometers out from the dacha, walking alongside a string of curbside shopping centers and taking pains to check through the storefront windows of each as they moved. For whatever reason, the undead could remain immobile for long periods of time, just standing in place, or lying against a wall. Human sounds, the steps of the living, would rouse them in a heartbeat, so one had to take precautions in areas where the zombies assumed people might be.

"This has all been picked clean, Vasily," Fyodor said as they came to an intersection and scanned the open space for the undead, the store fronts all broken open. "We're going to have to walk farther if we're going to find anything."

Fyodor stroked his beard and looked around. He hated having a beard, but procuring razor blades was one of the things that rarely occurred to him while he was out foraging for supplies. He kept the growth clipped close with scissors, but for some reason he was still drawn to stroke it as if it were some obsessive-compulsive disorder.

"What are you thinking, Fyodor?" Vasily asked.

Fyodor shrugged and watched as Nikita slowly walked to the edge of the sidewalk curb, moving her shotgun in small arcs as if she were searching for something at which to shoot. She might have some talent at this, he thought.

"I'm thinking we need bicycles, Vasily, but I haven't a clue where any might be."

"What for?"

"So we can cover more ground more quickly without making any noise," Fyodor said matter-of-factly. "It's not like there's any gasoline anymore. Not that you can drive anywhere with all the fucking car wrecks on the roads, but if we're going to have to keep going farther out each time, we're going to need to expose ourselves for less time."

"Bicycles," Vasily said, letting the word just hang in the air and sag under its weight, as if such a contraption were an indicator of poverty or powerlessness. He looked around the intersection, paused a moment on Nikita, who had made her way off roadway and was poking through some rubble near a crumbled wall, and turned to Fyodor.

"How long until they nuke us?"

Fyodor shrugged. "We're near Moscow. I think that probably still means something to them, even if it's mostly burnt to the ground. But if somebody doesn't figure out what's going on with these things, and how to kill them or cure them or whatever the fuck you have to do to them, well, it's only a matter of time."

"Unless the dead walkers get to them first," Vasily said with a sniff of a laugh He glanced at Nikita. "Look at that girl. Nineteen years old, perfect body, tight ass, and I'm tired of fucking her already."

Fyodor rolled his eyes. "You fucked her this morning before we came out here."

"Only I wasn't fucking her, not in my mind, anyway. I was with that redheaded coat check girl at the club who would never give me the time of day, only a stub for my coat," Vasily said. "I wonder where she is these days."

"You're not missing anything with Karena," Fyodor said, focusing on Nikita as she walked across the street, her shotgun held at her waist, ready for use.

"You didn't."

Fyodor barely shrugged. "I did. A couple of times. She's a sloppy fuck."

"You never told me you banged her."

"Yeah, well, it was before you told me you wanted to, so I didn't want to prejudice you."

"Looking out for me?"

"Not really," Fyodor said. "You didn't miss anything."

Vasily stood there in silence for a moment and watched as Nikita looked through the broken store front windows on the other side of the street. "How did you get in Karena's pants? I tried every time I was there."

"It was easy, Vasily, I was a little drunk and she was chatting me up about my coat and I asked her if she wore panties with words on them, and she said all panties had words on them and then I said -- before she could explain, because I knew she meant the label -- that I had seen a catalog with a pair of panties in it that said 'Wild in Bed' and I asked her if girls who wore such underwear were subject to truth in advertising laws."

"And that worked?" Vasily asked.

"I nailed her in the back of the coatroom twenty minutes later," Fyodor said. "I keep telling you that the way into a girl's pants is through misdirection. If you talk about a girl's underwear with a girl who will talk about her underwear, both of you are talking about fucking, not underwear. You've just got to recognize the indicator of interest in you. All women who are interested in you do this, send you a signal that they're into you, and if you know what you're doing, you can figure out what they're about pretty quickly and then it's just about negotiating the time frame."

Fyodor paused and stared at Nikita as she walked to the other side of the intersection. "Vasily, all women want to fuck, it's in their DNA just like it's in ours, they just want to fuck the right guy at the right time, and you have to know how to make them think you're that guy and that time is now. It's not foolproof, but you get to a point where you can tell which girls are fuckable and which aren't."

Suddenly Fyodor noticed Nikita jumping up and down, pointing to a hole in a building on the other corner of the street. She turned and waved at him, urging him and Vasily to come to her.

"She's excited about something," Vasily said, his voice a monotone.

"Not the size of your dick if her silence this morning means anything."

Vasily smiled. "I'm going to guess it's not a bag of dry dog food we can moisten with rain water."

Fyodor laughed out loud, a belly laugh he hadn't experienced in many weeks, and he realized that mirth and happiness were not lost in the new world of the zombie apocalypse, that a friend could still make you laugh with a comeback quip. Nikita was jumping off her toe-tips, pointing to her side, the smile on her face wide, a jubilant look. Whatever she had just discovered changed everything in her life, made it somehow better, made it worth telling Fyodor and Vasily about.

And then three runner zombies erupted from around the corner and tackled Nikita to the ground, one of them immediately biting into her shoulder. At the same moment Nikita's last dying impulse was to squeeze the trigger on her shotgun, the recoil from the blast causing it to jump from her hand and skitter across the sidewalk, the shot pellets briefly pinging off the wall of a nearby building. If she screamed, it was drowned out by the blast of the gun, and, anyway, an instant later she was inert flesh on the sidewalk being torn apart by the undead.

The two men glanced at each other briefly before raising their weapons and firing on the walking dead, a round from the Desert Eagle splintering the head of a middle-aged male zombie while Vasily's shotgun bursts swept the other two off Nikita's body and into the gutter along the sidewalk, where the body of a young man twitched for a few moments as the death seeped out of his living corpse. Fyodor walked quickly to Nikita's body and knelt down, slipping his pistol into his waistband and grabbing the idle shotgun from the ground. He stood up, aimed at the girl's head, and disintegrated it with a blast from the weapon.

"What a waste," Fyodor said, looking down the roads connected at the intersection, scanning for the inevitable arrival of a shuffling horde of undead. He had no idea why gunshots attracted them with such intensity, but it was a fact of modern life that they did.

Vasily took a few steps down the road to where Nikita had been pointing and stopped. His shotgun sagged in his hands at what he saw.

"You're not going to believe this, Fyodor," Vasily said, "but somebody blew a hole in the side of the bank since we were last through here."

Fyodor walked up alongside Vasily and stared at the crumble of rubble, the interior of the bank's vault exposed. Fyodor walked up to the edge of it and looked into the shadowy darkness. Coins and cash were scattered everywhere amid the broken masonry, a small fortune for a person in a modern 21st Century nation. Fyodor turned and looked over his shoulder at Nikita's body and then glanced at Vasily.

"Probably the most cash she'd ever seen in her life," Vasily said.

"It's not even good for toilet paper," Fyodor said.

"Or eating."

Fyodor laughed flatly. "We better get out of here before more dead show up."

Just then they heard the booming of another round of artillery fire, the sky above them rent apart by the projectiles as they burrowed through the air. Several seconds of silence passed before the explosions reverberated back to them. Vasily and Fyodor turned and faced each other.

"The army's retreating," Fyodor said, letting the words hang in the air. They both knew what that meant.

"We're going to need more vodka and another girl," Vasily said, nodding down the road, his voice flat, the words emitting only facts.

"This world can kiss my ass good-bye, but it's going to do it on my terms," Fyodor said, the two of them listening as another round of artillery shells sluiced through the air, "when I'm drunk and laid."

THE UNDEATH OF ROB ZOMBIE

Norman, Oklahoma - Day 199

Robert Sebastian Colfax had been thirty-four-years old the day Marguerite Rosario Del Rio bit him on the calf. She had been undead for almost sixteen weeks at that point, a janitorial team member who cleaned the Catlett Music Hall on the University of Oklahoma campus five days a week. She had been bitten by John Kennedy Creighton, an undergraduate student with an undecided major but a more than a passing interest in the oboe. Marguerite had bled to death after stumbling away from Creighton and hiding in a janitorial supply closet.

Creighton had been killed minutes later by a state trooper. John Creighton's body had been burned with hundreds of others in a pit dug in the football field. In the confusion of the battle for the campus, nobody had thought to look for the third-generation Mexican woman, and she had undied in the closet and awoken to living death. She had no concept of time in the closet, sitting there against the wall in complete darkness, never making a single move to stand up and explore the oven-hot room she was in.

And then the door opened and Rob Colfax and Claire Benoit shined a flashlight into the room, neither of them concerned there might be an undead third-generation Mexican janitor waiting patiently for the opportunity to taste living flesh. So unconcerned about the prospect of a zombie janitor in the closet were Rob and Claire that Rob stepped into the closet and shined the light up, above the undead body of Marguerite, playing the beam across the shelves of cleaning supplies.

"Shit, nothing," Rob said.

And then he felt the pair of hands grab his right calf followed quickly by the bite of teeth. He yelled.

"What the fuck!"

He shined the beam down on Marguerite as she shook her head back-and-forth like a thresher shark tearing at a fish, biting flesh, blood trickling down his leg and foaming around Marguerite's lips. Marguerite's undead life ended two seconds later, as Rob quickly pulled his Smith & Wesson .357 revolver from its holster and squeezed a round into her skull, splitting it open and spattering brain matter everywhere. The sound of the shot deafened both Rob and Claire.

Rob stumbled backward out of the closet and into Claire, who had her hands up over her ears too late to muffle the sound of the pistol and just in time for her to lose her balance and fall down when Rob bumbled into her. She hit the ground hard, grimacing as she landed on her tailbone. She stared at the bloody bite on Rob's right calf muscle and then looked past him into the dark closet. Rob looked down at Claire and then turned the beam of the flashlight back into the closet, where the deathless, lifeless corpse of Marguerite Rosario Del Rio lay on its back, a pool of long-since dried blood blackening the floor around her body. Rob worked the beam up to the un-living woman's body and trained it on her split-open head, one of her eyeballs having been blown out of her skull and hanging by fibers to the socket, the contents of her skull moist.

Rob looked down at Claire, holstered his pistol and extended his arm. "Come on, let me help you up."

Instead of taking his hand, Claire pointed to the bite indentation on Rob's calf: it was deep, the flesh torn and seeping blood, but the zombie hadn't actually bitten anything out of him. Rob eyed the bite for a few seconds before shrugging off his backpack and rustling through it for a bottle of tincture of iodine, which he unscrewed and began dribbling over the wound. There was a rumor making its way through the town that not everyone bitten became infected and that iodine could help. Nobody knew anyone who had tried, but nearly everyone still alive carried some sort of iodine solution or pills.

"What the fuck was she doing in there?" Rob said as he pasted a large square Band-Aid brand bandage to his wound. "I mean, what the fucking fuck was a fucking zombie doing just waiting in a supply closet? That fucking doesn't make any fucking sense."

Rob shook his head in total disbelief. He wanted to cry at the unfairness of it all: he was careful when out scavenging and didn't make "rookie" mistakes. There was no reason for a zombie to be sitting in a closet waiting for someone to open it. None. That's not what zombies did.

"You okay to walk?" Claire asked.

Rob nodded. "Yeah, it's not that bad. It looks worse than it feels."

"I think we should call this a day and head back."

Rob muttered a small, plaintive laugh.

"What?" Claire asked.

"I can't go back. Not now, not with this."

"Sure you can."

"No. I can't. They'll put me in the quarantine yard and wait me out, and if I turn into a zombie, they'll kill me."

Claire tucked some strands of hair behind each ear. "Yeah. If you become a zombie. Do you want to become a zombie and have us not kill you?"

Rob laughed a chuckle of genuine mirth at that. He smiled. "I don't want to become a zombie and I don't want anyone to kill me either way, to be honest with you."

"Maybe the iodine will kill the infecting agent?" Claire said unconvincingly.

Rob shrugged. "Maybe. But I'm going to stay here for the next day or two and wait it out. I've got a couple of Power Bars and some water, so I'll be okay. If I turn, well, I won't turn in the yard, so I'll be out here and you can hunt me down like free-range zombie. If I don't turn, I'll just show up in a couple of days and knock on the door."

"They'll still put you in the yard," Claire said matter-of-factly.

"Yeah, sure, but if I don't turn dead in the next day or so, I won't turn dead, then, either, so I won't be out in the yard wondering about my fate."

Claire stared at him for a long moment and Rob looked down at the bite wound. Nobody had ever recovered. They'd both heard stories, rumors really, of people who'd been bitten and not transformed, but neither they nor anyone they knew had ever known such a person. In the world of the undead, being bitten meant becoming one of the living dead.

"Go, I'll be okay," Rob said. "I'm sure the iodine will help."

Claire nodded sadly, looked him in the eyes, a look Rob interpreted as farewell, and she backed a few steps away from him, trying to smile confidently. Rob nodded his head and shouldered his backpack, all the while watching as Claire made her way down the hall to the stairwell. He had to watch her, she was armed with a 9 mm Colt Defender and he knew from shooting with her that she'd be able to plug him in the skull from inside 15 yards with ease.

After the door had creaked shut, Rob slid down against the wall and put his head in his hands, tears of disbelief finally welling in his eyes. Fucking zombies. Why the fuck was a zombie chick hiding in a closet in the music hall? What the fuck did her zombie brain think it was doing? It made no sense, and the unfairness of it all bewildered Rob into a teary rage of whimpers, shouts and weeping. He didn't want to become a zombie. He wanted to go back to the house, open a basement-cold beer and make love to Barbara Zane, his girlfriend of two months since he and Claire had rescued her from the overnight lock-up in the Norman Police Department. She'd been arrested for DUI the night before police had been ordered to the outskirts of town with various fire departments and the nearby National Guard unit to form a skirmish line against a horde of undead coming down North Flood Avenue from Oklahoma City. That was three months ago.

After a while, he got hold of himself, wiped his eyes dry and blew his nose out on the floor, wiping it with the back of his hand and then onto the seat of his shorts. Why hadn't he worn jeans today? It was only 104 Fahrenheit outside, and a dry heat at that. He shook his head and made his way out of the building and along the sidewalk running parallel to College Avenue, strolling beneath the shade trees and turning absent-mindedly onto West Boyd Street, past a series of cars frozen in a multiple rear-end car crash. He crossed the empty street and almost forgot that he needed to be aware of zombies - this area was frequently overrun with them (former students turned undead, Rob and others figured they came back to campus out of habit) - and walked up to the carcass of The Library, a once-popular bar and restaurant that had been ransacked and looted months ago. It was full of broken glass and overturned tables now, the front doors long-ago pried off, the windows broken. Rob missed the quiet comfort of the place on a weeknight in the summer, when there were fewer students to deal with and it was easier to get a seat at the bar and watch television over a beer.

Zombies. Why were there even zombies in the first place? How was that even possible? Why didn't the re-animated dead bodies continue to deteriorate and become dust in the wind? What made them walk and seek out living humans? And why? Zombies were like mosquitoes in that they seemed to serve no observable purpose in the ecosystem except to feed and spread disease: the world would miss neither if either suddenly blinked out of existence.

"Why?" Rob shouted up into the sky at the cumulus clouds rolling by.

"Why what?" said a voice from behind him, and Rob spun quickly, his hand falling to his holster.

A man in his fifties was standing behind him with a boy of about ten, both of them wearing cowboy hats. The man idly held a Winchester rifle in his hands, more-or-less not-exactly pointed at Rob's gut, while the boy had a small .22 caliber Ruger pistol in a hip holster. Rob smiled and moved his hand away from his gun.

"Was just asking God why this happened," Rob said, shrugging, scanning the area for the sudden appearance of the walking dead.

"Get an answer?" the man asked.

"Nope."

"Need any help?"

Rob shook his head. "Nah, just picking through the bones one more time looking for stuff that might've been overlooked. You?"

The man tapped the brim of his hat with his pointer finger and made a brief nod. "Just passing through. You be careful, there's a horde of about ten-thousand dead-ones out by Westheimer Airport. No idea why, but they're strung out like they're waiting for something to come and land."

"Thanks," Rob said, watching as the man and boy walked down the street, each of them turning their heads to constantly scan the properties lining the street, looking for the undead. They turned a corner and Rob was alone.

He walked up onto the disheveled patio of The Library and sat down on a chair. He ate a Power Bar, drank some water, and stared around at the world. He wished there were some way to charge his iPod so he could listen to his Life Sux mix, a playlist he had started when his last long-term pre-zombie-apocalypse girlfriend had broken up with him. He'd edited it many times since then, adding two other short term girlfriend specific songs to the mix, but the playlist had long since morphed into a general purpose "bad day" mix: until Barbara Zane had come into his life, he hadn't had a girlfriend in more than a year. The women who had originally inspired its creation never crossed his mind when he listened to it, and today would have been a perfect day to listen to it while drinking a six-pack of beer, seeing as it would likely be his last chance to drink beer as an alive human.

His calf throbbed with a dull warm pulse, and he looked down at the bandage. Not everybody got zombie-itis that got bit, did they? Someone had to be immune. Someone had to be resistant. Somehow, there had to be at least a natural chance that the disease didn't get passed on to the bitten, right? Some people could survive an infection, he thought, because not even the plagues in Europe in the Dark Ages killed everyone. Right? Some people survived. Somewhere, someone had to be working on a cure. Right?

"Not in this town," he said under his breath, looking around for anyone who might be in earshot.

The town was quiet, though. Only bird noises and the sound of the wind. If there was anyone in the country -

the world - working on a cure, nobody he knew had any knowledge of it. There was nobody on the roads, nobody roaming the land, nobody with knowledge of anything outside a day's walk of Norman, Oklahoma.

Nobody but maybe that man and kid in the cowboy hats.

He sat up in his chair and realized he had been crying, and wiped the tear streams from his face. Shit, he thought, two people passing through town and he hadn't bothered to ask them anything about the outside world, or even if they were from somewhere farther away than a day's round-trip. He left the bar's remains and walked in the direction of the cowboy hat duo, feeling a dull ache forming in his calf, as if he were succumbing to a cramp, tightening up, becoming less limber. He shook it for a second and increased his gait.

He turned onto South Flood Street and began walking north, the last point he had seen the cowboy-hat-wearing man and boy. There was nothing on the road aside from abandoned cars and skeletal remains. He walked cautiously on the side of the street until he reached the intersection with Main Street, which was clogged with vehicles, abandoned by owners long-since dead or undead. Nobody who fled lived, so far as he knew. Anybody who had ventured out in search of a safer haven had either been killed by zombies, become zombies, or been killed by the military or law enforcement in the last ditch attempts to enforce curfews and quarantines.

Nothing had worked. Somehow, the zombies always got through, and only those who had hunkered down had survived. And not all of them, either. Rob looked up and down Main Street: the storefronts were all cracked open, long since looted and pillaged for anything and everything. He had been among those doing the pillaging and looting back after it was obvious neither the police nor National Guard were coming back.

He suddenly felt faint, a hot flash coursing through his body, the taste of vomit at the back of his throat. He pulled a water bottle out of his backpack and drank deeply, the luke-warm water doing nothing to cool him down. How long had it been since he'd been bitten? It had been late morning then, and now the sun was setting. Where had the afternoon gone? He looked around Main Street again: this had been a bustling city of more than 100,000 before the zombie plague, and now it was empty. Where were the people?

His fevered mind told him they had gone somewhere, that a hundred-thousand people don't just vanish or turn into zombies that vanish. And, there weren't that many corpses in the town, though they were everywhere. Maybe there was an escape?

He stumbled through town for several blocks, increasingly feeling like he was drunk. He was losing his balance and his ability to see clearly. The world was taking on a fog-like shroud. He felt almost good in the same way as a late-afternoon beer buzz at a barbecue cook-out. After a while, he stumbled onto the grassy lawn of Wells Andrews Park. He stared around at the high grass and didn't realize it hadn't been mowed in months. But he knew where he was, and for no reason he could know he made his way to the amphitheater. He was burning hot, and he had run out of water on the way. But he wasn't thirsty. Or hungry. Just ... sleepy.

He made his way into the amphitheater and walked up into the seating area, not looking for anything, no longer aware of anything, just trying to find a spot to sit and sleep it off. He found a spot in the lower left-third of the seating area and plopped down unceremoniously. He wriggled out of his backpack and stared up into the sky, the sun nearly set, the sky filled with a riot of violets and indigos, still waiting for the arrival of the stars. After a moment, he saw the first star and shivered. He could feel the sweat on his body pooling. Nothing was right. He was drunk. Mightily so, and everything in him said "sleep."

And so he closed his eyes for the last time as a member of the living.

THE THIRD TIME IS THE HARM

Chippewa Falls, Wisconsin - Day 654

Milton Kempf worked his way along the hillside, keeping his eyes on the band of shuffling undead trudging down the road. For months, little groups of zombies had been making their way into Chippewa Falls, slowly forming in the Northern Wisconsin State Fairgrounds into a gaggle that resembled the swaying of tall grass on a windy day. Milton had no way of knowing why that location drew them. At first, he surmised it had to do with the proximity to the Calvary, Hope and Forest Hill cemeteries and all of the potential new recruits in their graves. And then he had made his way around those cemeteries and realized not a single grave had been disturbed. Anyone buried in them was still below ground. Whatever had killed and resurrected the undead had had no effect on the previously dead.

He sighted his compound bow at the trailing zombie and watched it over the tip of his arrow, feeling the gentle breeze and compensating for windage. An arrow through the skull would drop it to the ground and the others wouldn't know they'd lost a member of their group. On the other hand, if he shot it with the Desert Eagle strapped to his hip, the entire group would turn on him, and every zombie within hearing range of the report would start shuffling his way.

He relaxed the tension on the bow and stowed the arrow into his belt quiver, watching the undead shuffle off around a bend in the road. He picked up the three rabbits he'd bagged earlier in the afternoon, keeping his eyes alert for any errant undead that might have found its way into the backwoods. For whatever reason, the walking dead didn't often find their way off the beaten path.

"You're getting pretty good at that, but you messed up and established a rhythm, Eli," Milton said, turning his head over his right shoulder and smiling at his 14-year old son. "Remember to step carefully when you walk through the forest and to change your step pattern ever-so-slightly as you do so that the noise your feet make always sound like the vagaries of nature, not the patterns of a creature."

Eli rolled his eyes and quickened his pace to match his. "I so thought you were going to put an arrow in that fat zombie chick's head, Dad, but then you didn't. What happened? You had the bow drawn and ready."

Milton harrumphed low and shrugged. "Just because you can kill something doesn't mean it's a good idea to kill it."

"I thought we wanted to kill all the zombies."

"We do."

"But you didn't take the shot."

"I know."

"Why not?"

"The situation didn't warrant it. There's no reason to risk our lives killing a zombie when we don't need to. No telling what could've happened had I taken the shot. Could've missed and let the whole group know we were here. The longer the undead don't know we're here, the better it is for us. Just be patient, son, and we'll get everything sorted out."

Eli nodded an held up three rabbits.

"Rabbit? Tasty. Good hunting, Eli."

"I want a hamburger."

Milton smiled. "Me too. Ain't any burger shops 'round any more."

"There's those cows we saw the other week on the old dairy farm."

Milton looked at his son and nodded. "We're doing just fine on game. No reason to risk that. Not with all the undead moving through the area. Maybe someday, if they're still alive."

Their compound was a mile into the woods from the road. It was a former farm that had stopped being a farm sometime in the 1950s or 1960s, judging from the leftover equipment still inside the barn. The house had been boarded up sometime after farming had stopped, and forgotten. Until Milton and his group came across it while living in the woods after escaping the city earlier that first year. Nature had recaptured much of the farmland in the decades since it had been abandoned, but with some effort and creativity, Milton had planted an acre with a variety of crops. There was a chicken coop, two dairy cows and a half-dozen pigs, as well. They hadn't eaten any of the farm animals, yet, although there was fresh milk and eggs.

"What'd'ja get?" Nancy asked as father and son walked into the kitchen.

Nancy was Milton's fiancée. They would have been married by now had there been no zombie apocalypse. They wore rings anyway, figuring there might never be any "authority" to marry them, having pledged themselves to each other five months ago in front of his son, longtime friends Roy and Sara Campbell, and their two daughters.

"Three rabbits are out on the stoop, Nance," Milton said, closing the distance and kissing her. "Undead were all over the streets today, making their way for town, so didn't want to risk it to get more."

"Rabbits, huh? Haven't had those in a couple of weeks," Nancy said, smiling and rolling her eyes.

He smiled back. "There's only three of them, so I'm gonna guess we're gonna have a lot of potatoes and carrots with 'em."

"One of these days, we're gonna find out what the hell happened."

Milton looked over at Roy. They were sitting in the barn at "the bar," drinking home brew. Roy's passion from before the end of times had been making beer in his basement, small batches of whatever recipe entertained his fancy. Milton had always thought Roy's hobby pre-apocalypse had been too labor-intensive, but now he was glad they had spent those days the previous summer scavenging for the equipment he needed. "Beer is food," Roy had said then to settle the argument about how to provision their farm.

"I dunno 'bout that, Roy," Milton said. "There hasn't been a government to speak of since the last of the National Guard boys pulled out with the police and that convoy of school buses last year. And it's not like we get people moving into the area that could tell us anything. Everyone I come across is headed south before winter comes. We might be stuck in this world for a long time."

Roy nodded. "You know, when I used to think about life with no government, I never really meant zero government. I like to think that we'd have had the kinda government that could actually deliver the mail, fix the streets and do your basic police and fire work," Roy said. "But, then, I shoulda known that if government couldn't deliver the mail or fix the streets, it was never goin' to be worth a shit with dealing with the undead."

"On the upside, there's no taxes anymore."

"Yeah, there's that," Roy said, a wry smile accompanying a roll of his eyes.

They both sipped their beer for a while in silence, each man inside his own head. Almost like when they would go fishing and not talk for hours, just sitting in the boat casting, reeling in walleye or perch. You didn't need to talk to each other when you both knew what to do. They had rebuilt the farm largely in silence, too. Each man had taken over a specific aspect, Roy working on the structures and Milton on the livestock and garden, each man working to his strengths, helping each other when necessary. Sara and Nancy had gravitated equally naturally to the cooking and family-raising aspects of life, and though life was significantly more difficult absent everything technological that humanity had done to make life easier, they were, for the most part, happy.

Except for the kids. Life without cell phones had totally demoralized Roy's daughters, which confounded Roy since there was nobody to talk or text. Eli occasionally despaired over his inability to play on a PlayStation. The sudden descent from modernity had shocked the three teenagers in ways their parents hadn't imagined, and Milton got the sense that the kids felt they had been robbed of some birthright. They did their chores around the farm without too much complaining, but it was obvious they expected things to return to normal at some point. None of them expected the world to remain two-hundred years in the past for long.

It didn't help that they weren't without modern conveniences. The group had several solar powered battery chargers which they used to recharge the batteries to the walkie-talkies, GPS devices, mp3 players and assorted other electronic gadgets they had on the farm. Rechargeable batteries were still rechargeable and the crank-handle emergency radios they had could still - on a clear night - pull in a signal from somewhere from some lonely soul who was broadcasting on a ham set. They all knew they weren't alone, that there was still life out there on the fringes.

"Eli wants to see if we can take a cow from that dairy farm off County Highway S," Milton said.

"We already have two."

"He wants to eat it."

"Are they still worth eating? Last time we went by there the few that were around to look at were pretty skinny."

"He wants a hamburger," Milton shrugged. "I'd like a steak, come to think of it. Rabbit, deer and turkey are getting kind of old."

"Ayup," Roy said. "Lots of dead ones around, now, though."

Milton nodded.

"I don't know that we should be risking our young on hamburger. Not with so many of the undead so close to that place."

"I ain't arguing in favor of it, I'm just sayin' maybe it's worth considering," Milton said. "We could scout it and make a decision then."

"The last two times we tried something like that we nearly got eaten alive by the dead walkers," Roy said. "I think we should just stay put, stay out of the way, and learn to like living in the 1800s."

"We ain't going to live long that way," Milton said, thinking about the prospects. "And our teeth will fall out."

The sun outside had set, and the small propane lamp sitting on the floor between them cast a circle of light around their legs, exaggerated shadows and made them realize the direness of their current situation. Each man finished his beer and went to bed. The night watch was manned first by Eli, then by Roy's daughters until the wives woke to prepare breakfast. Even this far off a road, one had to be ready for zombies. They had no rhyme, no reason, no predictability, a lesson Milton had learned in the early days of the apocalypse when foraging for the necessities of a life he hadn't ever - really - anticipated living, and he had anticipated a lot of end-of-the-world scenarios.

But all of them had been based around the actions of people and what people would do in the event of a once-in-a-thousand-year natural disaster or sudden nuclear attack. It had never occurred to him to prepare for Night of the Living Dead. And, anyway, he had never watched zombie movies, so he had no idea.

Milton, Roy and Eli were on their knees in the scrub brush watching five undead mill aimlessly around the barn that housed their four-wheelers. They kept the vehicles a mile away from where they lived so that the sounds of the engines wouldn't draw the walkers to their actual home. It had been almost a week since they had last used them, and Milton thought it odd that there was a squad of zombies standing around the structure.

"The cost of these steaks just got a bit more expensive," Roy said.

Milton turned to him and nodded.

Eli looked at them with incredulity. "We can take them out easy from this distance, Dad. They'll never know what hit them."

Milton looked at his son and gave him the "patience, son" face. His son was always too eager to take a shot, to claim the victory, to walk home with the game.

"That doesn't make a whole lotta sense," Roy said, watching through binoculars. "They can't know what's in the shack, since they weren't anywhere around here when we locked 'em up last week. But, there they are, almost as if they were told to guard it."

"You know, from all we've seen them doing the last year or so, it's starting to make me wonder if maybe they're not completely dead inside, like there might be some small bit of the person left inside," Milton said, watching the undead mill about and scanning the horizon for some sign of something intentional. "Maybe they're aware of the world? Maybe they remember things? Maybe they have some intelligence?"

Roy looked at him and shrugged. "Let's hope not. On the plus side, they're slow. But on the other side, they usually come in packs."

Milton nodded in thought. "I'm starting to wonder if they're some sort of pack-hunting ... species. They can't succeed well individually, but as a large group, they have a good chance of surviving an encounter through attrition."

"Let's just kill 'em," Eli said, pulling the arrow back-and-forth in his bow.

"Eli, relax," Milton said, waving his palm toward the ground. "We need to get a sense of the situation before we do anything."

"You two hold here," Roy said, "I'll flank 'em from the right side and get a view of what's goin' on behind the structure and down the road towards town. If they've started figuring out how we're operating, we're going to need to start adapting. Just plain killing them might not always be the best first option if we want to figure out how it is they operate."

With that, Roy melted into the underbrush and made his way off, following a dry creek bed and disappearing into the earth tones of the landscape. Milton watched his friend and then turned to his son. Eli resembled him, was almost a duplicate, and yet had the personality traits of his ex-wife: stubborn, impetuous, too quick to make a decision that would turn into a mistake. He had spent years in the woods with Eli, trying to teach him the patience necessary before taking a shot, the importance of doing nothing but observing for long periods of time. But Milton suspected the electronics lifestyle Eli had gravitated to more readily influenced his actions: his son wanted a button to mash, a joystick to move and instant gratification or a re-spawn point for another try.

But out here on the cold, windswept countryside, there were no re-spawn points. And less instant gratification.

After a while, the walkie talkie clipped to Milton's belt clicked twice, a double-hiccup indicating Roy was about to initiate transmission. Milton held it up to his ear and adjusted the volume downward.

"Whatchya got?" Milton asked, his voice low and calm.

"Just what you're looking at, nothing else around."

"Alright, then, I'll start with the one on the far left and move in, you take the one on your end and do the same, and Eli will shoot the center and then cover wide in case we miss anything," Milton said. "Thirty seconds and let loose."

Milton turned to Eli. "Take the one in the middle, then pay attention to everything else but the zombies in front of the building, got it? We don't want any surprises while Roy and I pick off the last ones."

Eli nodded and readied his bow.

It was over in seconds. The two zombies not hit in the initial volley had no reaction to the sudden demise of their comrades. They just stood there and stared at the fallen ones until they were felled by arrows seconds later. Eli started to move and Milton grabbed him by the shoulder and pulled him back.

"Wait. Just to make sure, we wait."

Eli bent down on a knee, readied an arrow in his bow, and scanned the desolate countryside. Nothing. Milton looked at his son and wondered what he was thinking, if he was here in this moment or if he was somewhere else, thinking of whatever it was his son thought about but didn't talk with him about.

The walkie clicked twice.

"What do you make of it?" Milton said into his walkie.

"Seems clear."

"Alright," Milton said, tapping his son on his shoulder, "let's go get some hamburger."

Twenty-minutes later they had stashed the ATVs in a dry storm water ditch and made their way on foot the half-mile to the farm. They moved slowly, in a staggered formation with about ten yards between each of them, Milton in the lead and Roy in trail. All had an arrow at the ready and were scanning the landscape. They made the road bordering the farm and each man and the boy took a knee, Milton setting his bow down and looking through his binoculars across the farm.

"Well, there are two cows still alive, and I don't see any undead," Milton said.

Roy took the glasses from Milton and scanned the farm. "Looks like grass-fed free-range beef."

"Maybe we could take them back to the farm?" Eli asked suddenly, his voice filled with optimism.

Milton looked at his son and shook his head. "That we can't do. We're too far away from home; we'd be exposing ourselves out here for too long. There's too many walkers on the roads to risk the time it'd take to get them back."

"I have to agree with your dad on this one, Eli, those two cows aren't worth it." Roy said. If we're going to do this, we need to get in and out."

Eli sighed. "Why don't we just kill one of them and take back what we can, then? It's got to be better than squirrel."

"You know, Milton, we are here. They are cows. And if we don't eat them, they're just gonna die when the winter really hits, so we might be doing them a favor if we take them out and get what we can.," Roy said.

"Alright, alright, you've got a point, both of you," Milton said. "We might as well take them both while we're here."

Two hours later, Roy and Milton were mostly finished with cleaning the two cows, each man pleased with the decision to risk the journey. This meat would get them through winter easily. Eli stood watch near the entrance to the barn, standing in the shadows and scanning the outdoors for undead.

"How's it looking, Eli?" Milton said, wiping the blade of his Dozier K-7 knife and slipping it back into its sheath.

Eli shrugged. "Haven't seen anything since that foursome walked down the road an hour or so ago."

That group had stopped for a while on the road and given Eli the creeps. He couldn't tell for sure from the distance, but it had seemed to him the foursome of undead were looking at him. And then they had trundled along five minutes later.

Milton didn't know what to make of the way the zombies organized themselves or how they decided to move. Mostly, they congregated in population centers, accumulating new members over time until they reached some sort of density that caused them to disperse. Almost as if they knew, somehow, that the size of their group was now no longer good for hunting the living. There was no way to predict it, but downtown had seen the zombie hordes infest and abandon it several times, so Roy and Milton constantly monitored the activity in town for the times when it was empty. It was then they made raiding trips on the stores for supplies.

Right now, the zombies seemed to be in a building phase, collecting at the state fairgrounds for whatever reason, and one had to be careful when moving through the world because there was no shortage of groups of undead making their way to the collection point. He and Roy had come across a group of seven a month ago after a day of fishing on Tainter Lake. They were standing around the ATVs and he and Roy had had to pick them off with bowshots before returning home for the night's fish fry. They now hid the ATVs when they weren't on them.

"They know we're here," Milton said suddenly.

"Who does?"

"The zombies. That's why they were guarding the shack. Somehow, they know people are using the ATVs to get around," Milton said. "And those people are us."

Roy gave him a curious look. "We killed all the zombies guarding the shack. We hid the four-wheelers in a ditch under branches so they can't be seen. We're good."

"I dunno," Milton said. "We need to get out of here, soon. I think they know we're out here somewhere and they're looking for us. I mean, they keep changing their pattern. Sometimes they're a large group somewhere, like they're trying to draw us in to kill them, and then they're everywhere in little groups, roaming the landscape. I think that's a pattern, like they're trying to figure out how to find those of us in hiding and trap us somewhere we think is safe."

Just then a runner zombie turned the corner of the barn and skip-hopped past Eli into the middle of the barn, its mouth foaming, its teeth sharp in an elongated mouth. It growled, not groaned. It took a few steps closer to Milton and Roy, who were stepping away from the cow carcasses, their eyes tracking the undead monster, both of their bows on the ground several feet away.

An instant later an arrow pierced the shoulder of the zombie and it turned quickly to face Eli. He fumbled the next arrow out of his belt quiver and it fell to the ground as he tried to string it, fear seeping quickly through him now that he knew he had missed the first shot at its head. It raced at him, spittle flying from its mouth as it closed the ten yards between it and Eli.

And then the zombie's head exploded in a mist of blood and skull bits, the creature tumbling forward to the ground at Eli's feet. Eli looked over at his dad and saw him wielding his Desert Eagle .50 caliber pistol, the sound of the gunshot echoing through the barn.

"You okay, Eli?" Milton asked, stepping toward his son and looking through the open doorway.

"Yeah, it didn't even touch me," Eli said, his voice shaky with adrenalin.

Milton turned to Roy. "Let's get what we can and get the hell out of here."

Just then the back door to the door to the barn splintered open and a stream of undead staggered into the room, fanning out as they stumble-walked into the main area of the barn floor. Roy picked up his bow and let loose an arrow at the closest zombie, felling it. He reloaded and downed another.

"Well, Milt, the menu just changed from beef to human. Get Eli out, I'll hold 'em back for a few more seconds," Roy said, lacing another arrow into his bow and letting it fly into the skull of a zombie as he stepped slowly away from the undead.

Eli had already run out of the barn and was standing in the dirt parking area readying an arrow in his own bow. Milton glanced at the meat from the two cows, frowned for a micro-second at the loss, grabbed his bow and ran toward his son. As he ran, he saw a shot from his son miss a zombie, the arrow flying through the air into the distance. His son was flustered, frightened, and was quickly becoming combat ineffective. Milton raised his pistol and put a round into the skull of a zombie.

"Run, Eli, run! Get to the vehicles!" Milton shouted at his fear-paralyzed son. "Start moving!"

Milton exited the barn and stopped, bow in one hand, pistol in the other, and surveyed the landscape. Several dozen walkers were moving on either side of the barn, enveloping it. Something inside Milton told him it had been a trap. He looked into the barn and saw Roy backing out steadily, having dropped his bow and changed over to his sidearm, putting rounds into zombie heads. The slow walkers were about to close off the barn door when Milton caught a smear of fast-runners tearing through his peripheral vision toward his son.

"Roy, run!" he shouted, wondering what was making his friend down zombies instead of flee.

He glanced at his son: Eli stood motionless, his eyes wide with fear, watching two fast-movers close on him in their ghoulish skip-hop stride, his bow held at his side. Milton looked back into the barn, at Roy ejecting a clip from his pistol as a runner zombie raced from the back of the barn. He checked Eli, who was shaking trying to lace an arrow into his bow and then Milton flicked his eyes back into the barn and saw the runner almost on a backpedaling Roy, his friend pulling the slide of his pistol. Milton had to make a decision which zombie to shoot

Milton raised his pistol and fired two quick rounds, bringing each runner down just a yard shy of his son. Eli looked at him.

"Run. Get to the ATV, go home. Run!"

Milton turned and looked into the barn and saw only zombies.

"Roy!" he shouted. "Roy!"

There was no shortage of zombies with their attention set on him. He had only three rounds in the pistol and another clip of seven on his belt. Nowhere near enough to do the job, including the five arrows he still had. He looked quickly for any more runners and started backing away from the barn. He kept his pistol up and pointed at the undead, their shuffling gait an irresistible force. A dead man in his forties in a tattered blue business suit made a few steps ahead of the pack coming toward Milton, the undead man's face mottled-gray, the skin taut across the chin and cheek bones. For a brief second, Milton thought it smiled, a malignant upturn at the corner of its lips, as if it knew what it was doing and knew that its side was winning.

Milton squeezed the trigger of his pistol and the zombie's skull erupted in the back with a spray of brain matter, the body collapsing to the ground. The rest of the horde paid no attention to the newly dead undead, its group attention solely focused on Milton and the fresh meat he represented. They had been hunting, too.

Milton turned and ran after his son, catching up to him at the ditch where they had hidden their ATVs. The undead coming at them from the barn were far enough away they would never catch up, but they were still coming. Milton looked at his son and thanked god Eli was still alive.

"You never talk about this. I'll tell Sara and the girls what happened," Milton said, throwing the branches off the vehicles.

"Dad, I'm sorry, I don't - " Eli started.

"Shh," Milton said, moving and embracing his son in a hug, holding him close. "It's okay, Eli, it's not your fault. You did exactly what you were supposed to do."

He turned and looked at the cluster of zombies swarming around the barn and wondered if he were someday going to have to kill his best friend, or if they eaten enough of him that he wouldn't come back from the dead. He climbed onto his four-wheeler, started the engine, and nodded to the road, "Now, let's get out of here."

WHAT ARE LITTLE ZOMBIES MADE OF?

Enterprise, Alabama - Day 596

Trace Brewer squinted at the three runners as they skip-hopped toward him, a weird gallop he'd never quite gotten used to. Why they just didn't outright run made no sense to him, but, then, neither did the fact that they were living corpses. These wretches had been alive humans at some point, capable of actual running, but death had transformed that aspect of them, too. He took a few steps back, spat some tobacco juice in a nice, looping arc, and felt the reassurance of the stock of his Mossberg 500 shotgun against his shoulder.

Trace retreated a few more steps as the undead closed on him. He sighted down the barrel of the shotgun and picked off the middle-aged black lunch-lady-looking woman with a blast to the skull from fifteen yards, her head shattering into a thousand pieces of flesh and bone. He dropped to a knee, swiveled to the other side of the zombie group and pumped a round into the chamber. He raised the shotgun and put the sights on the teen-age skate-rat's mid-section and blew a hole through him, collapsing him in a heap. And then he chambered another round and watched down the length of the barrel at the fifty-ish fat dude still hop-skipping toward him. Trace waited for the zombie to take three more steps and fall through the camouflaged net that hid the tiger pit, spat out a dollop of tobacco juice and stood up.

A moment later, the weights-and-pulleys attached to the ropes connected to the net yanked the undead man out of the pit and up into the air, where he bobbed and moaned beneath a street lamp while Trace turned circles nearby, waiting for stragglers. There were always straggler zombies with the runners, and a moment later two thirty-something brunettes covered in blood and mucus pushed through some hedges and stared at him. He popped each in the head without giving it much thought, sucked hard on the tobacco in his mouth, and spit onto the ground.

"Fucking zombies are so stupid."

The fat man in the net above him moaned what almost sounded like "brains," and Trace shook his head: zombies didn't have any, so maybe that's why they always sounded like they were moaning about them. He drove his red Ford F-150 pick-up from its hidey-hole nearby, positioned the bed under the net, and lowered the fat man into the truck, banging the undead man's head on the metal floor and causing it - him? - to snarl for a few moments.

There was a groan from beside the tiger pit, and Trace walked over and looked down on the teenage skateboarder, a hole blown through his stomach, his backbone broken. His body was little more than a sack of undead flesh, now, but he wasn't dead in any normal sense of the word. He scraped at the ground with his arms, trying to drag himself somewhere, his legs useless behind him. Trace spat a bullet of tobacco juice onto the zombie's face: it would live like this for weeks, slowly drying out on the inside and mummifying. Trace had no idea if that killed it or just put the zombie in some sort of suspended animation.

He drove through downtown Enterprise, zig-zagging around the car crashes and ignoring the destroyed business district. The buildings on the west side of Main Street between College and Adams were burnt to their foundations, an attempt the previous year to burn the zombies to death en masse. The zombies had largely left downtown after that incident, but there were still plenty around, and Trace made it his job to find them. He turned onto Highway 27 and headed north out of the town and pulled off into a driveway near Lake Charles. He got out of the truck, opened the gate to pull the truck through, then closed the gate behind him. He had raided a fence supply company several months ago and hauled away a couple thousand feet chain link fence - he had been truly surprised to find the store completely stocked and untouched: every other place of business he'd seen had been looted to the shelving. But, then, you couldn't eat fence.

Holly and Charles were idling on the front porch to the house and watched with dispassionate interest as he closed in on them. They had been part of the group harvesting the year's peanut crops from the surrounding farms, and the yard was full of sacks of green peanuts, ready to be roasted or boiled. The farmers wouldn't mind as they were either dead, fled or zombified.

"What'd jaget?" Charles said after Trace had popped out of the truck.

"Fat white dude. Probably a banker or a teacher before," Trace said. "Dag still around?"

"Naw, he'n Mark went out a coupla hours ago to look for salt," Charles said.

The fat white zombie in the bed of the truck began rustling in the net. Charles walked over to the side of the truck and looked at the living corpse. It stank of death.

"Whatcha gonna do with this one?"

Trace smiled. "Gonna bleed it out and see what happens. C'mon, help me get it out to the barn."

The barn wasn't a real barn, but a large garage that was painted red and had a black shingled roof. Someone's idea of an aesthetic joke; probably the rich couple that had lived in the house alongside the oversized pond called Lake Charles. Molly and Wallace Cheever had fled or died last year like everyone else in the Wiregrass region of Alabama, leaving behind a richly-appointed McMansion that Trace and Dag had turned into a squatters hellhole before saving Holly and Charles from a group of zombies in the spring. Those two had taken to keeping the home in decent order, which would've struck Trace as odd for teenager behavior had he ever bothered to think about it. He hadn't noticed that the house had been falling into squalor nor that it had become neat and tidy on a daily basis since their arrival.

"Alright, now, le's be careful when I open the net, this one's a fastie, so he might spring up right quick and try to bite you," Trace said as he tilted the wheelbarrow onto the concrete floor and the zombie rolled onto it with a thud. It snarled and wriggled inside the net.

Trace grabbed the noose pole from a hook on the wall and readied it for action while Charles slipped his hands into some thick canvas gloves that came well up his forearms to just short of his elbows. Holly hefted the shotgun and made sure a round was chambered and the three of them all quickly looked between each other to ensure they were ready. Charles undid the fastening at the top of the net, pulling it down quickly and creating a large opening, exposing the fat zombie's head and shoulders. The creature writhed more quickly sensing its freedom was at hand, but it came to naught as Trace quickly slipped the noose down around its neck and tightened it, maneuvering the pole while Charles continued to undo the net.

"Now get the other pole on it right quick afore it gets all stood up," Trace said.

A moment later, the man and teenager had the fat zombie double-noosed and were fighting him back toward a barbershop chair Trace and Dag had removed from Atkins Barber Shop three days earlier and bolted to the floor of the garage. The zombie was strong and struggled against them. That was the only advantage Trace had yet figured zombies had - they were incredibly strong. And durable. If you didn't take the head off in some manner, they were more-or-less indestructible.

They were almost to the chair when the zombie stopped fighting against both of them and inexplicably set all its weight and momentum against Charles, pulling Trace off-balance and adding his weight to the maneuver, as if the zombie remembered some Judo training from its life of being alive. Charles had been a skinny kid before the zombie apocalypse, and his diet since then had only made him leaner and weaker, a disadvantage the zombie was now exploiting. Trace could see the fright in Charles' grimace as he watched the zombie claw the air between them.

"Hold calm, Charles, he can't get at you even if he pushes you up against the wall. You got five feet a stiff ash pole between you an' him, so jes keep ahold of yer end and ya'll be jes fine," Trace said.

Trace yanked back on his pole and the zombie stumbled, and within a few moments, the two had pushed the zombie into the chair and were pushing him against the seat back. Trace nodded to Holly and she rushed up behind the zombie and whipped a nylon tie-down strap around its chest and biceps, ratcheting the strap tighter until the zombie was cinched to the chair. She then strapped a rubber ball gag into its mouth while it was looking at the strap across its chest. Within a minute, the trio had the zombie completely immobilized.

Trace hauled out a white five-gallon plastic bucket and a length of rubber tubing with a needle attached to one end. He slipped a folding knife from a sheath on his belt and cut open the zombie's left pant leg, ripping a long cut in it and pulling the sides apart to expose the thigh. The zombie wriggled in the chair.

"Sit tight, you're 'bout to become a famous part a zombie lore," Trace said, checking the rubber tubing's attachment to the bucket was secure. "Today we fine out if yer kind can live without blood in yer body."

Holly walked over and tapped the bucket with her toe. "Whatcha gonna do to it?"

"Drain the blood out."

"How long will that take?"

"I dunno, but there's only a gallon or so of blood in a man, maybe more in this fatso, so it shouldn't take long."

Trace shoved the needle into the femoral artery and the zombie twitched, but otherwise made no notice of the event. Blood began slowly pumping out into the bucket, a reddish ooze with the faintest of yellow hues. Holly gave Trace a curious look.

"What's the yella? I ain't never seen any yella in blood before."

"Beats me. Maybe it's what makes 'em zombies."

Charles walked over and peered down into the bucket. "That's a glow, not a tint."

Holly and Trace looked at him.

"The blood in there. It's glowing yellow, not tinted yellow. You mix yellow and red you get some kind of orange. That's red with a yellow glow, and I've never seen a red that glowed yellow."

Trace looked into the bucket and shrugged. "Fucking zombies are just fucking amazing, ain't they? I wonder if their shit smells like lemons? That'd be a yellow glowing turd, wouldn't it?"

Trace looked at the two with a big grin. Holly and Charles both gave him weak smiles and walked out of the garage, Charles telling Trace to let them know how the experiment worked out. Trace closed in on the zombie and stared at it for a long moment.

"Come to think of it, do you even take shits?"

Trace grabbed the recliner lever on the side of the chair and shifted it, straightening out the zombie in the chair and causing it to gurgle against the rubber ball in its mouth. A trickle of blood and mucus slicked over the black ball. Trace looked at the former man and watched as his eyes fluttered and closed. He pulled the wad of tobacco out of his mouth and dropped it into the bucket with the blood, swished spit around his mouth to move the tiny flakes into a ball, and drooled that into the bucket.

In the backyard by the lake, Trace passed by the cage with the skinny blue-eyed blonde video store clerk in it. She had been in the cage for nearly two months, stripped naked and exposed to the sun from dusk to dawn in an attempt to determine what extreme sunburn did to a zombie. He paused and looked in at her: once upon a time, she'd have been considered pretty, albeit small-chested with pencil-thin legs, but some guys dug that look. Now, she was covered with bodily fluids, her skin the same shade of dull gray it had been when he had locked her in there. He looked in the bottom of the cage and then back up at the undead woman.

"Come to think on it, you ain't ate nothin', so why would you?" He walked away, listening to her shuffle to the front of the cage and bump into the bars.

The last few months had been strange months for Trace. Strange not in the sense that he'd had to learn to live with zombies, that had taken some time to get used to, but strange in the sense that he had realized he had an overwhelming fascination to see what made them tick. Or, more accurately, die. Initially, he had taken to figuring out how to shoot them to death, quickly concluding that only headshots actually finished them off. Anything else left something that could still move.

But he and Dag had also realized that ammunition might get difficult to come by, so shooting was limited to actual necessity, and they had taken to capturing the undead and finding other ways to kill them. Zombies could be burned, drowned, and decapitated. Poison didn't kill them, although it did fundamentally alter the undead's ability to function, usually by blinding them. Injecting them with various chemicals produced similar results, but only acids seemed to incapacitate them.

He stopped briefly at the burn pit, a twenty-by-twenty square hole that was ten feet deep. Inside it were the burnt remains of a dozen of the walking dead, maybe a few more, that had been put through some experiment or another by Trace. Several of the undead hadn't actually been dead-dead when put in the pit, and Trace had found their screams... of pain? ... to be curious and disturbing. Clearly, the undead didn't want to die, and they felt some sense of pain, at least when lit afire. When you shot them or chopped something off, they seemed to barely notice the wound and just kept coming at you: it was the damnedest thing.

Trace heard whine of Dag's 2005 Honda CRF250X dirt bike and turned to watch him ride in over the hill on the other side of the lake. There should have been two whines, as Mike rode a 2004 XR400R, but Trace just watched as Dag rode up to him and killed the engine, slipped off the side and steadied the bike on its stand.

"Some fucking Army sergeant zombie got Mike while we were poking around Rucker," Dag said, fishing a pack of cigarettes from his pocket and lighting one quickly. "Fuckin' thing came outta nowhere and fucking bit a hole in his head. I heard him scream, turned around, and shot the fucker."

Dag brushed the hair out of his eyes and tucked some loose strands behind each ear. "Then I put a round through Mike's skull and just got the fuck outta there."

Dag took furious puffs on his cigarette. "On the way out, I noticed the whole fucking army was hanging out at Cairns field, just moaning and shuffling and whatever. When the hell did they come back?"

"How many?" Trace asked.

Dag shrugged. "I dunno, a couple thousand, at least. They were just standing there, where they haven't been in weeks."

Trace scratched his forehead. "We're gonna have to see if we can make these things talk."

"Talk? You're lucky if you can listen hard enough to figure out if they're saying 'brains,'" Dag said.

"Yeah. But one of the things I've learned is that they know what they're doing even if I haven't figured out exactly what it is they're trying to do. They know to come at us, not dogs nor cattle nor horses nor nothin' else," Trace said. "They know we're what they're looking for, and we know it 'cause they's lookin' fer us."

Dag shrugged, took a deep drag on his cigarette, and spoke a cloud of words. "Trace, I don't think we're ever going to find out why there are fucking zombies or what they want. The world's gone and I don't think it's ever coming back."

Trace looked down into the burn pit and thought for a moment about the 40ish housewife zombie that he had burned alive just to see what zombies did when on fire. He had doused her in charcoal lighter fluid and then lit her clothes on fire before pushing her into the pit, which he had already lined with dead branches and scraps of wood. The ropes around her hands and ankles had burned off and she had gotten to her feet and thrashed about in the pit as the branches caught fire, but she eventually fell onto her side and burned to ashes as he tossed in more firewood. She had been the first in the pit, and he had wondered what her life had been before she had been turned, what her kids had been like and if she had been happy.

"Dag, it jes can't be possible that the entire world is now zombies, that the entire fuckin' planet is now filled with walking dead people who want to turn the rest of us who are living into zombies. I mean, what the fuck happens when everyone on the planet is a zombie? What do they eat? How do they live? What's their purpose? Shit, we're alive and we're killing them, so you know we're not the only ones."

"Yeah, but there's now four of us and a couple thousand of them out there at Rucker. It's probably like that everywhere. There's not really much we can do."

Trace shrugged. They had only known Mark about six months, but still it hurt to lose a friend, and plain old living people were hard to come by anymore.

"Sooner or later, Dag, we're gonna to figger out what the pattern with these things is, because there has to be one," Trace said. "Until then, we keep capturing them and putting them through whatever tests we can think of. Eventually, we'll find a way to kill them all in one big swoop, jes like how they all got made in one big fashion. We know we can kill them, it's only a matter of time until we figure out the easiest way to kill them on a large scale."

"Trace, we're just a few guys living in the middle of Alabama. We're not the government or some huge corporation: we don't have any assets. Even if we figure out that diesel fuel mixed with arsenic kills zombies when they breathe the smoke from it when it's burning, well, hell, we don't have diesel fuel or arsenic or any way to get anything we might come up with to spread it on a large scale. We're fucked, Trace.

"We're fucked, and we're going to have to live in hiding the rest of our lives."

"That might be true right now, Dag, but you can't know what tomorrow holds, because it wasn't too long ago that the world didn't have zombies," Trace said. "If that can change that quickly, you better sure as hell believe it can change again. And I don' see no reason not to keep killing them before they kill us. I'll kill a hundred, a thousand, a million, all of them. Or they'll kill me. But I'm never gonna stop killing them or trying to figure how to kill 'em.

"Dag, man, we used to change oil every day and rotate tires. We used to want something meaningful to do with our lives other than go to work, pay bills, and fucking hate on chicks who wouldn't give us the time of day. Now we don't have any of that shit. No work. No bills. No fucking chicks thinking they're too good for us. We've got a calling. We've got something to live to do. For the first time in our lives, there's meaning. "

Dag sucked the last smoke out of his cigarette and dropped it to the ground.

"Our lives have 'meaning?' Shit, Trace, I can't even fuck Marcia Brewer on the weekends anymore after we been drinking for a couple of hours at the bar. I can't eat hamburgers and French fries for lunch. I can't go to the movies. I can't do anything, anymore. I never really hated my life, Trace, I just wanted a little more than I had.

"Now, I got nothin'."

Trace smiled slightly. "And when we kill the zombies, Dag, and you get back all that; you'll feel like a king. Trust me: zombies ain't the future, we are. And we'll be some of the people who fought back, who won the war. Shit, we might even end up heroes."

Dag cocked his head and rolled his eyes. "Trace, I ain't never cared to be a hero. I just wanted to live a normal life."

And then Trace laughed boomingly, suddenly realizing his friend had been holding out on him about something important to him. "And, shit, Dag, Marcia Brewer's living in Daleville with her brother on the second floor of some apartment the flight students used to rent. And she's skinny, now. I thought you always thought she was just a good fat fuck, I didn't realize you liked her."

Trace laughed again and slapped Dag on the back. "Hell, we can drive down there tomorra mornin' and see if she remembers you.

"Now, let's go see if this fat-fucker I'm drainin' has bled out yet. I'm kinda curious how much blood they need to stay alive."

COMEDY OF HORRORS

Plano, Texas - Day 90

    Jessica Heatherington stared down the barrel of her H&K P30 pistol and watched the final zombie collapse to the ground, its head blown open by the weapon's .40 caliber round. Behind her, her teenage daughter Belle was breathing out tears in Morse code, fear of imminent death having paralyzed her after the three zombies had broken down the front door of their home and sauntered in. For a few moments, there was no sound but Belle's sobbing and the scrabbling sounds of Bob Crighton on the tile of the foyer as the last moments of his zombie death-life eked out of him.

Jessica looked over her shoulder at Belle and saw her daughter standing still, her arms slack. Jessica wasn't sure what she should do: smile? Shrug? Nod? The imminent danger was over. But Belle needed some assurance that only a parent could give, and Jessica couldn't rely on the age-old stock admonition: monsters were now real, so she couldn't very well say they weren't.

"Everything's going to be okay. Throw some clothes in a backpack and get ready to go, we have to get out of here, now," Jessica said, her voice chirpy with adrenalin.

She turned and looked at her daughter. "Come on, we need to get moving. It's not safe here anymore."

"Dad was right."

Jessica winced inside. Just days ago, her ex husband had tried to convince them to come with him out of the city, that it wouldn't be safe once the plague got into town. But she wouldn't listen to him, telling him the police and government would keep them safe. He, on the other hand, had never made her feel safe. He had always been too cautious, too uncertain. He was a poor handyman, unskilled with automotive repairs, and as far from an outdoorsman as a Texan man could be. On the other hand, he knew how to cook, could pair wine with a meal, and could talk about the most obscure details of pop music and current literature with anyone. He was a whiz at cocktail parties.

Which is why she had divorced him after starting an affair with Bob Crighton. Crighton was raised a country boy, hunted and fished, followed college and pro sports, and could fix anything. He was the consummate man's man. He was now lying on the floor of the foyer with a bullet in his neck. Bob had said everything would be fine if they stayed put, that the government would handle it, and then had gone out to fish the day before and come home with a bandage on his left arm.

Now her ex-husband Ken was safe in their cabin near Lake Bridgeport with her dog Beau (she had begged Ken to adopt the dog for her years ago, and it had repaid her by preferring Ken's companionship), a safe full of weapons and six months of canned goods. He always said you had to be prepared for the worst, but she had always taken that to be the insurance salesman inside of him talking. The boring, nine-to-five working, bicycle-riding, online-poker loving "I prefer single malts" man with whom she had grown bored during sixteen years of marriage. She had wanted something more than his routine ordinariness, and Bob Crighton had been sitting next to her on a barstool one night while she was out with her girlfriends and had provided the spark she thought she needed to get through the second half of her life with the happiness she felt she deserved.

But that spark had faded after a couple of months, and she had found herself trapped in a new relationship with a balding, slightly-less-than-bright "nice guy" with his own ex-wife issues. When Jessica had found out that Bob's marriage had ended because he had cheated on his wife, Jessica had realized the mistake she had made in filing for divorce, but pride wouldn't let her admit she had been wrong and apologize to Ken and ask for another chance. Ken had settled into his own new single life in the cabin, having sold his insurance business back to the company and written a novel, the dream he had always talked about over weekend cocktails but had never begun. Now, Ken had an agent in Manhattan who told Ken he was certain he could sell his manuscript.

When the plague had started spreading across the nation several weeks earlier, Ken had urged her to let Belle come stay with him, but Jessica had refused because school was still in session and Bob had convinced her "the plague" was just a media scare story. When people had started wearing surgical masks around town, she had wondered what the hell was going on, remembering stories she had seen on television from years earlier when people in Asia had gone nuts over some bird flu scare.

When the plague hit Dallas last week, Ken had driven in from the cabin and begged both of them to come with him. He had traded in his Acura for a used tan GMC Hummer, which he had left idling in the driveway of their home in the cul de sac of Melanie Lane.

"Just grab a bag and stuff it with some t-shirts, underwear and jeans," Ken had said, "and get in the truck. I need to get you guys out of here before the government shuts down the roads and quarantines everybody. You're not going to be safe here."

Jessica had stood in the foyer looking at her ex-husband and thought for a moment that he knew what he was doing, so assured, self-possessed and calm. Had he always been this way?

"Mom, come on, let's do it," Belle had said from behind her. "We can always come back if it turns out to be nothing."

Jessica had almost said yes.

"No, honey, we need to just stay here and let the authorities take care of it," Jessica had said.

But the authorities hadn't taken care of it. Just like Ken had said, they'd closed the city and quarantined everyone to their houses. At first, there were constant police patrols, the city government even using fire engines and ambulances to drive through neighborhoods and use bullhorns to keep the people inside their homes. She hadn't seen any authorities in two days now. She'd woken up before dawn that morning and found Bob not sleeping next to her and made her way downstairs to find the back door open and the patio furniture overturned.

By mid-morning, some of her neighbors had loaded up their cars and driven off, but she and Belle had stayed indoors and watched cable news, trying to make sense of the coverage of the plague. None of the anchors or reporters actually used the word "zombie," but the images of the infected people certainly made them out to be such creatures. And then the power went out and she and Belle had no way of finding out what was going on in the world other than looking through the windows of their home.

Bob showed up before sunset the next day, his pajamas covered in blood and mucus, two other infected people with him, a twentyish man in a Quick Lube oil change uniform, a barbed-wire tattoo curling up from his left arm and around the bottom of his neck, and a middle-aged blonde woman wearing a lab coat and a torn skirt. Jessica watched them come onto the lawn and try to open the front door of the house before they started circling the house, trying to find a way in through the other doors.

Jessica got her pistol from the safe in the bedroom - it had been a gift from Ken on the last wedding anniversary they had celebrated (she had gotten him a silver money clip with his initials engraved on it) - and told Belle to stay in her bedroom. She had fallen asleep on the couch after watching Bob and his new pals shuffle off down the road, but the splintering of the front door this morning had awoken her and Belle at the same time, and each had run to the foyer to investigate.

And there was Bob with a crowbar, blood-infused drool trickling down his chin, staggering into the foyer in his pajamas and bare feet. He was pale, too, as if the blood had been drained from him. The look in his eyes was a mixture of sleep and hate. Curiously, she thought she heard him moan "brains" as he lurched into the house, the other two groaning behind him as they filed in.

"MOM!" Belle shrieked from the stairs as the zombies approached.

Jessica raised the pistol and put a round into the wall of the house, the recoil of the pistol surprising her. She pointed it at Bob again and squeezed the trigger, the bullet piercing his chest and staggering him momentarily.

"Shit," she said under her breath, trying to remember all of the things Ken had tried to teach her about shooting. Ken had told her he wanted them to go a range on a regular basis as something for them to do together as a bonding element for their relationship. It was to be a new version of "date night," and she had almost rolled her eyes at the idea that Ken had thought shooting a gun before cocktails would turn her on.

The zombies moved through the foyer and she took several small steps backward, now looking through the sights of the pistol at Bob's head. She pulled the trigger and sank a bullet straight through his mouth, splintering his neck bone and collapsing him to the floor.

Jessica stepped back a few more feet, paused, and fired four more rounds at the other two, watching with fascinated horror at the eruptions of blood from the backs of their skulls. Her ears rang from the gunshots. Bob wasn't dead, but all he seemed able to do at the moment was move his head slightly as blood pooled out of his neck on the floor.

"Move it, Belle, we've got to see if we can get to your father," Jessica said.

She felt weird having said those words. She now realized she needed Ken, needed him in a way she never knew she had needed a man before: he would know what to do. But, then, he had always known what to do, she had just never wanted to do it his way.

"Five minutes and we're out of here," Jessica said. "Get moving."

Twenty minutes later, she and Belle were backing the Toyota Land Cruiser out of the driveway. The sun was up and the sky was littered with a scud layer of clouds below a high overcast sky. A few tendrils of black smoke reached into the air from the direction of downtown, but she wouldn't be heading that way so she shrugged off the significance. Minutes later, she braked the truck to a stop at the corner of Sailmaker Lane and Mission Ridge Road. A five-car pile-up filled the intersection and automobile fluids pooled around the vehicles.

"Shit, that's Claire and Pete's Benz," Jessica said as she looked at the cars. She put the truck in park and popped out onto the street. "Stay inside. I'm gonna see if anybody's hurt."

"Mom, don't," Belle said.

Jessica walked up to the black Mercedes station wagon and looked in through the open driver's side door. It was empty, the air bags deflated. There was luggage still in the back and a small black clutch purse sat on the middle of the front seat. She moved away from the Benz and around a Toyota Prius that was crumpled under the nose of a Ford pick-up, the eco-car's front windshield shattered by the truck's bumper, a white air bag dangling from the steering wheel.

A cocker spaniel was wedged under the front passenger side wheel of the truck, and Jessica wondered if the crash had been caused by someone trying to avoid hitting the dog. She looked around at the nearby houses of the neighborhood: all was quiet. Nobody was in any of the cars and the chirping of birds mingled with the hush of the breeze.

And then she heard a weird stutter-thumping on the pavement and turned to see five blood-stained people skip-hopping toward her. Lurching, almost, but attempting to run. Their arms pumping, spittle foaming out of their mouths, their faces a mixture of rage and intense concentration. It took another moment for her to realize they were coming for her, not toward her before she started running to her own idling vehicle. She could see Belle's look of incomprehension as Jessica closed on the car, her daughter's eyes wide and flitting between her and the group behind her. Jessica banged into the side of the door, yanked it open and slid inside.

Moments later, the five deadened people slammed into the side of the car and began pawing at it. The electric locks slammed down as Belle hit the button.

Jessica turned and regarded her daughter. "Good idea."

One of the men on the outside pulled at the handle on Jessica's side, jerking it violently and leaning his head against the window, his face filled with rage, spittle flecking the glass, bloody drool pooling out of the corners of his mouth. His left arm looked dislocated and his clothes were soaked in a mixture of mucus and vomit.

"Mom! Drive!" Belle shouted as a pair of twenty-something women pounded at the passenger side door her daughter was staring through.

The truck peeled out, spinning the infected assault group to the pavement as each lost whatever grip it had on the vehicle. Jessica drove across the lawn of a house, snapping a mailbox off at the base before losing control of the truck as it jumped over the curb on the end of the lawn and skidded sideways across the street, slamming into a UPS truck sidled up to the curb.

Jessica's head banged into the window. She rubbed it for a moment, trying to regain her wits. What was going on in the world? She turned and looked at Belle, who was staring through the various windows, her head swiveling quickly.

"Mom, they're coming after us, we've got to go," Belle said, careening to look over her shoulder. "Mom! Go!"

Jessica turned her head and looked through the rear window at the five-some she had just left, each of them again skip-running toward her vehicle. She took her foot off the brake and touched the gas pedal gently, easing the truck forward, not wanting to panic and floor it again. She drove through the neighborhood slowly, alert for other panicky motorists and new groups of infected individuals, unsure of which to be more fearful.

The drive down Colt Road chilled the blood in her veins and let her know that not everyone had remained calm in their homes to wait for the authorities to deal with the situation. The shops in the strip malls near the intersection with Spring Creek Parkway were all busted open, the parking lots littered with abandoned burnt cars and a scattering of bodies. The Wal-Mart Super Center bled smoke into the sky. Belle turned the car radio on and tuned through the stations, all of them set to the emergency broadcast outgoing message.

"This is the emergency broadcast station. All citizens are urged to remain in their homes during the outbreak of influenza in the greater Dallas-Fort Worth region. The virus is highly contagious and causes those infected to become extremely aggressive and dangerous. Remain calm and indoors until local officials contact your neighborhood with the all-clear and tune to this station for further updates. This is the emergency broadcast station."

It was the same message on every station, a message as vague and unhelpful as could be.

"They give better updates for thunderstorm warnings," Jessica said absently.

"What's going on, Mom?" Belle asked.

"I don't know, honey, I don't know," Jessica said, steering her way around a car crash and onto the parkway. "Let's just get to your dad's and figure things out."

The intersection with Highway 289 was a nightmare littered with smashed vehicles. Jessica pulled the Land Cruiser over to the side of the highway and stared at the mass of cars, suddenly unsure about whether it would be smart to try to drive around the dead vehicles and down the roadway. The parkway she was on had been lightly traveled for the short distance she'd been on it, and she'd seen almost no traffic in the neighborhoods before then.

Everyone, it seemed, was bugging out of town at the same time. Probably, she thought, since yesterday or the day before, and she wondered how long some of the people on the highway had been sitting in the traffic jam, going nowhere, slowly.

"Let's see if the Dallas Parkway is any better," Jessica said, steering around an abandoned car and back onto the road.

"It's going to be like this everywhere, Mom," Belle said. "We should go the back roads."

"We might have to, but let's just check and see first."

It was even worse there. Tractor-trailers were jackknifed in the intersection. Sedans and hatchbacks were crumpled into each other like lovers embracing in their final moments. Four-wheel drive trucks and SUVs were abandoned in the fields around the gigantic intersection. A recreational vehicle was upended onto its rear end, the front windshield pointed to the sky, its tires all blown out, a pair of police cruisers crunched nearby.

And everywhere, bodies.

"Jesus Christ, the world is ending," Jessica said. She looked up into the sky at the scud clouds moving quickly beneath the high gray overcast.

There was an explosion of glass behind her and the Land Cruiser was suddenly catapulted forward, the tires squealing for a brief moment against the pavement before Jessica's body jerked against the seatbelt and her foot slipped off the brake pedal. The world moved in slow motion, and Jessica watched as an abandoned mini-van spun across her windshield and T-boned the nose of her truck, the quick pop of the airbag suddenly cushioning her as the truck settled into the mini-van.

For a moment, she was confused, the punch of the airbag having knocked the sense out of her. But as the air seeped out of the fabric she found the brake pedal and moved the gear lever into park. She looked over at Belle, a bead of blood forming at the base of her left nostril, her eyes focused on infinity.

"Belle, are you okay?"

Belle's head lolled for a moment and she rubbed her palm over her forehead, blinking reality into place, trying to recognize the world around her.

"Belle?"

Belle nodded slowly. "I'm okay, Mom."

Jessica looked quickly through the rear window of the Land Cruiser and saw a smashed up yellow Ford Mustang near the spot she had just been in, a thin line of white smoke oozing from the beneath the bent-up hood. She slipped out of the truck and stood in the intersection and regarded the damaged car: how had the driver hit her? She was sitting in the middle of the road in plain sight. She walked toward it and the driver's side door creaked open, a twenty-ish man with long thin blonde hair pulled back into a pony tail and a wispy mustache staggered out of the vehicle. He was pale, ghostly, and his eyes turned uncertainly in his head, as if they were not capable of fixing on reality. He moaned and turned his head to look up into the sky, his head wobbly as if he were drunk.

"Are you okay?" Jessica said, taking a few small steps in the man's direction, just enough to make sure her voice traveled the distance between them.

Her voice caught his attention and his head lowered, wavering on his shoulders as he tried to concentrate on her. His eyelids kept dipping down, heavy with sleep. He took a step and nearly fell over.

"Help me," he said softly, his voice thick as if his tongue were swollen.

He tried another step and bent down to the ground, holding himself steady with a palm on the asphalt. He made a desperate little pitchy noise in his throat, a gasp of accepting his fate, and curled onto the ground. Jessica turned in place, staring at the tableaux of devastation around her: this is how the world ends?

Belle popped out of the truck and stared at the mash of vehicles in the lanes of the intersection, then looked to Jessica with a bewildered expression. "Now what do we do?"

Jessica wanted to shrug, wanted someone else to tell her what the next step was, but the world provided only an approaching green Subaru that slowed to a stop a hundred yards shy of the intersection and turned around, driving away.

"We gotta get a new car," Jessica said, eyeing the Enterprise Rent-A-Car sign in a parking lot on the north side of the interchange. She looked at the Land Cruiser and thought of the supplies in it and shook her head. "Get your backpack, honey."

They walked off the highway and into the parking lot of the rental agency. Everything appeared in place, as if in the final moments of order and clarity in the world, nobody had thought about needing to rent a car. Where would you return it to after the apocalypse ended, Jessica thought, and smiled. The door to the office was locked, but Jessica smashed the glass pane with a rock and undid the bolt from the inside, unafraid there might be an armed employee of some sort waiting inside. Everyone had abandoned their posts and fled in the last few days, but judging from the major roadways, few had made it far.

"Try and find the keys," Jessica said. "I don't care to what; we'll drive anything."

After several minutes, Belle pulled open a cabinet door and stared at a collection of keys on pegs, each with a small laminated paper tag attached.

"Found 'em, Mom."

"Grab one."

"We really don't care?"

"No, honey," Jessica said, "just grab a set and we'll walk through the lot clicking the clicker until we hear a horn. We don't have time to find anything specific; we need to get out of here."

Walking through the parking lot, Jessica felt relief. Soon, they'd have a new set of wheels and a new plan to drive on the back roads as much as possible, at least until out of the urban network. And they'd retrieved a half-case of bottled water from a back room in the rental agency, a boon to replace some of what they'd had to abandon in the Land Cruiser. Not that they'd need much for the two hour drive to Lake Bridgeport, but it was nice to have. Ken would be proud of her situational awareness. Jessica clicked the button in her palm again and a horn sounded two short blasts off to her right. She turned her head and saw the parking lights blinking on a Nissan Altima. She smiled at her daughter.

And then frowned at what she saw in the background. The sound of the horn had alerted a pair of overweight, jeans-and-flannel shirts-clad bearded truckers that she and Belle were there. At least, what else could have caused them to suddenly stand up from behind a row of cars and turn around until their glazed-over eyes pointed at her and her daughter? The two men began shuffling toward her, a relentlessness to their motion. They were nowhere near as fast as the crowd in the intersection a while earlier, but they were no less fixated on her.

She pulled her backpack off and rustled the pistol out of the front pocket. The two walkers were still 40 yards away, way outside her shooting ability. Shit, she thought, if only she'd let Ken take her to the range any of the times he'd tried. But she'd lost interest in Ken by the time he'd given her the pistol, and spending "quality time" with him - shooting pistols, Scrabble-playing or drunken fucking - had become something she'd avoided. Now, when a monthly trip to the range would've come in useful, she found herself staring through the sight of the pistol trying to remember what Ken had told her about shooting and wondering what Bob Crighton had ever brought to her life. Orgasms, but she'd had those off-and-on, depending on the guy, since losing her virginity to Walter Stubbs at a party in her junior year of high school. She had never understood why orgasms were so important to men.

She squeezed the trigger at what she figured was just inside twenty-five yards. Missed. Shit. The two truckers lurched forward drunkenly, assuredly. She put the sight on the middle of the left-one's chest, remembering something Ken had told her about "center mass," breathed in, paused, exhaled slowly and pulled the trigger. The zombie staggered back, coughed up some blood, and shook its head as if it had been poorly insulted at a cocktail party. And then came toward her. She sighted on the zombie's head and fired again, missing. They were now inside twenty yards. She fired again and missed.

"Shit," she said, holding the pistol at full arms length and sighting again on the undead man's head.

She pulled the trigger back again and heard a click.

Empty.

Fuck.

She'd forgotten to reload the magazine. She rummaged through the bag and quickly realized she had forgotten to bring the spare magazine or the box of bullets. She stared at the gun in disbelief, a lump of metal, now. Useless.

"Mom, we gotta go," said Belle from behind her, her voice chock-full of fear.

Jessica nodded and stood up, dropping the gun into the bag and zippering it quickly. "Let's get to the car, quick."

She turned to look for the Altima as Belle started walking when Jessica heard a weird slapping off to her left: a skip-hopping rage-faced twenty-something man in a torn-apart blue business suit, a yellow tie cinched way too tightly against his neck at an angle that suggested it had been wrenched by someone. Fifty yards behind him a gaggle of slow-moving shufflers were moving toward her. She dropped the bag and sprinted a dozen steps directly into a rental agency clerk covered with blood, mucus oozing from his mouth. She bounced off of him and the key clicker went skittering across the asphalt as she spun her arms wildly to regain her balance and remain upright.

Jessica could see Belle turn at just that moment. The look on her daughter's face was pure horror, her eyes wide, her mouth forming an O.

"The key," Jessica shouted, and saw the movement of her daughter's eyes as Belle caught sight of it sliding on the asphalt toward her, but nowhere near her.

The rental agent groaned something and stepped toward Jessica when she was hit from behind and wrapped up like a Dallas Cowboys quarterback getting tackled in the backfield by a Pittsburgh Steelers linebacker who had correctly gauged the snap count. The air burst from Jessica with a gasp and she could feel the bite of teeth on the back of her neck as she was pushed into the side of a gray sedan.

"Mom! No!" were the last words she ever heard as her face was pressed against the driver's side window and she stared into the car at the steering wheel and dashboard, her left arm suddenly pulled out of its socket as another pair of teeth tore into her.

She felt warm wetness spreading over her shoulders and down her chest and back, could hear the grunted rage of her attackers as they bit into her again. A moment later her legs were lifted up and her jeans were being shredded from her body. She knew she was moments from death and something in her made her stop struggling and wait for it. She thought of Belle for a moment, a flash of an instant really, praying Belle had gotten the key and was driving away, then momentarily remembering holding Belle on her chest moments after she was born, how happy that day had been. Then she remembered meeting Ken for the very first time at a tailgate party before an OU-Texas football game, drinking beer and laughing with him. He seemed so easy-natured then, so full of confidence and optimism that she spent the entire day with him. And then most of the rest of her life.

Those were a good memories.

THE WAR ON HORROR

Atlanta, Georgia - Day 274

Chief Petty Officer Daryl "Sandman" Grecich floated down beneath his parachute, his eyes scanning the ground of the Druid Hills Golf Club below him. He'd seen the video footage, read the intelligence reports, knew everything there was to know about what to expect when he and his team hit the ground, but still didn't believe it. On the other hand, he was glad to not still be in Afghanistan, where it had suddenly seemed that the war on terror had lost its meaning. The jihadis he had been killing had given up fighting months earlier, retreating into their compounds and caves shortly after the United States closed its borders to everything.

It had taken Grecich and most everyone else in the military in Afghanistan by surprise when the US government announced it was closing its borders, and that included to them, too. Higher command had assured the troops there was plenty of food, ammunition and other supplies to stay without worry for many months, but Grecich figured that's exactly what the higher-ups would say. Thousands of miles from home, surrounded by Islamist radicals, no reinforcements and no recall to home port. Grecich figured he and his men were as good as dead. But then the local jihadis gave up on fighting them, retreating to their caves or melting into the civilian population, ending their guerrilla warfare. Another SEAL team captured a jihadi a few weeks later and it turned out the Islamists thought Allah was finally punishing the West for its sins, so they were content to wait it out and see what God's Plague made of the infidels.

The men in Fire Base Coldstream did nothing for months. Patrolling yielded no actionable intelligence, and there was precious little information filtered down from above. According to the news, a highly infectious contagion was spreading the globe through every means available and turning people into something that resembled zombies, although most news reports simply called them "the infected." Grecich's commander figured they were probably in as good spot as any to wait it out, seeing as Afghanistan was still stuck in pre-history and infected people weren't likely to travel there.

But after many weeks of inactivity, a helicopter had arrived from the USS Dwight D Eisenhower with orders for all of the SEALs on base to board it for evacuation. Once aboard ship, they had been briefed in full about what was going on in America and across the world. Almost every major population center in the world had been hit with the contagion, and much of the United States' military had been rendered combat ineffective, the exception being most of the Navy's ships that had been at sea at the start of the pandemic. The president was apparently on board the USS Ronald Reagan in the waters off the coast of Maryland.

"Well, D, it seems like the war on terror has been supplanted by the war on horror," said teammate Petty Officer First Class Henry "Quacker" Duckman after they had exited their first briefing on the state of the world.

Grecich shrugged nonchalantly. "Taliban ... zombies ... I dunno, it seems like either way we've got a lot of killing to do."

And now Grecich found himself floating down through the Autumn air above suburban Atlanta, his mission to determine if there was anyone working on a cure for what the Navy was officially calling the Zombie Plague. It was the first time in Grecich's fourteen years in the Navy anybody had bothered to name anything what it was, and Grecich was sure it was zombies after watching the video.

His feet touched the ground and he yanked on the control cords to his chute, braking to a halt and running a few feet to slow his momentum. He unclipped from the harness and let it drop to the ground, unslung his rifle and took a knee, quickly scanning the area while the rest of his team hit the deck behind him. A few seconds later, they reported in to him over his radio headset.

"Garbo, able."

"King, able."

"Quacker, able."

All were down and in position. He keyed his mic and spoke to mission control, "Motherlode, this is Kellogg, we're a go."

"Roger, Kellogg, proceed to objective."

Grecich made the smallest hand gesture and the team dispersed into a well-rehearsed formation, moving forward as naturally as cogs in a machine. They all knew they were in a new environment, a different threat envelope, and they knew they had no idea what the threat was capable of doing. It was a known unknown. Out there, everywhere, were infected humans - zombies - that intel said would attack them on sight. There were no known tactics to counter or prepare for.

The golf course hadn't been mowed in months and was overgrown and riddled with weeds. A yellow flag rippled in the breeze a hundred yards ahead of him, an easy nine-iron shot, Grecich figured. It was surreal.

"Contact left, 100 meters," Quacker's voice sounded in his headset and Grecich turned his head until he saw a teenage girl swaying on a street corner, drained of color and her chest covered in mucus. He lifted his rifle and looked at her through the 4X Day Scope.

"Weapons tight," Grecich said, watching the girl, her mouth deformed with what looked to be sharper, longer teeth. Her hair was a tangled mess and her skin was mottled gray.

She was someone's daughter. Had been someone's daughter. He had a daughter, somewhere in North Carolina with his wife and son. He hoped, still. The girl in his sights was maybe eighteen and acted as if strung out on drugs, just standing still, swaying, her sorority sweatshirt covered in grime. Grecich made a hand gesture and the team moved off away from the girl.

They moved cautiously into the street networks of Emory University, bounding in small moves and covering each other as they progressed. The college was deserted. There were car crashes in some of the intersections, evidence of a mad dash to get out of the area that had failed, utterly. Decomposed bodies filled the quadrangle as the team moved alongside it and past the Candler Library. Grecich paused the team and surveyed the dead: they were laid out as if awaiting removal, some still covered with blankets or weighted-down plastic sheeting. Most were bones covered with remnants of dried-out flesh and tattered clothing.

"Yo, Sandman, what the fuck happened here?" whispered into his headset.

Grecich looked over at Garbo and drew a slash across his neck. Garbo shrugged and nodded. Grecich stepped toward a row of the dead and looked down at them. College kids, he guessed. Probably penned up on campus to keep them safe and in one place while somebody somewhere figured out how to get them home.

And then one of the bodies ten yards to his right sat up and turned its head at him. Grecich almost startled. Almost. He took a half step back, training his M4 rifle on the figure. It was a young man, maybe twenty, covered in sputum and devoid of color, his body dehydrated to the point it reminded Grecich of photos he'd seen of World War Two German death camp victims. It stood up.

Grecich raised his rifle and sighted down on the ... creature. Grecich wasn't nervous, he was certain every man on his team also had the shot.

"Keep your eyes out, I've got this one," Grecich whispered into his microphone.

Grecich flitted his eyes around the area quickly, checking for other suddenly re-animated corpses. Nothing. He watched the young man stagger toward him, murmuring something under his breath.

And then a crossbow bolt pierced the man's skull and the zombie collapsed to the ground. Grecich dropped to a knee and turned toward the point from where the arrow had been shot, looking for the archer.

"We've got armed locals, be aware," Grecich said into his mic.

Just then a man in gray urban camouflage cargo pants and a black T-shirt dropped out of a tree at the edge of the quad and waved at Grecich to come toward him. Grecich pointed his weapon at him, but the man only waved at him and looked around the area nervously. Grecich figured he was a twentyish Asian man, probably Japanese, armed with a crossbow and a quiver of bolts.

"Keep frosty, I've got a civvy to deal with," Grecich said, standing and making his way quickly to the archer.

"I'm guessing you're not here to save us, so what are you here for?" the man said, pulling a bolt from his quiver and readying it in his crossbow.

"Not here to save you?" Grecich kept his rifle at the ready, but pointed downward. "Why do you say that?"

"You're the third team of military I've seen come in and try to get to the CDC, and not one of them has tried to help any of us," the man said. "So, you're probably just another team trying to get something from inside the building."

Grecich was irritated that he hadn't been briefed about previous attempts, although it was possible command was unaware of what the people stateside had been doing while they had been at sea.

"Well, I'm not here to rescue you," Grecich said, "you're right about that. What happened to the other two teams you saw?"

The man shrugged. "No idea. But if they sent you guys here, they must've been killed by zombies before they got what they were looking for."

Or after, Grecich thought, which pissed him off. Whatever intel he was supposed to get could now be anywhere.

"What the hell was that about?" Grecich said, nodding at the body with the quiver in its head.

"Saving you," the man said. "Wasn't sure if you guys knew what was out here and what to do about it."

Grecich glanced at his rifle.

"Not a good idea, man, gunshots are like dinner bells for zombies," the man said, and stuck out his hand, "I'm Hideo Watanabe."

Grecich looked at the hand for a second and back up at Hideo.

"You can call me 'Sandman'," Grecich said.

Hideo let out a short laugh. "Hey, just like-"

"Yeah, just like it," Grecich said. "So, what can you tell me about these zombies?"

Hideo looked at the mass of corpses. "The fuckin' zombies pull that one all the time. They put themselves somewhere where there's lots of real dead people hoping you won't notice, and then they get you when you're not paying attention. I was afraid you were going to shoot it, so you gave me no choice. I still gotta live here, so dealing with a couple of hundred extra undead in the area would've made that kinda difficult.

"And for whatever reason, the undead seem to know there's something important around here, so they haven't gone and joined the super-group that's downtown."

Grecich nodded.

"We get lots of people coming in looking for the CDC," Hideo said. "They mostly get eaten by the zombies."

"Really? What's lots of people?"

Hideo shrugged. "Hard to say. I've seen a couple of dozen people in different-sized groups come in over the last few months. I guess they figure there must be someone working on a cure in there, but nobody can get in and nobody ever comes out."

It took some effort for Grecich to keep his composure to ask the next question. "What's the zombie situation like between here and there?"

Hideo shrugged. "There's thousands of them spread out across campus and in the nearby neighborhoods. Lots of 'em act dead like this dude was, but there's groups of twenty-to-a-hundred of them in pockets. You gotta be careful, the slow ones are real quiet and can sneak up on you. But the fast ones can come at you at a pretty good clip and get you before you know it if you don't have somewhere to get to pretty quickly. And you gotta pay attention to what they're doing, because sometimes the slow walkers are trying to distract you from the fast ones, and sometimes it's the other-way-around. You'll figure it out after you've seen it a couple of times."

Grecich regarded Hideo for a moment and was impressed by the young man's ability to suss out what appeared to be zombie tactics, such as they might be. "Anything else I should know?"

"You know you have to shoot them in the head, right? That's the only thing that kills them," Hideo asked.

Grecich nodded and patted Hideo on the shoulder. "Thanks for the help. Now, you get to wherever's safe and leave the rest to us."

Hideo's face clouded over. "You don't want my help?"

Grecich smiled in the most practiced, friendly way he knew. "You've already given it, Hideo. But we need to be just us."

Grecich moved away from Hideo and called his team in with a hand gesture.

"What's up?" Quacker asked.

Grecich told them what Hideo had told him, and they screwed suppressors onto their weapons. Grecich wondered how loud the sound had to be to attract attention and hoped he wouldn't find out.

They moved slowly through the campus of Emory University, silent as ghosts, steering around the pockets of undead. The undead were everywhere, swaying in intersections or standing near the entrances to buildings. The team passed Sorority Village and crossed over Facilities Management Drive and halted in a copse of trees, each man assuming a well-rehearsed position. Grecich stared across the railroad tracks at an abandoned protective cordon set up by the Army. Up and down the railroad tracks were thousands of bodies reduced mostly to bone and dried flesh.

Grecich whispered into his mic, reminding the team about zombies hiding among the real dead, and sent Garbo and Quacker out to examine the checkpoint on the other side of the railway. Ten minutes later, the team was outside the headquarters for the Centers for Disease Control, a carpet of bodies spread across the streets and a nearby parking lot, evidence of a massive firefight at some point months ago.

A roll-down protective metal screen over the front doors had been exploded and peeled open. Grecich sagged inside: someone had already gotten in. He motioned to his team to enter the building, and Garbo and Quacker made their way quickly to the breach point, paused at the opening, and then disappeared inside. Grecich turned to King. "Let's go."

Inside, Grecich turned on his night vision goggles and led the team into the lobby of the deserted building: a half-dozen bodies moldered on the floor, dead for maybe a week or two. Nearby, two more bodies with headshots lay in heaps, the corpses desiccated, the flesh flaking off their faces. Whoever had blown their way in here hadn't made it any further than the lobby. The SEALs cleared the first floor room-by-room and then made their way back to the lobby. Grecich flipped his NVG goggles up and looked at his teammates in the half-light gloom, ignoring the bodies on the floor. He knew they were dead.

"Alright, King and I will head downstairs and clear each floor, you two go up and do the same. There's not going to be any people in here, but there might be an infected, so don't get complacent. Report in every ten minutes with a location update and scoop up anything and everything the higher-ups might think is useful intel," Grecich said. "We don't want to miss something and have command send another team into this place."

Going down, Grecich could tell the building had been abandoned, not evacuated. Files, paperwork, everything was still in place. Work stations were at rest, still with work to be done. The labs they checked were undamaged. Nobody had run rampant through them, or looted them. They were just ... empty. Whatever work had been done here had just ended.

"Sandman, I think you better check this," King said.

King was standing by a door in a hallway with rooms for patients. Or cells for subjects. Grecich couldn't know which.

"What is it?"

"There's a person in this room," King said. "Or a something."

Grecich walked over and looked through the window, his NVGs showing him a gaunt man standing in the far corner of the room, facing away from the door.

Grecich flipped up his goggles and toggled on a flashlight. The person in the room reacted to the light and turned and moved toward them, bouncing off the furniture on the way to the door. The infected man pressed his face against the reinforced glass and snarled. King gave Grecich a confused look about the person on the other side of the door. Grecich shrugged, looked around, and found the medical folder in the sleeve next to the door. He pulled it out and read the cover page.

PATIENT: HRISTO GRUEV

And beneath that: Preserve Patient At All Costs

Grecich shined the light in through the window. An emaciated man covered in blood and mucus swayed drunkenly, trying to maintain his balance, his skin taut and deathly gray, flaking in points where it bent around bone. Grecich read the cover page inside the folder and shook his head.

"Holy shit," Grecich said softly.

"What?" King asked.

Grecich laughed. It was a short, bitter laugh of disbelief. "The fucking government actually had the guy who started this whole plague in custody before this all started ... and it all started anyway."

"That guy?" King said, shining his own flashlight through the window of the door onto Gruev's face. He turned the beam through the room and saw that it had been totally upended, that nobody lived in the room in any normal sense. "Should we put him down?"

Grecich closed the folder and looked through the window. "No. Somebody somewhere probably needs him alive for tests or something. There has to be somebody on this planet working on curing this."

"Yeah, well, this was the place for that," King said. "And there's nobody doing anything here. Or in Europe or Asia, so far as we know."

"Yeah: so far as we know. And we already know nobody higher up really knows anything concrete, which is why we're here in the first place."

"So, what's the call?"

Grecich shrugged. "We take this folder, mark this location, and set up a passive defense line inside the hole in the exterior wall upstairs, marked so nobody gets curious and anybody who does gets dead. Someone up the chain gets to figure this problem out."

Just then there was a bang against the door. The two turned and shined their flashlights through the window and saw Gruev shoving his face against the door, a thin line of blood-tinged mucus dribbling out the right corner of his mouth. Gruev banged into the door again.

King smirked. "I think he wants a piece of us."

Topside, Grecich was glad to be in the sun. Dark didn't frighten or unnerve him. He spent so much of his professional life operating in it that it was always a welcome relief to be able to operate in the light of day. It was, almost, unnatural to be working in broad daylight and out in the open. Grecich updated Motherlode with the information he had gained and was told to move to the extraction point.

"Contact! Thirty-plus zulus on our right, 100 meters and moving toward us," Quacker said.

They all looked at the same time while also moving into new positions, each man finding a defensive location. Where had the zulus come from? How did they know Grecich and his team were there? He lifted his rifle and looked through the scope, moving it from zombie to zombie, barely pausing to notice the undead faces of the infected. He had long ago learned to turn off any feelings for the targets in his sight, he was just trying to see if he could sense something of the group dynamic, get a feeling for what three-dozen undead might be up to.

"Weapons free, but only shoot if you need to. We're moving to the extraction point, bounding overwatch," Grecich said. "I don't want to get bogged down plunking infecteds and wasting rounds we might need later.

"Quacker, King, move!"

Grecich lifted the rifle back up and looked through the scope again and wondered how zombies had managed to take over the world. And not just any world, but the modern world. Ethiopia, North Korea, anyplace in Central America, sure, zombies could take those places over with ease. But America? Europe? Places with advanced medical systems, omnipresent police forces and first-rate militaries? Afghanistan hadn't had any zombies when he'd left it.

One of the zombies moved out from the group and turned its attention toward him and Garbo, its head lolling as if it were suddenly thinking while scanning them, figuring out something. Grecich looked through the scope and squeezed the trigger on his M-4. The head of the fortyish man dressed in pajamas spouted blood, his body collapsed in a heap just like any jihadi he'd taken down. Everything dies, even the dead.

"Garbo, let's move!"

They made the dash past Quacker and King and took up positions. Grecich scanned the area around them, waiting for the other two to bound past. He looked back at the pack of zombies following them and noticed they'd changed from a mob to a skirmish line, ragged and barely formed. He lifted his rifle and looked through the sight, panning it up and down the new formation.

"Sandman! We got two fast-movers running at us from two-o'clock," Garbo said loudly.

Grecich turned and took his eye out of the scope, finding the two skip-hopping undead coming at them from an oblique angle from the group. Weird. "Take 'em down, Garbo."

A moment later the two zombies collapsed in cartwheeling tumbles. Quacker and King zipped by them seconds later. Grecich scanned the area, looking for some sense to the scenario. Sprinting zombies? Zombies that lay in wait? Zombies that moved in a large group that changed formation? There was a pattern in there, somewhere, he was sure of it.

He heard the arrhythmic poofing of a pair silenced M-4s and turned to look: Quacker and King were laying down fire on a small mob of undead, knocking them down one-by-one, each man as calm as if he were spending a day at the range. At least the infected didn't shoot back, Grecich thought as he watched.

A shadow suddenly covered Grecich and he turned quickly to see an undead woman in a restaurant waitress outfit looming over him, bubbly saliva foaming over her lower lip, a clump of her brown hair torn from above her mangled left ear, exposing lacerated flesh that had dried into leather. Grecich swung the butt of his rifle up quickly, cracking the woman's jaw and sending her stumbling back several steps. He knew he should have just busted her jaw to bits and caused her to collapse to the ground in pain, but she recovered quickly, the foam on her lips now filled with blood.

He raised the rifle quickly and put a round through the middle of her forehead. She took a step forward, a last signal from her brain to her body, and fell on her face with a dull thud on the pavement.

"Where'd she come from?" Garbo asked.

"I dunno, but we gotta get out of this place before it turns into zombie Mogadishu," Grecich said. "Let's get going."

They bounded past Quacker and King, and the SEAL team kept at it for twenty minutes to the Chappel Park baseball field. All the while, Grecich was trying to figure out what the pattern with the zombies was, guessing their next move, convinced they weren't just ambling around uncertainly. The sound of aircraft engines began to fill the silence, and Grecich let his eyes roam up to the sky and track the Osprey as it made its way down toward them, the propellers switching the aircraft from fixed-wing to rotor-craft.

"These aren't your daddy's zombies," King said.

They took up position around the pitching mound, each man focused outward. Hundreds of undead were stacking up behind the fences that encapsulated the field, spreading out and lining it on the other side, probing for a way through it.

"They seem almost like they're up to something," King said loudly, the roar of the Osprey's engines rising as the aircraft settled onto the grass in center field.

Grecich nodded. "Yeah, I get that impression, too."

The loading ramp let down and Grecich motioned for the team to move to extract. He turned to King after watching Garbo and Quacker make it to the aircraft.

"Whatever it is we're up against, it isn't just your normal zombie flick zombies. This infection has changed the people with it. I think we're up against a whole new predator species."

King looked at him. "Species?"

Grecich nodded and turned for a last look at the mass of undead piling up against the fences all around them.

"They aren't humans, not anymore," Grecich said. "They're preying on us."

DETROIT MOTOR CITY

Detroit, Michigan - Day 397

Keyshawn Merriwether watched through the scope of his police-issue Remington M24 sniper rifle as several rage-runners tore into a pair of the living on the street below him, the dead running out from an alley and tackling the living to the ground, biting into them and breaking their arms. He had his finger on the trigger and considered pulling it, maybe putting a round into the skull of a soon-to-be-dead living person, saving them the last moments of horror of being eaten alive. But bullets were hard to come by; fools, not so much. It would only be a matter of time until the walkers showed up to finish eating the couple, leaving behind another pile of humanity that would freeze into a lump until spring.

The zombie apocalypse had come as a complete surprise to Keyshawn. He had never followed the news on television nor read newspapers. He hadn't lived the kind of life that needed to know what went on in the world outside of his Osborne neighborhood. He had always just assumed that what he saw on television shows or movies reflected accurately on the state of the world in general, and the things he knew from zombie movies had never caused him to think there might someday be zombies.

Of course, the movies had gotten the part about the head shots right, so they had to be based on something real. He wondered if maybe something had gone wrong in some voodoo ritual somewhere, with some priestess casting the wrong hex and instead of creating just one zombie, had made it so everyone could become a zombie. It was either that or something had gone wrong in a laboratory somewhere, and a monkey with some genetic-enhancement-gone-wrong had escaped and started biting people. He figured he would never find out what had caused it all to happen, and he wondered if there was anybody working on trying to fix it. There were still lots of living people in the world; one of them had to be a scientist. Of course, there were two fewer people in the Detroit than there had been just minutes ago, so the odds seemed to be shifting in favor of zombie domination.

"You gonna find us somethin' to eat or jes sit there and stare out the winda all day?"

He rolled his head backwards and stared at the ceiling for a moment before turning it over his right shoulder. Shacelia was standing in the doorway, arms akimbo, mouth puckered. She wasn't going to take no shit.

"You ain't the only one hungry," Keyshawn said flatly, "but I seem to be the only one who gets food. That bein' the case, I'll go when the fuck I'm ready to."

Shacelia had been Burdo's girlfriend, but Burdo had gone out to pick through the Wal-Mart Supercenter in the Fairlane North Shopping Center five months ago and never returned. Two months later she had turned into his girlfriend, and since then she had gone from adoring him as her savior to hectoring him over their situation and his duty to keep them fed.

"Key, we been eatin' pretzels and Cheerios for three days now," Shacelia said, unexpectedly softening. "I know it's cold out there. I know it's scary out there. But there's six of us here and you're the only one who can do the job."

He nodded slightly. He knew the math. Him, Shacelia, Burdo's-and-Shacelia's two-year-old daughter Kayleece, Edith and Marcellus -- the elderly couple he and Burdo had helped back to their - this - apartment the day the zombies showed up, and Luke, a nine-year old kid he and Burdo had scooped up and brought in with everyone else, closing the steel security door just seconds from the arrival of hundreds of hungry, angry undead.

"I know," Keyshawn said softly.

There wasn't any food left. Not in the stores in the city, anyway. Nothing to loot or pillage or raid. Entire neighborhoods for blocks-on-end had been gone through and hollowed out of everything with calories before the end of last summer. You had to keep going farther and farther out into the wilderness of the suburbs if you wanted to maybe find a can of something, but you had to be careful where you went because there was no shortage of shotgun-wielding white guys. Zombies weren't the only worry.

"I'll see what I can get."

Shacelia nodded and walked down the hallway to the communal room where they all spent most of their time. He leaned forward and looked down on the street and shook his head: five walkers had moved in on the couple and were tearing the flesh from their bones.

He hoped Burdo hadn't met a similar fate, that he had suddenly decided to head out on a whim and had made it. Burdo had always wanted to live in Florida because it was always warm there, but Keyshawn always wondered why Burdo had left that day on his without telling him. They had a rule against that. But Burdo had told Shacelia he'd heard a rumor about there being food locked in a storage room in the shopping center and had left while Keyshawn had been putting together a charcoal grill on the roof with Kevin and Marcellus. After that, human nature had changed Keyshawn from Shacelia's comforter into her lover.

Three hours later he was sitting on a bench in Palmer Park, a frigid breeze steady down Seven Mile Road, a low layer of scud clouds slipping by above him. But he was warm in a yellow North Face Himalayan Suit he had rescued from a store in Grosse Pointe in the fall when he and Burdo had decided to head out of the city and raid upscale neighborhoods for gear and provisions. Burdo had laughed at Keyshawn when had tried it on - it had been a warm fall day in the low 70s, and putting on the snowsuit made him instantly too-hot, but he had somehow known it would be colder than normal come the winter.

He stared absently at a group of deer that walked onto the far end of the park near Pontchartrain Boulevard. You saw lots of deer in the city, anymore, and he'd heard rumors of bear sightings. Deer had been wandering through some of the deserted neighborhoods of town for years, especially in some of the parts of town where people had taken to planting large gardens the size of small farms. He'd heard there were chicken coops on some of them. He smiled: farms in the city, inside Detroit motor city, car building capital of the world.

And then it hit him: you can eat deer.

He slowly slid off the bench and took a kneeling position, raising the rifle up and looking through the scope at the deer. None of them had antlers. He wasn't sure why that mattered, but he knew antlers meant a better deer. He scanned the length of one and wondered where you were supposed to shoot it. Did it matter? He placed the crosshairs on the head of the deer farthest on the right of the group, took a shallow breath, calmed himself, and squeezed the trigger. The deer collapsed into the snow while the others scattered quickly, bounding into some nearby trees and vanishing.

Keyshawn stayed kneeling and pulled his head away from the rifle, turning to scan the area around him, watching for zombies. Gunfire attracted them for some reason. So did running motors, food being cooked, music, talking, and a dozen other common things. They must remember something about their living experience and homed in on the sounds of things alive people did, Keyshawn figured. Although, in his experience, most people ran in the opposite direction of gunfire, so that was weird.

He waited several minutes before moving, giving the zombies time to get to the park. After none arrived, he tramped through the snow, rifle held at the ready, his eyes roving. Zombies might be dead people, but they still had some sense of what they were doing, and it wasn't unusual to see ragers and walkers working together to trap living people. The walkers would set themselves up to block escape routes while the ragers would attack. He'd seen it too many times, though he couldn't tell how they coordinated it. It just was.

It was going to be a waste of a lot of meat, he realized, because he had walked and could only carry so much back. Maybe it would freeze and stay okay for a later trip for more? He bent down and took out his Buck 105 Pathfinder knife and began cutting off the rear leg, wondering how real deer hunters did this kind of work.

Keyshawn made it back to the apartment building just as the winter light was getting flat. He was exhausted. He entered the apartment and put the front and back left legs of the deer on the counter. Propped his rifle against the cupboard and grabbed a pitcher of melted-snow water. He drank deeply.

"Holy shit, Key, what happened to you?" Shacelia said, her voice panicky.

"What?"

"You're covered in blood! Did they get you out there, baby? Are you okay?"

Keyshawn looked down at himself and saw his snowsuit was stained with blood.

"It's deer blood, I'm okay." He turned and pointed with his thumb at the two legs on the counter. "We got meat tonight."

He looked down at his snowsuit again as he pulled his gloves off and, for a moment, felt disappointed that he had ruined his North Face snowsuit. The thing was expensive even if he hadn't paid for it, and it was ruined, in a sartorial sense. Not that anyone he knew would have ever been impressed had he worn it around them: he'd have been laughed off the block in the old days and he smiled thinking one of the guys would've probably called him "Big Bird" for the rest of his life if they'd ever seen him in such a getup.

"Ya gotta cook it up on the roof. Too many dead around for the courtyard. The wind will carry the smell everywhere," Keyshawn said, settling onto the floor and pulling off his boots. So far as he knew, zombies didn't eat cooked food, but they sure knew the living did.

He walked through the apartment and pushed through the blanket covering the doorway into the living room. The others were sitting huddled under blankets, a half-dozen pillar candles burning in the room. The walls in this room and the two bedrooms were covered with pink R-13 insulating foam that he and Burdo had salvaged from a The Home Depot when the weather outside had started turning the apartment cold inside. It was a ramshackle job of gluing it to the ceilings and the walls, but it kept the main living areas of the apartment tolerable. They had pulled in area rugs from other apartments to line the floors, and each of them slept under blankets and comforters scavenged from the other units after the first frost when they realized their shared body heat wouldn't be enough for survival, much less comfort.

He and Burdo had looked long and hard for propane and sterno stoves when they had finally realized there would be no heat in the building come winter, but everyplace that sold them had been picked clean. The two of them had been amazed that so many people had thought about it before they had, and they wondered what else could be used to provide some sort of heat - and light- for their winter home. They had stood in the parking lot of the Eastland Shopping Center and wondered about alternatives.

"Candles," Burdo said suddenly, "but we'll need a shitload of 'em."

"Candles?" Keyshawn said.

"Yup."

They stood in silence a moment more and Keyshawn perked up.

"There's a Pier One like two blocks from here. Dated a girl who liked their candles because they had scent to 'em."

Burdo chuckled. "We need candles with scent, then. The apartment startin' to smell skanky now that the showers ain't workin'."

They drove over to the store and parked in the street without worrying about blocking traffic. Keyshawn had a Beretta 9mm at the time and kept watch for the undead while Burdo broke open the front door with a crowbar.

"No alarm," Burdo said flatly.

"There's no electric."

"I know. Jes' sayin' is all," Burdo said. "Never even thought there'd be a time wit' no alarms."

"Or wit' zombies."

"Tru dat."

Inside, everything was fully stocked, as if the clerks had just closed up shop like normal and gone home expecting to open the next day. Burdo had joked it had been left alone because there was nothing to eat and nobody needed wicker furniture or bamboo rugs to survive the apocalypse.

"'least not yet: maybe zombies is allergic to wicker and bamboo," Keyshawn had riffed back.

They came out of the store with a duffel bag of candles and stepped smack into an ambush of five men with weapons pointed at them. It wasn't anything special to see, given Keyshawn's pre-zombie lifestyle, but it was something he hadn't expected to have to deal with again: hold-ups.

"Yo, homies, jus' show the sky the palms o' yer hands and you'll be walkin' 'way from here with no extra holes," said a large black man wearing a navy blue watch cap and pointing an MP5 submachine gun at them.

"Toker?" Burdo said incredulously as he stared at the big man.

Toker tilted his head to the side, squinted at Burdo. "Burdonne Watson? You still alive? My man, congrats on that."

"Why you takin' from us? There's a whole town wide open for the askin'," Burdo said.

"Not lookin' fer yer takin's" Toker said, motioning for the others in his group to move forward and search him. They took his Sig Sauer pistol and looked in the bag, showing a candle to Toker and dropping it back in the bag.

"Candles?" Toker said, bored.

Burdo laughed. "It gets real dark at night anymore."

"It do."

Toker's gang took Keyshawn's Beretta next and backed away around the corner. They hadn't crossed paths since.

Burdo picked up the duffel and turned to Keyshawn and shrugged. "I guess we ain't done with the old ways of living, yet."

They walked down the street with their senses wide-open, looking and listening for the approach of the undead. Unarmed, they had only a sporting chance of getting away. Burdo shoved the duffel into the hatchback of the banged-up Chestnut brown Kia Rio they had liberated from an authentically dead white couple caught at the tail end of a traffic pile-up at the corner of Warren Avenue and Dickerson Street earlier in the summer, when everyone had been trying to escape town. Keyshawn had long since grown tired of the taste of gasoline, but neither he nor Burdo had figured out a way to get gas out of a car that didn't involve a siphon. But driving still beat walking.

"Why the fuck they take our guns?" Keyshawn said, shaking his head.

Burdo settled into the driver's seat, fastened his seatbelt and turned to Keyshawn. "Prolly 'cause they di'n't have no bullets in theirs. Shit, Key, I only had three rounds in mine, what'd you have in yours?"

"Five."

"So do the math," Burdo said, starting the car. "They coulda wasted two bullets on us to get our eight, or they coulda just figgered we'd give up our guns wit'out a fight and the zombies'd get us on the way home. Either way, they get ours."

"The world ain't s'posed to be like that no more," Keyshawn said, rolling his window down and resting his hand on the outside of the car door. "We gotta stick together, look after each other. It's the end times."

Burdo laughed. "End times? Yo, Key, time still goin' on, jus' like before. Ain't nothin' can happen to change the way people be. People is people. Some work for a livin', some steal. Jus' the law decide which is which. Nature is nature."

Keyshawn and Kevin walked up the stairwell and pushed through the door onto the roof of the four-story walk-up. The smell of deer meat cooking on a charcoal grill spun around them in the churning wind as they entered the fresh frozen evening air. Keyshawn's mouth watered and Kevin looked up at him.

"Smells good," Kevin said. "Ain't never had no deer before."

"Me neither."

Keyshawn walked to the edge of the roof and looked down into the shadow-darkened street below him, searching for any undead that might have caught the scent of the meat. Nothing but the lump of couple from the morning. He looked over the skyline of the city, the buildings becoming silhouettes against the blackening sky, and wondered if the lights would ever come back on in them. A year ago, he hadn't realized how many stars were in the night sky, hadn't known they were drowned out by the lights of the city, and had never made the connection why he had never seen many stars before. But the night sky was beautiful.

Life had been hard before the zombies, but he had always been able to get an order of fast food or a slice of pizza. Somebody always had a joint to smoke. Fortys were cheap at the corner store. Nobody expected him to put his life on the line every day finding something to eat, even though he had put his life on the line all-too-often. But now he had a girl to keep happy and a make-shift family to feed.

It was different, now. He put his life on the line for a reason, and it was always a good feeling to come back home with something for them, proof that he could do the job of providing for them: it made him feel like a man in a way he had never felt before, and Shacelia showed him a gratitude he'd never experienced from a woman before. What he did mattered, now.

Shacelia turned from the charcoal grill and grinned at him. "Smells good, don't it?"

Keyshawn smiled and nodded. "It sure do."

"You done good today, baby," Shacelia said.

Words of affirmation. They filled his soul and made everything worth doing. Until he had started taking care of these people, he had never known what it was to be praised, to be appreciated for his ability. It felt good, and he wondered - almost wondered - why his father had never visited and why his mother had always gotten high. There had been a life for them that they had refused to take hold of and he had turned to the streets and the life it offered because it had a set of built-in friends and rules. Home life had never had anything to recommend it.

But now he had a family.

He stared up into the night sky and smelled the venison on the grill, his mouth watering. Family. The word turned through his mind in a way he had never thought of it. These people weren't his kin, he wasn't related to any of them, but they had come to mean more to him than any other grouping of people he had been apart of. They were family.

His family.

And he loved them.

FIGHT CLUB

Thatcher, Arizona - Day 483

Garth Davies held his katana before him and stared at the five undead shuffling toward him from the R&R Pizza Express parking area. A little more quickly than normal, he thought, as he watched them approach. He had lured them down West Thatcher Boulevard from the spot nearby the Infamous Bar and Grill, where they had been hanging out for several days. Former patrons called home to their watering hole of choice by some leftover memories buried deep in their zombie brains and activated as a potential hunting spot? He looked around for a sprinter zombie. You had to be careful about the sprinters. They came out of nowhere fast and took you down quick.

Not that he was worried. Just concerned. Bobby was in a homemade ghillie suit off to his left with an AR-15 rifle and Jose was behind the dumpster to his right with a Remington shotgun, although he was using a camcorder at the moment. Garth shrugged and adjusted the football shoulder pads, shaking them against his body and making sure they fit right. He was covered in sports padding: baseball catcher's shin guards, rollerblading knee and elbow pads, and a skateboarding helmet on his head. You didn't want to take unnecessary chances with the undead.

The zombies closed on Garth and he whirled the blade before him, reassuring himself of the weapon's balance point. The undead took no notice of the danger he posed, ignorant or uncaring of the blade Garth held. Bullets worked, but gunshots attracted more of them. Arrows worked, but none of them were any good with a bow. So, the katana. He had a 9mm Ruger just in case, too, but he kept that in its holster in the small of his back.

For the last few weeks they'd been scouting the town for loner zombies or small clusters of walking dead that could be busted up and the individuals taken down one-at-a-time. Each of them needed practice and there was nobody to teach them how to kill the undead, so it made sense to find singletons and gang up on them.

It had taken them a while to realize they were on their own, that after the police had disappeared and the National Guard had never shown up their safety was in their own hands. None of them was older than twenty-two and suddenly the future of the world was in their hands.

They also realized that the supply of ammunition was mostly locked up in gun stores, and getting in any of them would be tough. So far, it had been impossible as none of them had any explosives to blast off the reinforced doors on the gun shops they'd tried to enter.

So, they turned to swords of various kinds they had collected at Renaissance fairs over the years and realized they had no idea how to properly use them, not to mention that putting edges on them had been a steep learning curve. They had learned quickly that you couldn't just swing them like baseball bats as the momentum would leavie you off balance and exposed if you missed.

That's how Ray Durham had gotten bitten their first time out at the end of last summer. There had just been three of the undead, and the group had them cornered out by Bark Avenue on the outskirts of town. Ray had moved in quickly, but with poor footing, his balance off. A fortyish woman wearing a grimy bra, jeans and athletic shoes had stepped forward toward him from out of the group, and Ray had swung. Missed. The sword tip had buried into the ground, and he had pulled it out in a panic, throwing himself off balance some more, and stumbling backward.

None of them had thought to be holding a firearm at that moment, and in the next instant, the woman had grabbed Ray and bitten him on the shoulder, blood oozing from around her mouth as she moved her back and forth, sawing at the flesh. Garth had quickly pulled his Ruger and put several rounds into the two undead men accompanying her. Jose had moved in on the undead woman and cut her right leg off. Both of Ray and the zombie had fallen to the ground as a result, and Jose had buried his sword into the zombie's head.

"Jesus, that was close," Ray had said, massaging his shoulder wound. "I thought I was a goner."

They had buried Ray the next morning in the woods behind Garth's parent's hunting lodge after Ray had died from the infection twelve hours later. They had been having a dinner of canned pork-and-beans when something had begun scratching at the back door.

"Probably a raccoon," Bobby said.

Garth had walked over to the sink in the kitchen area and peered through the window and had been totally surprised at what he had seen pawing at the back door.

"Holy fuckin' shit," Garth had said, "Ray's out back trying to get in."

"No, no, no. We all saw him die," Bobby had said, walking over to the sink and looking through the window at his undead friend.

"We've seen lots of people die."

"But none of them came back to life."

Jose gave him a queer look. "None? The whole state is full of dead people.

"Infected people," Bobby had said. "News reports from the government all said it was a virus of some sort, not that it brought people back from the dead. I thought it just made them look like they were zombies."

Jose and Garth regarded each other and turned to Bobby as one.

"Dude, really?" Garth had said. "It doesn't put people to sleep for a while and then wake them up as zombies; it kills them dead and turns them into the undead."

"He died. We buried him."

Garth shrugged. "Who knows how it spreads? Could be lots of ways. But we now know being bitten is a way. So let's not any of us get bitten going forward: Note to self."

"Keep his attention on the back door," Jose said, picking up his snub nose Smith & Wesson Model 42 and checking it to make sure it was full of five rounds.

"What are you going to do?" Bobby asked.

"Put Ray down for good before he attracts any more like him."

Jose had gone out the front door and around the cabin, with Bobby and Garth watching through the kitchen window.

Jose came to a stop ten feet away from Ray.

"Hey, Ray," Jose said.

Ray turned, groaned something beneath his breath, his thick tongue pushing out against his teeth, thick mucus oozing out of the corners of his mouth.

"Sorry, man," Jose had said. He put a round in Ray's head, and then they buried Ray again, only this time deeper and with a layer of rocks mid-way down.

Garth began stepping to his left, the sword held out before him, his eyes focused on the first zombie as it shuffled inexorably toward him, its eyes locked on his, full of rage. For a moment, Garth thought he saw a sense of something alive in the visage of the undead monster, as if it were calculating some course of action of its own. Garth changed his focus and watched the four behind the leader as they trudged toward him, each one separated by about three or four feet and in a ragged line that drifted to Garth's right. Garth took another couple of steps left and watched the lead zombie separate further from the pack.

And then when the space between them had closed to ten feet, he took several purposeful, measured steps forward, lifting the sword higher, juking quickly left once more and striking the zombie's neck quickly with a powerful slash, separating the undead man's head in a spray of foul blood, the body collapsing to the ground while the head rolled off to the side.

Garth moved quickly to his left and took several small steps backward, watching the other zombies as they readjusted, oblivious to the loss of the first of them. The second in line was a girl in her late teens, her blonde hair grime-streaked and matted to her head. Her jaw had been dislocated at some point in the past and she had trouble opening it as she moved toward him. But still she moved toward him. Garth could sense his heart rate increase slightly. He had never killed someone so young before, and he felt bad for the girl until she made a feral snarl and small dribble of blood-flecked drool oozed out of the corner of her mouth. This was no girl; this was monster.

He moved toward her as he had the previous undead walker and sliced for the neck, but at the last instant the zombie's stutter-walk had changed her position, altering the angle of attack from the blade. It cut only half-way into her, lodging deep into the girl's neck bone, blood weakly trickling out onto her chest.

Don't panic, he thought, and pulled the sword quickly out of the creature, changed his footing and counter-sliced from the other side of the girl with a level blow that finished the job. The girl's head popped off and rolled on the ground while her body fell sideways, dark red-yellowish blood gurgling from her exposed neck arteries. Garth took several meaningful steps backward and surveyed the other three zombies as they came at him.

Garth glanced over at Jose, who was pointing the video camera at the girl's body before turning it back on Garth. Garth smiled when Jose gave him a thumbs-up and mouthed "don't get cocky, kid."

"We got two runners coming at us up the side alley," Bobby said flatly. "You got about twenty seconds to finish these three off before I have to shoot."

"I got it. You wait," Garth said.

The talking had made the zombies start looking around, now aware of more potential food. Garth rushed toward the closest one and easily cut its head off, yelling "the vorpal blade just went snicker-snack" as he paused to center himself on the next undead walker. He moved quickly toward it in measured steps, aware of his footing, keeping his feet near him to maintain a center of balance at all times

But the fourth zombie stuck its arms out toward him as he closed on it, as if it had maybe learned something from the deaths of the previous three and was attempting a defensive posture. Garth had already imagined such a scenario many times and changed his stance and swung the blade through the zombie's right hand, stepped with the momentum of the sword and then chopped off the zombie's left arm just short of its elbow. Blood oozed from the stumps but the zombie took almost no notice of the damage done to it and stepped toward Garth.

"It's a black knight," Garth said, moving to his right and slashing the katana through its neck.

But in the commotion of the last few seconds Garth had lost sight of the fifth zombie and he turned too quickly to his right to acquire it. Then it was on him, both arms squeezing the shoulder pads with enormous pressure, keeping his sword at stomach height and forcing him down and backward. He looked up into the face of an enraged thirtyish man, his jaw deformed into an intense biting apparatus, the teeth thicker and sharper, the mouth wider.

Adrenalin flooded his body and fear rushed through him. Garth slashed the sword sideways into the fleshy middle of the zombie. He wrestled the sword out for another chop when he heard a shotgun blast and the zombie's head popped open and blood splattered everywhere. Zombie blood stank to high heaven, and Garth fell to the ground under the dead weight of the undead creature. He pushed it off and rolled over onto his feet just as the two sprinters came into the fight zone and Bobby took each out with a head shot.

"Yo, Garth, you okay?" Jose asked.

Garth nodded and breathed deeply. "Yeah. ... Yeah, I'm okay. We should probably get out of here before any more show up. I'm sure a hundred probably just heard us and are shuffling this way right now."

The other two nodded in agreement and they quickly piled into Jose's Jeep and headed away from the town toward Garth's cabin. Garth sat in the back removing the helmet and shoulder pads, making a disgusted look at the fetid zombie blood that clung to the plastic and coated his fingers. He rustled around for the bag of wet wipes and pulled a few out and wiped his face and hands clean. He prayed to god that none of it had made it into his eyes or mouth, although nobody knew if that was a way you could get the living death, though it made sense that you could.

After all, if being bitten and getting some zombie saliva in you could turn you, blood in a wound was probably a guarantee of being turned. He shook his head at the thought: who the hell had come up with these creatures? He paused, breathed deeply, and told himself he was okay. He'd gotten zombie blood on him before and had never turned. All of them had.

He picked up the katana and wiped it clean, taking care near the edge so as not to cut himself. That scared him more than fighting the zombies, just the fact that he could nick himself cleaning it and the zombie blood could commingle with his and he'd turn. All because of dumb luck. He'd thought about that a lot, and he was more than certain that there was no shortage of people turned into zombies by sheer, random bad luck. Hell, anybody not just killed and eaten by a zombie was evidence of bad luck: they'd escaped certain death for imminent undeath. He wasn't sure which outcome was the better one.

"Probably death, dude," Bobby said later that night, as they sipped on warm beer in the glow of a propane lamp. "Who knows what it's like to be one of them? Dead, I can imagine, because I don't exist anymore. Undead? What if it's like being totally paralyzed and unable to move or talk, but having full consciousness? Just staring out of your body while some other force caused it to move and eat people? Kill me, that happens to me."

"I don't know, man, what if they can cure this?" Jose said. "I know we have to kill them because that's the only option - kill or be killed - but what if they can come up with a cure and turn them back into the living? You know the government has got to be working on this right now in one of its labs. It's only been like a year or so since Phoenix fell."

Garth snorted. "Yeah, right. The government. Let's see, first they tried to keep us locked up in our homes under quarantine, and then the first responders and police all disappeared and the National Guard never showed up. Those are all government people, so I'm going to guess the government told its people to go somewhere the government people could be kept safe until this whole thing blows over and we're all dead or zombies.

"And whenever that moment finally happens, the government people are going to come out and kill everyone of us out here because they aren't going to take the risk those of us still alive aren't infected."

"They're probably all at Fort Knox. I hear that's the most heavily defended fort on the planet since it holds all the gold," Bobby said.

They were all quiet for a while, sipping on their beers, each in his own thoughts.

"Is it even worth staying here? Maybe we should get the hell out," Jose said. "My dad's cousin has a small cattle farm outside Imuris in Mexico that would be able to take us. It's not that far from here, maybe two-hundred miles. We could make it in a day."

Bobby laughed. "Right, because Mexico isn't filled with a hundred-million zombies between here and there, and if we made it, your cousins wouldn't just kill me and Garth just because we're white guys."

"No, not if I was with you. You'd be fine," Jose said.

"Jose, it's hard enough siphoning gas to get around here," Garth said. "How much harder would it be to do in a third world country? We can't go anywhere south of the border, we wouldn't last a day. Hell, we're lucky we last each day here, and this is the middle-of-nowhere."

Jose sagged as if the weight of the world had finally been placed on his shoulders.

"This can't be the future, it just can't," Jose said. "I was goin' to school to learn how to be a machinist. I was supposed to be able to get a job earning real money. I wasn't supposed to be scrounging food from abandoned houses and killing the undead."

He paused. "I just don't get it."

Bobby shrugged. "Yeah, but at least I ain't stockin' shelves at the store no more. That was boring, man, and it was the only job I could get."

"Nah, man, you could have totally worked in fast food," Garth said, adding a small laugh for effect.

Bobby gave him a limp-wristed middle-finger and rolled his eyes. "Ooh, a zinger from the comic-book-store guy."

"Well, we're going to have to figure out something more to do with our lives than what we're doing now," Garth said. "There aren't any actual rules anymore other than survive, and we aren't going to live a helluva long time in this cabin just doing what we're doing. And while killing real zombies is almost as much fun as it was killing them online, we aren't going to respawn if one of them gets us. Well, we might respawn, but we'd come back like Ray did."

Bobby brightened and sat forward on his chair. "We could just work on clearing the town out of them. A couple a day, just go in, chop their heads off, shoot 'em, whatever, and come back here. Maybe in a couple of months we'd have killed them all off and we could live in town."

Jose furrowed his eyebrows. "And then what?"

Bobby shrugged. "I dunno, man. Hunt deer? Plant a garden? Try and find some girls to move to town?"

"There's a thousand zombies in town, Jose. We're three guys with replica swords, a couple of guns and about 300 rounds of ammunition. Those are some long, long odds," Jose said.

"What are our odds now, Jose?" Garth said softly, dropping his head and staring at the floor. "We can't survive like this forever, and we're not the only ones around scavenging for dry goods and canned food. But if we can take maybe - what'd we take down today? Seven? - If we take down seven a day, on average, we can clear out the town in about a half-a-year or so."

"And then what?" Jose asked.

"I dunno. Maybe we can find a way to start letting the other people know what we're doing and maybe they'll come join us. Gotta be people out there with working walkie-talkies; it's still the twenty-first century and there're plenty of batteries nobody is using. If the people come, we can start over," Garth said. "If we can get enough of us who are still alive together, maybe we can fight off the zombies the next time, now that we know what we're up against."

The three were silent for a moment as each thought over the idea. Fight or flight. Neither seemed like a good option, but those were the only two options, ingrained in their DNA as the essential survival choices. Choose one.

"Alright, Garth, let's do it. Let's take the town back," Jose said. "We know we aren't the only still alive people out here, so we can't be the first ones to come up with the idea. Which means we might not be the only ones doing this after a while, but until then, we're going to have to get real good at using these swords."

Garth nodded. "Yeah, our vorpal blades are going to go snicker-snack quite a lot over the next few months."

THE ROAD WARRIORS

Perth, Australia - Day 169

The sun was just up, casting long shadows across the road. Duncan Wiltshire stayed in them, taking careful steps, his eyes constantly searching for the infected. Behind him in other shadows were Gannon Hardcastle and Katrina Blandon. They were waiting on the military helicopter a kilometer away to move off so that they could continue on their way out of the city.

Which was illegal, as the government had issued an official "bug-in" policy, requiring everybody to remain in their homes until the military and government agencies had contained the outbreak. That had worked until the power had gone out almost two weeks earlier, causing a massive panic when nobody could watch the news on television or tune in a radio station. With the sudden disappearance of any information about the plague, everyone had assumed the worst and had been fleeing the city.

"Okay, it's gone," Duncan said, his voice a loud whisper. He fished a small pair of binoculars out of his messenger bag and scanned the road. "There's a couple hundred of 'em down to the left, but the right is clear."

The road was knotted with fender benders in both directions, the doors to many of the cars open, evidence of sudden flight. Duncan figured almost nobody had driven out of town, and guessed a large percentage of those that had been in the cars were now in the mob to his left.

The three of them had been five just two days earlier, but Gina and Roger Cavalleri had been eaten by a group of twenty-plus undead yesterday afternoon, Roger swinging a cricket bat at a fast-runner zombie that had latched onto his wife. Fatal mistake, as two other runners had set upon him seconds later while a gang of shuffling walkers moved inexorably down the road toward the whole group.

Duncan had put two rounds center-mass in one of the zombies just before it bit into Roger and been stunned the creature hadn't collapsed until Gannon had said, "Head shots, Dunc," and used his own .38 to blow its skull open. Which was too late to save Roger and had caused the zombie horde to realize there was more fresh meat on the menu: they had barely managed to get inside a building and barricade the door before the dead had tried to pry it open.

They crept down the street in a loose formation, the two men with their pistols and Katrina wielding a gardening hoe. They worked their way slowly through a couple of blocks, carefully checking each car as they passed it, constantly scanning for police or military personnel. The authorities had orders to shoot-to-kill anything moving, but they were obviously overwhelmed with dealing with the zombies. The undead were everywhere. So were the remains of their victims.

Duncan heard a grunt off to his left and startled. He turned quickly and raised his pistol and saw a man trapped between the bumpers of two cars. Not a man-

man, but a was-a-man, a human figure turned a deep gray, its mouth deformed and with larger, razor-sharp teeth. It stared right at Duncan and struggled in its predicament.

"Sorry, mate," Duncan said as he lowered his pistol. "Hey, Kat, you wanna come over here and clobber this fella?"

Katrina stopped alongside him and looked at the undead man struggling to free himself from the grip of the bumpers. His mid-section was pinched closed: he should be dead-dead. But, he wasn't.

"That's just...," she paused, reconsidered. "Nobody could live through that."

"I don't think he's 'living' through it," Duncan said, "but I can't say as I know what state of life a zombie is. But we can de-animate the reanimated."

Katrina took a few steps closer to the half-zombie, positioned her hoe above its head for aim before raising it and cleaving deeply into the zombie's head. The zombie torso went silent and motionless between the bumpers.

Gannon walked up and said, "Great, one down, twenty million more to go."

"You don't think it's that bad, do you?" Katrina asked.

Gannon shrugged and looked at Duncan. Gannon pointed. "Over there, look."

Duncan and Katrina both looked.

"What?"

Minutes later they were inside a sporting goods store, trying on protective gear. Gannon slipped an Obo Robo throat protector around his neck and adjusted it while Duncan snuggled himself into an Atlas Pro Body Armor hockey torso suit. The two men looked at each other while Katrina grabbed a trio of Cambelback hydration backpacks and headed to the back of the store in search of a sink to fill them.

"Isn't that a bit of overkill?" Gannon asked, eyeing the foam armor Duncan was adjusting.

"You saw how those fuckers bit through Gina and Roger the other day," Duncan said. "Every little bit has to help."

Duncan caught sight of himself in a mirror and chuckled. "When do we mod some cars for driving in the Outback?"

Gannon smiled. "Not cars, Dunc, bikes."

Minutes later they were pedaling down Graham Farmer Freeway, weaving around grouplets of walkers caught unaware of the silently moving trio of living. A pair of runners had given them chase but had been easily left behind when they switched up gears and pedaled harder.

They came upon an Army blockade at the edge of the city that had been abandoned, and stopped. There were no dead or undead around, just clusters of sand-bagged emplacements and some automatic weapons positions minus the machine guns. They dismounted and poked around the position, looking for anything useful the Army might have left behind when Duncan noticed that the roadblock seemed designed to keep people inside the city. Whatever its purpose, it had been abandoned without apparent use, the Army choosing to fight elsewhere.

"You know, it seems to me that a modern Western democracy with a first world military force ought to be able to defeat hordes of zombies in short order, seeing as they're out in the open and don't move very fast," Gannon said, "but instead, they fly combat patrols over the city and warn the uninfected to stay inside or we'll be shot."

Duncan shrugged. "I don't think the government knew what it was up against. Zombie plague? Really, mate? I don't think anybody really knew what to do and they tried to deal with it like fighting an influenza outbreak. But the zombies didn't act like normal sick people, instead of staying in bed, they went out and started making more of them."

Katrina nodded. "And, they might be working on a cure and not want to kill so many of them, only the ones they have to. Maybe they figure if they kept us in quarantine, we'd be safe while they worked on a cure."

Gannon laughed. "Only idiots would choose that course of action. Have we cured the common cold or AIDS or cancer? And look at how much money the world has spent trying for as long as it's been trying. Nah, Kat, the government isn't going to go all-in on funding a cure that will save everybody from turning into a zombie. I'm honestly surprised that they haven't started nuking cities by now."

As if on cue, a flight of eight RAAF F-18s streaked by at low altitude, and the three turned their heads quickly to follow them toward the city. Moments later, explosions rippled back toward them, columns of dark smoke rising in the air.

Gannon smiled sheepishly and shrugged. "Thank god we don't have any nukes."

Duncan walked over to his bicycle and turned to the others, "Let's just ride. We need to find somewhere to stay before nightfall."

The road out of the city was littered with car crashes, evidence of mad dashes from civilization to a hoped-for zombie-free wilderness. Where there were few people, it stood to reason, there should be few zombies. By mid-afternoon they were walking alongside their bicycles, none of them conditioned for long terms sitting on narrow, gel-padded seats. Gannon had been the first to complain about the discomfort he felt, but when he had made mention of it, Duncan had braked to a stop and gotten off his bicycle and made a series of weird, goose-steps trying to restore the sensation to the area of his body that had been pressed against the most narrow part of the bicycle saddle.

"Shit, I think my nuts are numb," he said, reaching into his pants and re-adjusting his private parts. "How the fuck does anybody do the Tour de France? No wonder that Armstrong guy got dick cancer. This ain't how you're supposed to sit for any length of time."

Duncan looked at Katrina for a moment and bobbed his head. "Sorry, Kat, but it's the truth, and I had to say it."

She laughed. "What? I'm supposed to be offended because you were talking about how your penis is sore from sitting on a bike seat for a couple of hours? Please. My ass hurts something fierce."

So they alternately walked and biked until late afternoon, when they came upon a make-shift barrier of cars pushed together in a line to form a wall blocking the road. It was obvious the placement of the vehicles was intentional, to keep anyone moving down the road from going any further. The cars extended off to either side of the road to points where no automobile could drive around.

The insides of the cars were stuffed with a variety of things, but mostly pillows and blankets. Atop the cars were anything and everything that could be set upon them to make a barrier: lawn chairs, charcoal grills, garden gnomes, sand bags, assorted pieces of masonry and uprooted shrubbery. Whoever had built it didn't want anyone looking through or over the barrier, or going over it. Around, on foot, was the only option.

Gannon looked at the other two, slipped his pistol out of his belt, and said, "Well, there's either living people or undead on the other side of this, and methinks neither kind are likely to welcome us."

Duncan pulled his pistol out.

Katrina looked at the two of them. "What? Are you going to just shoot them?"

Gannon smiled. "Only if they're already dead."

"Stay here with the bicycles," Duncan said, shrugging out of his backpack. "There's probably nothing on the other side, but you don't even have your hoe anymore, so, you're better off being here and riding in the opposite direction if anything goes wrong."

Duncan and Gannon walked around the right edge of the barrier, weapons at the ready. A dozen bloated bodies lay on the ground, melting into goo or mostly bones in clothing. On the opposite side of the road from them, a zombie with the flesh burned from its legs scrabbled against the ground with its hands, its eyes fixed on the two of them. Duncan and Gannon glanced at each other, unsure of what to make of the scenario: there was a second row of cars twenty feet beyond and identical to the first row, built up with the flotsam of suburbia to reinforce it.

"What the fuck, Dunc?" Gannon asked.

"Dunno, mate, but it's most definitely weird," Duncan said, stepping forward and examining the corpses near him. "Clearly, we aren't the first ones to try to get through here. Somebody doesn't want us to get past, at least not on the road. But going around seems easy enough." Duncan walked up to the next row of vehicles and started walking the down the length to the end.

"Who builds a double-fence out of cars and spare backyard objects? It's almost a mockery of being spooky," Gannon said, stopping by one car and looking through the windows. "This one is three-quarters filled with water and has a layer of footballs and tennis balls floating on top. Uh, why?"

Duncan turned and raised his pistol, stepping quickly to his left and aiming. "Duck!"

Gannon spun and dropped to one knee, bringing his pistol up just as Duncan's shot echoed inside the canyon of cars. The zombie's neck tore open at the Adam's apple and the middle-aged man in pajamas staggered backward a half-step.

Gannon pulled the trigger of his pistol and the top of the undead man's head popped into the air with spurt of blood. The zombie collapsed to the ground atop another body.

"Head shots, Dunc," Gannon said, "head shots."

"Shit, we've gotta see what's on the other side of this wall of cars right now," Duncan said, hustling to the end and turning the corner. Shuffling toward him down the road were hundreds of zombies, all now attracted to the sound of two gunshots. Gannon came up quickly behind him and paused.

"Well, we ain't going that way," Gannon said. "Let's go."

They ran around the first row of cars toward the bikes and a bug-eyed Katrina, who stared at them in anticipation of terror.

"What's going on?" she asked.

"Zombies. Lots of them about a half-click down the road, and coming this way," Duncan said as he got on his bike.

"Out here on the edge of the desert?"

Gannon was on his bike and made a quick circle around the other two. "Come on, let's get back to that town we just passed through and hunker down for the night.

They biked back into the little Shire of Brookton an hour before sunset. They rode through the small town for a short while, scouting it out, looking for the undead, before deciding that the entire place had been abandoned. The shops they had passed were boarded up, and the three figured there hadn't been any of the looting that had gone on in Perth in the mad frenzy after the authorities had lost control of the city. These people had vanished, perhaps with a plan to come back once the contagion had been contained.

"Crikey, I can't believe the entire town is deserted," Gannon said as they pedaled around the streets, looking for a house to break into.

"It's not a big town, Gannon," Duncan said. "Probably only a coupla hundred people lived here. I can see 'em bugging out of town if they thought it wasn't going to be safe."

Katrina made a dismissive laugh. "Really? A little town without an airport or any reason for someone to visit evacuates everyone, but a major city like Perth tries to quarantine us all in under shoot-to-kill orders? If there was anywhere this plague would hit, it'd be Perth, not here. These people should've been the ones to sit tight and wait it out. The Army could've probably saved them, here."

"Bingo, Kat, which is why they tried to keep us all penned in: they couldn't possibly get us anywhere safe 'cause there were just too many of us, and they couldn't just let us all leave willy nilly because here's where we'd come, and here we are," Gannon said. "Only, where are they?"

Duncan shrugged. "Maybe they knew something we don't?"

Gannon paused for a moment. "Yeah, but what? There aren't any bodies, no signs of looting, it's just as if they all packed up and left before anything happened."

"But where?" Katrina asked.

"Maybe they've all got family in Esperance like Gannon?" Duncan said with a laugh.

"Once you've tasted the clams from Pink Lake, you'll understand why I want to go there," Gannon said with a wink.

Duncan smiled and thumbed at a house. "Let's break in to this one. It's far enough from the main road that we shouldn't have to worry too much about any of the undead making their way this far into town, if they're still coming."

That night, Duncan took first watch, sitting up in the living room of the house and wondering if the light from the two votive candles was enough to alert the undead that he was alive, inside the house. The world outside was quiet. Too quiet. He heard noises in the breeze that brushed against the outside of the house, imagining them to be the palms of hands testing for weaknesses in the exterior wall. He swore he could hear trash cans being bumbled into, a shuffle of feet en masse moving down the sidewalk outside. And, for a moment, he thought he could hear a chorus of voices on the wind in a minor key, murmuring "brains."

There was a stir in the house and he tensed. The sounds of footsteps softly indenting carpet nearly roared through the house, and he turned his head and gripped his pistol.

"You're still awake, nice," Gannon said as he turned the corner into the room. "I was trying to be quiet so as to give you a start when I touched your shoulder."

Duncan smiled. "I heard you a mile away."

"Heard anything outside?"

"Not a sound."

"I wonder if that's a good thing," Gannon said, walking to the windows and pulling a curtain aside an inch. Duncan's eyes widened and his gut tensed. "Nothing out there."

"So, whaddya think we should do? Continue the plan to ride until we find a safe haven, or maybe hunker down here and see if we can ride things out?"

Gannon shrugged. "The people who lived here didn't see a future in staying here, and there's a couple-hundred of undead just a mile or two outside of here on the other side of a double wall of parked cars blocking the main road.

"Somebody tried something to keep the town safe, but nobody stayed. I'm guessing there's a good reason for that."

"So we keep riding for Esperance?"

"That was our plan."

"Then we have to spend tomorrow finding a four-wheeler and then find all the gas we can and mod out a vehicle," Duncan said. "This biking shit is going to get us killed."

It took most of the next day going house-to-house before they found the keys to a car that was acceptable to them: a 1979 Toyota LandCruiser

"You really want to risk our lives in this?" Duncan said. "It's almost a half-century old."

"Believe me, Dunc, this is what you want in the end times, not some fancy shmancy Beemer four-wheeler made last year for the tennis set," Gannon said, starting it up and listening to the rumble of the engine. "This was made for the wilderness, not for tooling around town with a bunch of kids in the back so you're not embarrassed to be driving a mini-van."

"Yeah, but if it breaks down, we're screwed."

Gannon shook his head. "No way, mate. If a modern car breaks down, now that we're in the apocalypse of zombies, then you're screwed. You can't fix a modern car on your own because of the way they're made: the engine's a square bit of plastic with wires coming out of it. You need a computer and a rocket scientist to fix 'em. But this you can fix with a wire hanger and electrical tape, and you can make spare parts out of metal cans, plastic tubing and spare coins."

Duncan raised his eyebrows querulously.

Gannon grinned. "But why the worry? Whoever owned this has kept it up. Ignore the mileage and it might as well be brand new."

Katrina came out the front door of the house next-door with a canvas bag and smiled.

"More food," she said.

"This town is a gold mine," Gannon said, getting out of the car and closing the door.

Katrina walked up to them and dropped the bag on the ground. "I figure we got a week or two's worth of food and water now, so we should be good."

"For a week or two, sure," Duncan said. "And then what?"

Gannon shrugged. "Well, hopefully everything will be peachy in Esperance. If not, we do like we just done here, stock up and move on. There's gotta be a safe haven somewhere."

Highway 40 southeast out of Brookton was mostly open roadway, with a few broken-down cars pulled off to the side. They had all expected zombie infestations, but each of the small towns they had passed through had been empty, as if the inhabitants had left in an orderly manner. Gannon slowed the LandCruiser down as they passed through them, hoping a living person would emerge with news, but nobody had, and they had goosed the speed back up exiting each place. They were all dead. Or undead. Or hiding.

Gannon lifted his foot off the gas pedal as they neared the intersection with the South Coast Highway, letting the vehicle coast the last kilometer with the engine idling. The three of them scanned the countryside. Duncan picked up the binoculars from the seat and looked through them at the intersection.

"Holy shit."

"What?" Katrina asked.

Duncan pulled the binoculars away from his eyes and handed them to her. She looked through them for several long seconds before gasping. "My god."

"Alright, enough with this, what is it?" Gannon asked.

Erected across the intersection, barring easy driving access to the highway toward Ravensthorpe was a make-shift barricade straight out of Middle Ages. It was fifteen feet high, constructed of hewn trees lashed and nailed together in five large Xs and braced with concrete barriers at the base to withstand attempts to ram through it. Tied to the Xs were undead, splayed out, alive in their undead state, moaning.

"I don't know what's scarier, this barrier or the thought of the mates who went to the trouble to construct it," Gannon said, hefting his weapon and walking around to the back of the gate, examining it. "It's not meant to be rolled aside, neither."

Duncan laughed.

"What"

"What the hell's the point of it?" Duncan asked. "It's not going to scare anybody off but somebody has now put up a couple of these fucking things. First the wall of cars, and now this."

Gannon shrugged. "Yeah, you really have to wonder why the fuck the drama? It's one thing to build a wall; another thing to tie the undead to it." He motioned with his pistol down the road: "Shall we, then?"

They motored slowly down the coast highway into Ravensthorpe, the road changing name to Morgans Street, giving anybody who might be watching a long time to scan them and realize they meant no harm. Inside the town limits, everything was quiet. Abandoned. There was some sign of pandemonium, but for the most part the town resembled the last: left behind in an ordered fashion, ready for repopulating.

The police station was ringed with sand bags four feet high, a measure of concertina wire topping portion where the defensive perimeter turned around the corners of the walls, the windows boarded over with small slits cut into them. No sign of a struggle to the end, however, just evidence of preparation for a fight.

"Hey, look, a pharmacy," Duncan said. "Maybe we should see if there's anything left inside?"

Gannon chuckled. "They bricked the front doors over with cinder blocks."

They stopped the LandCruiser and got out, each looking around at the structures lining the main street through town. All of them were securely boarded up, many with make-shift defensive positions built into the main entryway to the building or on a corner of the lot.

"I think these people were expecting a fight and then chickened out," Gannon said, scratching the stubble under his chin.

"Maybe they found a better option," Katrina said.

"Maybe," Gannon said. "But they didn't want anyone snooping in their stuff after they left, so we should probably just move on to Esperance. A couple of hours and we should be there."

Duncan pointed to the Eagle Fuel petrol station as they were nearing the fork in the road that exited town. "First, maybe we should fuel up. And maybe see if there aren't a few jerry cans around for extra, just in case."

"Just in case what?" Katrina asked.

"Just in case we have to go somewhere else all the sudden."

The drive had taken twice as long as it should have. Abandoned cars were parked behind car crashes that were sometimes a half-kilometer long, necessitating the pushing of cars to the side. Decayed bodies of the dead were everywhere, a mixture of killed undead and the dead living. Whatever had happened, the people in Ravensthorpe appeared to have fought a rear guard action down most of the highway toward Esperance, making little last-ditch stands here and there to gain minutes or meters for the rest.

They managed to scoop up a Weatherby Mk V Sporter bolt-action rifle and a pair of Sig Sauer 9mm pistols at one such defensive position, the owners of the weapons having been eaten to death. Gannon handed one of the pistols to Katrina along with an extra clip, giving her a twenty-second demonstration on how to use the weapon.

They drove the final twenty kilometers in silence, watching as the plumes of smoke in the distance grew thicker as they approached the coastal city. They were forced to stop as they approached Pink Lake on their right and Lake Warden on their left: a make shift fence of every conceivable vehicle and large object had been strewn between the two bodies of water, five-hundred meters of Toyotas, Audis, Hondas, cement barriers, tree trunks and construction site detritus. Bodies were everywhere.

Gannon brought the truck to a halt. He got out and started lacing on the sporting goods protective equipment they had picked up the day before.

"What are you doing?" Duncan asked.

"Getting my kit on," Gannon said. "You two should do the same."

"You want to find a way in there?"

"We gotta take a look. We're here."

Duncan and Katrina glanced at each other incredulously. From a distance, it appeared the entire town was afire, tens of columns of smoke boiling thousands of feet into the air before the winds aloft bent them inland.

"The entire town's on fire, Gannon," Katrina said.

He shrugged. "My brother and his family are in there. They've got a nice little house in the West Beach area, not far from the ocean. Nice neighborhood. We get there, we'll be okay."

"And if we can't get there?" Duncan asked.

"We go in as far as we can. If we can't get there ..." Gannon trailed off and cocked his head to the side. He gazed across the surface of the lake, the algae giving the heavy salt concentration of the water a pink complexion the color of a lipstick an ex-girlfriend of his had worn as her signature color. He had told her that pink wasn't a real color but an illusion, something the human brain concocted to make sense of red and violet wavelengths entering the eye at the same time. She had asked him why that didn't make pink things invisible instead? He smiled for a moment thinking about her and now, staring at the lake, he saw the beauty in the color's defiance of nature's water colors palette. He wondered if the undead appreciated nature, if they noticed it for its beauty, if they were somehow a part of nature, like insects, sharks and viruses, serving some vital element of the ecosystem, or if they were some cosmic joke.

He wondered if the dead could see pink?

Gannon turned and glanced at the smoke in the sky, could hear the faint whines of sirens in the distance. "If we can't get there, then we turn around. Go somewhere else. This isn't a bloody suicide mission."

They managed their way into town weaving between the shore of Pink Lake and Collier Road, Gannon steering the LandCruiser while Duncan kept watch for the undead. It didn't take long to run into them: near the intersection with Longbottom Lane, a thousand undead stood amassed, churning in place as if awaiting orders to deploy. Gannon stopped the truck.

Just then, a pair of zombies stepped out of the crowd, one on either edge of the mass of undead, and regarded the arrival of their vehicle. Each took staggering steps toward them, and the mob behind began to turn as well. Gannon rested his head on the steering wheel.

"Runner!" Katrina shouted from the back seat. "On the left by the building over there!"

Duncan looked out his window and saw a teenage boy skip-hopping furiously toward their truck, maybe fifty meters away, spittle flying from his mouth, a small, hand-held garden rake in one hand. Duncan glanced quickly over at Gannon.

"Mate, we gotta go, we got a tsunami of undead headed our way."

Gannon nodded and put the truck back in gear. He grimaced and shook his head. He turned to Duncan, "Where d'ya think, mate? Maybe the north coast? What's up there? South Hedland? Broome? Darwin? Can't be many zombies up there as there never were many people.

Maybe make a go of it there? If not, there's gotta be someplace else, right?"

Duncan nodded. "Never been to the north coast. Always meant to see the country on a driving tour. Now seems about the right time."

"We gotta go, this runner's almost here," Katrina said from the back seat. "I vote for whereverthefuck."

Gannon laughed. "Right, then, whereverthefuck here we come."

THE CORONER'S REPORT

Monclova, Mexico - Day 499

The thunderstorm crackled and popped, the wind howled and hurled sheets of rain against the building. From the ceiling in the room, a few leaks had started letting in a steady stream of water droplets which pooled on the dirt floor and made splotches of mud. Noelys Sanchez stumbled drunkenly across the floor, oblivious to the storm and the raindrops, her head lolling atop her shoulders, blood-infused drool seeping out of the corners of her mouth. She banged into a wall and paused, her eyes searching the room, unable to focus on anything. She took a few steps away from the wall, vomited a small measure of blood, and collapsed to her hands and knees.

She took a few more shallow breaths, paused, and sucked deeply on the air in the room before lowering herself to the dirt and curling into the fetal position. Noelys closed her eyes for the last time and Carlos Trejo looked at his watch: thirteen hours and nine minutes from the moment of infection to death.

Now, he had to wait to see if she returned to life. Well, unlife, undeath, nobody knew what state the infected resurrected into. Although there was a significant chance that she might remain dead: about thirty percent of those infected never arose again. Curiously, nobody had ever recovered from the infection; it was either death or undeath. He noted the time of death on the medical form and slipped the sheet into the manila folder with her name on it.

Carlos made his way through the mansion to his study, poured himself three-fingers of Herradura Reposado Antiguo tequila, and sat at his desk. The storm raged louder as the cell at its center made its way over the city, and the candles on his desk flickered. He looked at the hand-drawn spreadsheets he'd made on the nature of the disease, flipped through the various home-made charts detailing his scientific findings, and wondered if there was any way to make sense of the data. What he wouldn't give for access to a computerized data base that could crunch the numbers and maybe let him see some larger pattern at work. He wondered if somewhere in America or Europe there was a laboratory still capable of modern science, or if the entire world had fallen into a new Dark Ages.

Lightning rippled across the sky followed by a crack of thunder. So much for humanity destroying the planet. Now, Mother Nature was allied with the undead to undo everything man had achieved. Already, the earth was taking back the city as plants took root in places where men had once maintained civilization. Wild animals roamed the streets. He wondered what a world run by zombies would look like. Did they have some sort of purpose greater than killing? Would the zombies eventually die out when there were no living to feed upon.

Carlos awoke at dawn, the night's storm having given way to a normal day of blue skies. He looked through his bedroom window at the city and saw smoke in the distance, evidence of a building somewhere in the city having caught fire. There was no one to put it out, and he half-wondered when such a fire would consume the entire city rather than just a block. Time was not on the side of the living.

He made his way to the observation chamber and looked in on Noelys Sanchez. She was still curled up on the dirt floor, dead. He checked his watch - it had only been nine hours since death, so she was still within the resurrection timeframe. He made a note on her file and scratched the four-day stubble on his chin. Behind him, the door to the observation deck creaked open and he smelled coffee.

"She turn, yet?

Carlos shrugged and turned toward Federico, his assistant. Federico stepped to him and handed him a mug of coffee and looked down at Noelys.

"No, she's still dead," Carlos said.

"So, we're going to wait?"

Carlos nodded and sipped his mug. "We now know the disease is contagious through the air, but we need to figure out if this is a major pathway to infection or if there is some other mechanism at work. Not everyone infected can have been bitten, first, because the undead seem to prefer eating the living as to converting them. There has to be a reason why so many have been infected."

Carlos savored another sip from his coffee and looked down on the girl, wondering if she might recover instead of revive as undead. There had to be someone who was resistant to infection. If she came back to as living, her blood samples would be worth more than gold. He smiled at that thought. What was gold worth in a world where it could not be spent? Indeed, why had gold ever been considered a source of wealth? It was just a metal, and a soft one a that. And, yet, for the entire history of mankind, gold was a highly desirable commodity that people killed for. Gold? Carlos sipped his coffee. An ounce of gold was useless anymore. A can of tuna was priceless.

"You keep an eye on her and record any changes. Her file is over there on the table. I'm going to go out and see what I can find."

He hated going into the towns because that's where the undead were. It was also where the living went in search of the dwindling supplies of dry and canned goods that could be found in abandoned homes. Every trip could be his last as there was no way of knowing if that was the day a herd of zombies had moved through in search of living flesh. And every building he entered harbored the possibility of a loner zombie laying dormant waiting for an opportunity. Carlos often wondered if there was a structure to the zombie menace, if there were a hierarchy that caused some to form into raiding groups that roamed the landscape while others waited patiently in spots that only they could have determined to be strategic to their cause.

But they were everywhere.

He moved through the town cautiously, keeping to the shadows of buildings as much as possible while scouting his next move through the open. Most of the houses had been gone through in the neighborhood, their doors open. Some of them opened by him in previous trips. He sagged against the wall of a house and wondered at the futility of it all: with nobody producing any food, it was only a matter of time until everyone was either dead or undead. His work on a cure would be for naught.

"I don't think this is a good idea. Every time we stop in a town looking for gas we end up running for our lives. There's got to be another way to get out of this fucking country."

Carlos froze at the sound of an American voice speaking English. A female voice. He cradled his AK-74 in his lap and listened harder.

"Yeah, well, Kate, the only place to get gas in this third-world hell-hole is towns like this. So it's not like we have a choice. It's this or walking, and the last time we tried walking we all nearly got eaten."

A man's voice. Carlos started scanning the area: they were near. He moved away from the wall he was leaning on and stepped several feet closer to the sounds of the voices.

"Quit arguing, you two, there's a dozen or so cars still parked on this street. We can get the gas out of them and we'll be on our way."

A different man's voice. Carlos edged his way along the side of the house, getting closer to the road. He peeked around the corner of the house and saw four Americans standing at the front of a beaten up Ford pick-up. They were college kids. Probably stuck in the country since a spring break vacation just before the plague outbreak. None of them seemed armed with anything more dangerous than kitchen knives and camping axes. He was amazed they were still alive.

"Maybe we should check a couple of houses for food while the rest of us are getting gas?"

That was a brunette with her hair pulled back into a ponytail that fell to her mid-back.

Another young man nodded. "Why don't Gail and I check a couple of the houses for something to eat while the rest of us syphon?"

Carlos stayed still for the next thirty minutes, watching the Americans at work. He could tell they had been doing this for a while, syphoning gasoline from abandoned vehicles. Maybe all they needed to survive were knives and axes? The zombie apocalypse had had a side-effect he hadn't anticipated, which was that it honed the survival instincts of those who remained alive. In any case, four was more than he could handle, even with a machine-gun.

And then he noticed a pair of the undead stagger from between two buildings down the street, between the American's car and the De La Revolucion Mexicana highway. Carlos found it curious that after turning onto the street, the two zombies paused, swayed, their heads turning in what seemed uncertain scans of the area. Carlos looked up the street and saw the two Americans on syphoning duty comparing their take, discussing whether or not what they had filled into their plastic containers was enough. Talking too loudly, like typical Americans.

"Yo, guys, this neighborhood has been totally picked out," said a shaggy-haired blond man holding a can in each hand. "We've been in about fifteen houses and pulled out a can of pork-and-beans and some Chef Boy-ar-Dee beef ravioli."

One of the men with a gas can laughed. "Mexicans eat that stuff?"

"Holy fuck, runners!" said the other man, dropping his gas can to point down the street.

Carlos turned his head and saw the two undead skip-hopping madly toward the three on the street. These ones were fast. Without thinking, Carlos raised his AK and drew a bead on the zombie on the left, followed it for a few beats and squeezed the trigger. The bullet tore into the walker's shoulder and caused the creature to stumble into the one next to it. Carlos aimed again and put a round through its skull, breathed shallowly and plunked the other runner through the ear, shattering its skull.

Carlos kept the rifle snugged into his shoulder and took several steps out of the shadow he had been in, scanning down the road toward where the pair of zombies had come. He was sure there would be more. There always were more.

And there were. Within seconds streams of the undead erupted from between the houses, shuffling toward the street. Forty? Eighty? More? Carlos pointed his weapon at them and swept it between the groups for a moment, wondering if he should shoot. He looked over his shoulder at the Americans, all of whom were now armed with bladed weapons, and turned back to the zombies. The Americans would not be getting back to their vehicle today.

He backpedaled toward the Americans, weapon pointed at the zombies.

"If you want to get out of here alive, come with me," Carlos said in fluent English.

"Mike, what the fuck are we going to do?" Gail asked.

The shaggy blond man shook his head. "I think we listen to the guy with the gun."

The Americans stood still a moment longer, as if sizing up their ability to fight the horde and make it to their vehicle. Carlos was nearing his own panic threshold, staring at the streams as they formed into a horde and came at them. He focussed.

"Please. Come with me. My truck is two blocks away. We can come back tomorrow and get you on your way, but right now, we have to go," Carlos said.

A runner broke from the pack, spittle spewing from its mouth. Carlos shot, missed, shot again and brought it down.

"We have to go now."

"Mike?" Ken said.

Mike looked at Carlos. "Let's go. Lead the way."

Carlos looked them and motioned over his shoulder with his head, and then began a slow run toward his truck. He looked behind himself several times and was pleased the Americans were following him. The zombies had fallen far behind by the time he broke from a yard onto the street his Chevy Suburban was parked. He pulled the keychain from his pocket and clicked the "unlock" button, the car emitting a bleat to the world. He pressed the button on the fob for autostart and pointed to the car as Ken came from between the houses.

"There, the blue Chevy truck, go," Carlos said.

Ken stopped alongside him and turned toward his friends.

"Come on, we're almost there, the blue Suburban right over here," Ken said, waving his friends him and pointing toward the idling vehicle.

"Shotgun!" Mike said as he tore across the front lawn toward the truck. Carlos looked at Ken and saw he was smiling and shrugging. No gun was involved.

Moments after Mike rushed by him, the two women rounded the corner and followed Ken's direction to the truck, both piling through the same door and shouting for Ken to hurry up while Carlos back-stepped toward the vehicle, rifle raised. Carlos entered the truck and passed the rifle over to Mike, who put it on his lap and turned his head to look out the passenger side window. For an instant, Carlos wondered if he had just given up control of the situation, arming the American with the AK. He let go of that fear quickly and tapped Mike on the shoulder.

"You know how to use one of those?"

Mike glanced down at the gun, shrugged and smiled. "Just point and shoot, dude. I've had to use a couple of AKs in the last year. No worries."

This perplexed Carlos. "Why aren't any of you armed if you've had weapons in the past?"

"Guns are easy to find here in Mexico. Bullets, not so much," Mike said. "We got a boatload of guns in the back of the pick-up, but none of them have any bullets in them."

"Zombies right behind us!" Kate yelled.

Carlos glanced into the rearview mirror and started the car, peeling out on the gravel and fishtailing as he pressed down on the gas. Carlos eased up, calmed down and began to drive quickly through a few turns of city streets before taking a road out of the city. The countryside flashed by, a mixture of abandoned farms and empty landscapes. In the backseat, the two girls and Ken talked about how close a call that had just been, and Carlos smiled: he had saved quite a few people from the clutches of the undead, but never any foreigners. Perhaps his luck was going to change, and he'd make some progress in figuring out how the zombie plague spread?

They drove for about fifteen minutes before Carlos turned the truck off the main paved road and down a dirt driveway. As they approached a gate in a fence that extended off to either side of the road, Carlos pressed a button on a box attached to the sun visor and the gate slowly swung open. He sensed Mike looking at him and turned his head and smiled.

"My home, my new friends, is your home for the night."

Carlos parked the truck on a paved driveway in front of a sprawling mansion, alongside a blue Toyota Prius and a silver Porsche 911, both covered in thick dust. He walked away from the truck and to the front porch and turned to await the Americans as they exited the Suburban. He could tell they were dumbfounded by their luck by the way they stared at the house. He was happy they felt safe. They walked up to him as a group and stopped. Federico opened the front door to the house and stepped outside and gave a look to Carlos that only he would know meant Federico was surprised by the sudden arrangement.

"I still have hot and cold running water, but there isn't any electricity, so if you want to bathe, I suggest you do it soon, before the sun goes down. My assistant Federico here will show you to your rooms."

Ken looked at the others and smiled. "Hot showers? Rooms? I think we're finally on vacation!"

Carlos took the rifle from Mike and looked at the group of smiling Americans. He checked his watch and glanced at Federico.

"Cena en, digamos, una hora y media?"

Federico nodded and looked at the group of Americans, motioning for them to follow him. "De esta manera, por favor."

"Please, follow Federico. He'll come and get you for dinner in an hour or so, after you've all cleaned up."

Carlos walked through the house filled with joy. He stopped in his study and set the rifle in a corner, twisted open a bottle of tequila and poured two-fingers worth, swirled it and wished, for a moment, for an ice cube and sliver of lime. It wasn't too long ago Americans would've run from a Mexican armed with a machine gun, not to one. He smiled at his luck and left the study for the observation room.

She had risen. He looked down into the dirt-floored chamber and watched Noelys Sanchez stumble around, trying to gain her bearings. He wasn't sure about that. No zombie, not even the runners, were very certain on their feet. Autopsies had revealed nothing wrong with the muscles or ligature other than that it was dead tissue. Examinations of brain tissue had showed nothing obviously wrong, at least with what he could tell using the equipment he had on hand.

What the yellow-tinted glow he had observed in bodily fluids meant, he had no clue. He hadn't been able to determine a source in the samples he'd examined, but he was certain there was a yellow ... glow.

Carlos picked up the paperwork and looked it over. Noelys had been dead for fifteen hours, nineteen minutes before reviving as a member of the living dead, well within the normal range of resurrection. But now he had a clue as to the delivery systems of the virus: prolonged skin exposure to at least 60 milliliters of infected bodily fluids was enough to turn a person. He smiled: it was a good day for science.

Carlos heard the door open and turned. Federico entered.

"I killed two of the chickens to feed our guests."

"Good choice."

"Anything else?"

Carlos nodded. "Get out a couple of bottles of the 1998 Barolo and chill them a little, tonight is a night we celebrate. I want our guests to feel welcome. They got out of a narrow scrape today. They should be dead. They made it this far from some tourist resort on the coast by siphoning gasoline from cars and scrounging for food."

"What do we do with them?"

"Leave that to me. "

Federico served the chicken with a tamed-down mole sauce, uncertain if the American's taste in spicy food was as intense as his fellow Mexicans. They gorged on it and the rice-and-beans side-dish he prepared. So did Carlos. None of them had eaten such a feast in a while, and Carlos remembered when such a meal was commonplace for dinner. He nodded approvingly to Federico and with a motion of his eyes Carlos let Federico know he should help himself to the meal before it was devoured.

"I thought it was all bullshit, at first, Doctor Carlos," Ken said, drinking a glass of wine. "A pandemic? In this day and age? I mean, the CDC and the World Health Organization and who knows who else is out there watching the world, and then, suddenly, there's this fast-moving bug infecting the planet? I just ignored it and figured the government knew what it was doing, that it would fix it."

Carlos laughed. His government had never been able to fix anything, except, of course, who was in the government. He knew: he was in the government. Chief coroner for the city of Monclova."From what I understand, your government fled to West Virginia when the first infected were found in Washington, D.C.," Carlos said. "Apparently, there's a bomb shelter somewhere big enough to house your entire Congress so that it can continue to govern your country during a nuclear war. And your president is on an aircraft carrier somewhere. He broadcasts a radio message every Wednesday at noon and says your government is doing everything it can to work on a cure and keep your country safe. But he's still on the aircraft carrier, so I don't believe he's made any progress on either claim."

The four Americans turned and looked at each other. It was the first news of any kind they'd heard about what was going on in America.

"Do you know anything else?" Mike asked.

"About America?"

Mike nodded.

Carlos shrugged. He'd caught a couple of Mexicans returning from America after the plague had taken hold, and they'd all told him America - the border states at least - were in chaos. The rule of law had disintegrated and people were fleeing in every direction, nobody knowing where to go. By the end of the fourth month of infection, America had become a wild country filled with the undead and littered with pockets of heavily armed Americans who wouldn't take his countrymen into their newly formed tribal units, forcing them to hope for a better chance in their home country.

But the reactions of his people had been the same, closing down communities and shunning strangers. Carlos figured that only fools would trust the comfort of strangers in these times.

"America is not safe," Carlos said. "No place is safe where there the undead roam."

The room grew quiet and the Americans stared at each other glumly. Kate tilted her glass of wine into her mouth and drank it in three gulps, grabbed a bottle and poured her glass full.

"I thought there was hope, but there isn't," Kate said softly.

Ken turned to her. "There is. There always is. Kate, we're going to find a way through this and get back to our families."

"Or die trying?" Gail said. "We've been on the road for three weeks after a year of being holed up in a series of fucking hotels up and down the coast, waiting for a cruise ship or the Navy or somebody to come and rescue us. And we find out now that everyplace is just as bad? Where are we going to go?

"We're going to stay with the plan, Gail, and drive you and Kate home first," Ken said. "And then we'll figure out what the next step is. Doctor Carlos said there are groups of people still out there. All of our families could still be okay. Let's not assume the worst."

Carlos raised his glass and tapped the floor with his foot. "Look on the bright side, you lived another day in the zombie apocalypse, be proud of yourselves; not everyone can say that. Celebrate a victory and take the day off. Tomorrow, you can return to your quest."

He pushed himself away from the table and stood. "Please, enjoy the wine and eat some more. I have more work to do. If you need anything, Federico can help you."

Carlos watched from the upper level as the American named Ken awoke on the cot in the center of the observation area. Ken coughed roughly and shook his head a little, as if trying to orient himself. He realized he was on a cot in the middle of a large dirt-floored room and scratched his forehead.

"What the fuck?" he said quietly, calmly.

Carlos wrote down the time of his awakening on the medical form and watched. Ken sat still and looked around the room, located Carlos on the upper deck and stared. Ken blinked hard.

"Is that you, Doctor Carlos?" Ken asked. "What the hell is going on?"

"I'm just observing your awakening is all," Carlos said.
"Why am I here? I'm pretty sure I went to bed in one of your guest rooms."
"You did. We moved you here after you were asleep."
"Why? Is something wrong?"
"That's what I'm trying to observe," Carlos said. "You were exposed to what is an aerosolized amount of the zombie contagion, albeit at a lower parts-per-million content than I've previously observed. I'm trying to determine what the threshold level of airborne infection is, because this plague spread much more quickly than through bites from the infected. There has to be an alternate method of infection. The stories of people just suddenly waking up infected or becoming infected while at work are too great to ignore, so, somehow, the alternate methods of transmission need to be determined."
Ken stood and took a few steps, stopped, and tried to center his balance.
"Are the other guys okay? Is it just me?"
"Yes, they're just fine," Carlos said. "We're just going to watch you for a while and see what happens."
Ken nodded. "I feel kinda drunk ... or drugged."
"Tell me every sensation you are going through. It's important for me to know what's going on with you so that I can figure out how to stop it."
Ken stumbled a few steps and almost fell. "I'm hot ... I'm thirsty."
Ken's head rolled around his shoulders aimlessly and his body quivered. He suddenly coughed up a small amount of blood and mucus. He turned and stumbled back to the cot and fell onto it. Carlos wrote a note and motioned to Federico for them to leave the observation deck.
Inside the next room, Carlos and Federico took off their face masks and placed them on the table.

"That was half the dose of the last subject, and it was still as quick. Whatever this bug is, it moves fast. Keep an eye on him throughout the day and let me know if he revives."

"What about the others?"

Carlos shrugged. "They're not going anywhere. Just keep them locked in their rooms."

He walked through the laboratory and pushed through the office doors and sat at his desk. For some reason, the contagion took over a person much more quickly when a person was asleep and exposed to it by the air: almost twice as fast as by a bite infection or exposed blood contamination. It made no sense to him. Carlos looked at his watch and figured that if subject Ken reacted as previous subjects had, he'd arise as undead within six to eight hours. And his tests had all been conducted using his various guess-work concoctions as to what the pathogen might be composed of.

He was sure that for it to have spread so rapidly across the globe, and infected so many so quickly, there either had to be a better explanation because it hadn't infected everyone simultaneously. People in one house would arise in the morning like normal, looking for breakfast while the family next door would awaken to a life as the undead. It made no sense.

And then it hit him.

It was a learning virus. A retro-virus of some sort, perhaps, that couldn't infect everyone at first, but as it mutated through those it successfully infected, it began incorporating the differences in DNA of the human species into its attack sequence. He sat back in his chair and wondered if that made sense, if a virus could be so adaptable. And, especially, if it could alter itself that quickly.

"But it doesn't always change the host, it sometimes kills the host," he said aloud, softly, to no one. Killing the host was a mistake. The virus must have adapted early on to revive the host as something different. But if it didn't infect everyone through its primary delivery system then that meant there were humans who were resistant to the plague, at least until it evolved further. Which meant there was a cure. Or a vaccine. But there was hope.

He flipped through some of the paperwork on his desk and wished, again, he had a computer that could crunch data, analyze trends, spot outliers. This work could take decades done this way, and he wasn't sure he even had years. He was going to need to run more experiments. He was going to need equipment. He was going to need time.

And he was going to need more test subjects.

THE ROAD

Tulsa, Oklahoma - Day 204

The two were on horseback, now, having made the beginning of their trek across Oklahoma on foot under the searing summer sun. Carter hadn't wanted to use a motor vehicle of any kind as he didn't want to be tied down to the need for gasoline and maintenance. In the days they'd been making their way across the state, they'd come across countless little caravans of vehicles abandoned in the middle of the road, so he figured he was in the minority on this issue. The world had gone to hell more quickly than anyone could have imagined, abruptly ending thousands of years of steady progress toward air-conditioning and convenience store burritos, and most of the survivors were still clinging to the ways of civilization.

There was no civilization. Not anymore. Already, Mother Nature was taking back that which the humans had brought under their control, planting weeds and grass anywhere a seed could take root in a crack. It was only a matter of time until the tornados tore apart the buildings in Oklahoma City and Norman. In time, everything man had built would fall to the ground. Carter had no reason to believe the walking dead would maintain anything, seeing as they seemed bent on devouring the living. Whatever the future for man was, if there was a future, it would look a lot more like the distant past than the recent past. Carter figured that the people who adapted quickly to the fundamental change of how life would become and learned the skills sets of the outdoors would find themselves in a better situation than those who roamed the countryside in four-by-fours in search of a way to salvage what had been.

Like anything easy or fun, letting go of it would be difficult. People - Americans, he corrected himself (and, then, parenthetically, in his thought process, he guessed the West in general, and any advanced civilization on the planet specifically) would find it difficult to give up on the idea of electricity, automobiles, grocery stores and leisure time. For most of the lifespan of the human race, easy living had been the rarest of rarities, and those who had achieved it guarded it jealously. Most people had to eke out a subsistence and lived grubby, short lives of desperation and want.

Now the human race was back to that paradigm. The walking dead had seen to that. Why was a question no one might ever know the answer to. Not that it mattered. What was done, was done. Only now, humans weren't the only Alpha Predators on the block, so the road back would be much, much more difficult.

The whine of dirt bikes rose above the sound of the wind and traced its way along the landscape off to their right, a niggling whirr of noise that spent a minute moving east before fading into silence. Carter made no effort to look, although he knew the boy certainly was.

"Don't worry about it. There's no shortage of people roaming around. Long as we can hear them, we know where they are."

He lifted up his cowboy hat and wiped the sweat from his brow, pushed his hair back up and set the hat back down. The boy was probably right, though. It probably was the same pack of bikers, stalking them, now choosing to be brazen rather than stealthy. Whatever the boy had in his pack, they wanted it. They had killed his parents in an attempt to get it, and he had shown up however-many seconds too late to help them, arriving just in time to kill the two leather-coat-and-football-pad-encrusted thugs and save the boy.

He had asked the boy his name, but the kid - he guessed him to be about twelve - hadn't answered. Carter had shrugged and not told the kid his name, and the two had formed a unit that had made its way across Oklahoma in silence. Carter prodded his horse and it began walking, the kid saying "let's go" quietly to his horse a second later.

They kept the horses off to the side of route 51. The road was empty with the exception of an empty car or truck every couple of miles. They rode for hours without coming across another person - living or undead. Carter found that odd, and it rolled around in his mind, searching for a reason to stick to. This close to Tulsa, there should've been some activity. And then he smiled to himself and shook his head: just a couple of months into the zombie apocalypse, and he assumed he was already an expert at sensing the patterns of the new world. What the hell did he know? The kid probably knew more about zombies than Carter did.

They had seen the smoke pouring into the sky long before they got to the outskirts of the city, and Carter had figured Tulsa had fallen just as fully as every other city they'd been through. He had never really followed the news: pre-zombies he had been a Major League Baseball and college football junkie, so he had listened to sports talk radio and watched ESPN. By the time he realized he should find out what was going on with the world, it was too late.

"Over there," the boy said.

Carter looked over at the kid and saw he was pointing. Carter followed the trajectory outward and saw a knot of walking dead. They were milling around on the other end of the dam which made Keystone Lake, almost as if they were guarding it, but still too disorganized to be a coherent unit. He watched the undead stumble around and thought about the options. It would be easy to go a different way, and the time lost wouldn't matter, as he wasn't in any hurry.

But, still, the undead had managed a choke point? How would they have known to form as a group here, where there were no other living? The zombies were constantly moving, in search of new food or new converts. He had no idea what the undead really wanted, what they were up to, only that they seemed always hungry for human flesh. Not that he'd had the chance to study any of them up close, but he had yet to come across one of the undead that was not hungry or intent on killing the him. Carter was pretty sure a sated lion wouldn't attack something else and kill it just to kill it, although he nodded to himself that he didn't know that for sure, either.

"Let's not risk it," he said to the boy, motioning with his head to the east. "We'll head that way and find another spot to cross."

At the intersection of routes 51 and 97, there was a massive traffic jam. Hundreds of cars were wedged against each other, many crashed into each other. Four-wheel drive vehicles were bogged down in the nearly dry river bed, the water dammed up miles behind them to create the lake they had just left. The cars had done the same thing to those in the city, forcing people onto their feet for the flight from the city. Most hadn't made it:

bodies were strewn everywhere, torn apart and stripped to the bones of flesh.

"Keep your eyes moving, you know how the undead like to hide among the dead," he said.

"We gonna look for any supplies?"

Carter shook his head. "No. Going in there would be foolish. If there's any undead, you'd never be able to get out. We'll make our way across the river bed here, then skirt alongside the west side and make our way around the north end of the city.

"It'll be getting toward dusk by the time we get up there, so keep your eyes open for any place looks like we can put up for the night."

They came across a small farm that had been an equestrian training school an hour before sunset. Carter had knocked on the door of the farmhouse, rang the bell, and peered through the windows before deciding it was safe to break in, which only took pushing the door open: the owners had left without locking the place, figuring they'd never come back. Or, maybe they figured they might lose the keys in the time they'd be gone and wouldn't want to have to break in. He didn't know. He'd locked the door to his house before leaving. And he'd moved everything he thought would be worth stealing to the attic, figuring staples-focused looters wouldn't waste time on opportunity theft if there was nothing he valued laying around.

He and the boy cleared all the rooms in the house one-by-one, he wanting to make sure there were no living or undead inside. Then they checked the stables, an auxiliary storage building and a car garage. They grabbed some hay and littered two stables with it, filled the feeding troughs and put the horses in for the night.

"Now, we can eat," Carter said.

He rooted around the pantry at the bottom of a staircase connected to the kitchen, using a small flashlight to play across the shelves, which were stocked with canned and dry goods. Whoever had lived here left quickly to have abandoned so much food. But, then, everyone everywhere had either left quickly or been killed quickly. The news of the spread of the plague had gone from centering on the quarantine of Los Angeles the first month to the sudden appearance of it nearly everywhere a month or so later. After that, there was a national panic as everyone realized everywhere was unsafe and began to flee.

He had told his wife that no place was safe, so it was just as well they stayed put and waited it out. Neither of his sons thought that was a good idea, but he reckoned that was because they both had small children to look after. He had had a heated argument with his older son, Carl, when he had shown up on their doorstep to tell him they were there to take him and Jolene with them to his hunting camp outside the Mark Twain National Forest.

"Carl, it's not anymore safe there than it is here," he had said. "This plague is everywhere at the same time. Missouri's no more safe than Oklahoma. You know that."

"But Dad, it's out in the sticks, far from populated areas, so there will at least be less of them," Carl had said. "And food is going to get scarce. People are going to end up killing each other, too. It won't be just the zombies."

He had laughed at that. Zombies. "These aren't the dead risen from the grave, son, they're infected with something. Somebody will figure something out."

"Maybe, but nobody's gonna figure anything out soon. You and mom have to come with us, now," Carl had said. "Peter's already on the way. We have to leave now, though. When it hits Oke City and Tulsa, you won't be able to go anywhere on the roads. It'll be pandemonium just like LA and Chicago and New York. We can all wait it out together."

He had shaken his head at that, the thought that he would abandon the family farm, now his after three generations. Not that he had ever farmed it. He and Jolene had a large garden behind the house, but the rest of the 500 acres he rented out. He owned a small auto repair shop in Hammon and his wife worked as a dental hygienist.

"Listen, son, I know you mean well, but your mother and I are gonna stay right here and wait this thing out. We've got everything we need in the house to survive for close enough to a year," Carter had said. "Don't try to change my mind about this; your mother and I have already talked it through, and we're staying put."

Carl's shoulders had sagged and he stared at the ground. "Dad..."

"I understand you've got to do what you think is right by your family, so you do that. Meet Peter at the hunting camp, tell him we're fine, and we'll be here when the trouble has passed."

His son had just nodded a few tiny head movements. "Okay, but will you at least do me one favor? Will you both at least keep your cell phones turned on and on your persons? Especially if you decide later to come? So we can keep in contact and know where you are?"

Carter had reached out and placed his hand on his son's shoulder and smiled. "Carl, you'll know where we are, because we'll be here," he had said, "but we'll make sure we keep the phones on."

But he had left the phone on the desk in his office at the shop when a horde of hundreds of undead had swarmed through Hammon late one morning a month earlier. He'd grabbed the Remington 870 he kept in the corner of the room and shot his way to his truck, and then driven to the dental office where his wife worked, only to find it had been abandoned, the receptionist and a patient both eaten to death in the lobby.

He'd driven home to find an empty house. He tried calling Jolene on her cell, but all the calls rang through to voicemail. He'd spent several weeks holed up in the house, waiting for Jolene to come home. He had called Jolene's phone every day and left voicemail. And then he saw the beginning of a zombie horde making its way down the road toward his house from the window of the master bedroom and realized everything was much worse than he had thought it had been, and he would probably never see Jolene ever again. He spent five minutes throwing supplies into a backpack, grabbed his Winchester rifle and 9 millimeter Smith & Wesson pistol, and raced out to his truck, driving off furiously in front of the zombie phalanx.

Away from Hammon.

Away from his wife's dental office.

Away from the farm.

He was almost to Texas when he had realized he was driving in the wrong direction. He had made his way over to Interstate 44 and began the long drive north until traffic jams around Fort Sill had forced him out of his truck and on foot. He had made his way on side roads until coming across the boy in Chickasha.

Carter awoke to the sounds of several dirt bikes racing around in the early light of dawn. In the distance, the figures were shades of gray whirring up and down the main road adjoining the driveway. He was sure it was the same gang that had been inexplicably shadowing them for the past few days. Why?

He slipped his feet into his cowboy boots and went downstairs, surprised to find the boy already awake, eating a bowl of corn flakes with condensed milk from a can.

"They're back."

Carter nodded. "Any idea why they're following you?"

The boy shook his head and ate a spoonful of cereal.

"When you're done with breakfast, come out to the barn and help me finish saddling up the horses," Carter said.

Outside the whine of the engines rose and fell over and over again. Carter wondered what the hell they were doing on the bikes just as much as he wondered why. He knew it was the boy they were after, but what could the boy mean to them? Why would several men be interested in a boy who was maybe eleven or thirteen years old? And then he shuddered at the realization.

"There's no fucking way that can be the reason," he muttered as he cinched the saddle straps under his horse.

The whining of the bikes was getting closer, and it was only then that Carter noticed something peculiar about the rise and fall of the noise. It was as if the they were riding up and down the road in short bursts, getting incrementally closer instead of just riding up on the farm. They knew he was armed and that he would shoot, so it made sense they were keeping their distance. But they had to know he knew they were coming. He grabbed a pair of binoculars from the saddle bags and climbed the ladder to the loft, pushing through the loft doors and scanning for the riders on the road. They were, indeed, riding somewhat slowly back and forth. What for?

He glanced down at the boy. Normal kid. He put the glasses back up to his face and scanned the road some more. His jaw dropped: the bikers were luring a horde of hundreds of zombies up the road, racing to and from the horde and acting as bait. He looked back down at the boy.

"Hey, I need you to run back into the house real quick and get a backpack I left on the kitchen table. It's got food in it we'll need for the next couple of days of travel," Carter said, making his way down from the loft. "Hurry. We've got maybe five minutes left here before we have to start riding hard."

The kid nodded and sprinted out of the barn. Carter took the kids messenger bag off the saddle horn and marveled at its weight. The kid had been carrying this for days across the state. He dropped it to the ground and zipped it open.

It was filled with gold jewelry of every type imaginable: rings, bracelets, necklaces. He lifted a handful of it and stared at it in disbelief. Diamond engagement rings and gold earrings slipped from his hand. He dropped the jewelry into the bag and shook his head. The desires of the old world hadn't ended, not yet, not completely.

Outside, the whining of the dirt bikes grew closer.

The kid came back with the bag of food and stopped suddenly, his eyes flicking between the open bag on the floor near his horse and Carter. He dropped the food and his hand drifted to the pistol on his hip.

"That's my bag. You had no right looking through it."

"Son, you've done brought a hailstorm of a dilemma on us," Carter said. "I'm not interested in this bag of yours, but I reckon the men on the bikes are. I could tell you fine, go on and do that. It's yours and it's a free country, and if you weren't twelve or thirteen-years old and your parents were still around, things would be different. But they aren't different, because here is where we are.

"I don't know why you're carrying this bag of gold with you, and, frankly, I don't care. But the men out there that been following us do care. They think it's worth something and they want it, and for reasons we'll never know, they're going to some extraordinary lengths to get it.

"But I'm going to tell you that this bag of yours is never going to be anything but a source of trouble. You need to leave it here."

The kid stared at him for a moment and then dropped his eyes. "My Dad said gold is the money of all time. That if you had it, you would be okay in the future because you could always trade it for something."

Carter nodded. "That was the old world, the one the zombies are destroying. Zombies don't care about gold. You can't eat it. It's not useful for anything that isn't jewelry. And there's nobody who wants it."

"They killed my parents to get it."

"They're still living in the past. Right now, a lot of people are still thinking the lifestyle we had will return, but it won't," Carter said. "This world is done. The rules have changed."

The kid just stared at the ground.

"My Dad said to ...," the kid said, suddenly sobbing, tears dripping from his eyes onto the dirt floor of the barn. "He said if I had this, it would save me in the future."

The whirr of a dirt bike rolled close to the barn and then turned and circled the house before lowering to a putter as it made its way back to the main road. Carter had seen his own sons cry like this when they couldn't understand why what they had done was wrong, confused by the differences in what their consciousnesses told them was what okay and the reality that the world didn't work that way. As always, there was a compromise.

"Grab a handful and stuff it in your pocket, but leave the rest here," Carter said. "But we've got to leave, now. If it's ever worth anything again, what you can stuff in your pockets will be more than enough."

The kid stuffed his pockets quickly while avoiding Carter's gaze and then climbed onto his horse. Carter grabbed the bag and rode out the front door directly at the nearest man on a motorcycle, held the bag high and tossed it to the ground. The zombies were only yards behind him, and the rider looked over his shoulder, nodded back at Carter, and zoomed away.

The zombies paused for a moment and one of them stepped out from the crowd, then another, and began looking around. They settled on Carter and the boy on their horses and the group began moving toward them. Carter surveyed the hundreds of undead shuffling toward him, the sun now fully up and heating the Oklahoma morning. It was going to be hot.

Carter looked over at the kid. "It's going to work out just fine. One of the things you'll learn about life is that everything always works out in the end. Maybe not to your favor, but everything ends. And then something else begins."

He nodded toward the approaching horde. "Even this won't stay like this forever. It'll change, too, and maybe not to our advantage. Come on, let's get movin'."

THE ONLY WAY OUT IS THROUGH

Pittsburgh, Pennsylvania - Day 1349

Rain is cold.

The rain poured from the evening sky, drenching Will. He tried not to shudder, not to move, not to make a sound. For a moment, he remembered the first girl who had ever taken him for an intentional walk in the rain. Susan. Sue. Brown hair, brown eyes, the rain smoothing her clothing against her body into an hourglass of perfect desire. She had liked walking in the rain. He remembered it was supposed to be romantic.

Rain is cold.

He huddled against the crumbling cinder block wall, his P-90 machine gun clutched to his body, listening. The rain drowned out the ambient noise. Will cocked an ear and listened harder, trying to make out the sounds of a rhythm, of a zombie on the prowl. But the rain did just as much for the undead as it did for him: masked movement. He turned his head and looked through the darkness, wondering about his next move. He saw nothing. But, still, the dead could be anywhere.

He shivered.

He couldn't stay here forever. He couldn't stay here for long. The undead knew he was somewhere near. The undead were somewhere near. He summoned up what courage he had left in him and began to step forward along the wall, his weapon raised. There was a rally point, a place for them to meet if everything went to hell. Again. Or: as usual. The world was hell. Once upon a time, the world had been awesome, but that was a long time ago. There had been beer and steaks and women you could take home for a night. Where had that memory come from?

He shivered.

"Yo, is anybody still listenin' to this freq?"

The words sounded out in his earpiece. Olandis was still alive. Will smiled but said nothing. He looked around, again, saw nothing, and pressed the button on his walkie: click, click.

Will moved stealthily along the wall, testing the ground with each step to avoid kicking debris. The last thing he wanted to do was knock an old soda can over and cause it to ring out. For whatever reason, the zombies had learned to differentiate between the world's natural sounds and those made by man. He had watched zombies investigate the shattering of glass plates as they fell from downtown skyscrapers and ignore the scuff of a plastic trash can as the wind blew it down the street. They knew that motorized vehicles could only be operated by living people and moved toward the sound of the engines. Gunfire was like a dinner bell.

Lightning flickered across the sky and he crouched instinctively. Ahead of him in the parking lot was a zombie, silhouetted in the brief flash, facing away from him. He watched it as it swayed in place, its head lolling above its shoulders, ears listening for him, eyes looking for him. Will looked over the top of the wall at the rest of the parking lot, looking for any other undead. He knew there were dozens nearby, maybe hundreds.

He slung the P90 over his back and slipped the Ka-Bar Black Kukri Machete out of its scabbard. He stepped lightly on the the balls of his feet, his eyes fixed on the undead monster before him, and swung the blade through the neck of the zombie. Its head popped off and its body collapsed to the ground with a plop.

Bad idea.

He could hear the skip-hop before the undead head stopped rolling on the ground, the slapping of feet coming from the direction of the building off to his right. He turned quickly and saw a skeletal man in tattered clothing coming at him in what amounted to a run for a zombie. A trap. He cursed himself in his head: of course it was a trap.

He took a couple of steps to the side and began a slow retreat, making the undead monster change its course. They were easier to kill when they had to suddenly change direction, as it seemed to put them off-balance and you could move in quickly and kill them before they could adjust themselves for a new approach. Will watched in surprise as it veered off to his left and lurched to a halt a dozen feet from him, by the corner of the building.

Not good.

He looked around quickly, the uncertainty of the situation maturing in his brain's analysis: this wasn't normal. He turned and saw a slow mover only steps away from him, its arms out, mouth open, a woman who had been in her thirties and was now clothed in only dirt-stained threadbare bra and panties.

He turned the machete through the air and brought it down through the top of her skull, splitting her head open in two halves. She fell away from the blade to the ground and he turned his attention quickly back to the sprinter who had already closed half the distance between them. He stepped quickly to the side and slashed the zombie's right arm off at the forearm. It turned and growled at him but Will stepped in and slashed the blade through the creature's neck, its head falling backward and leading the rest of the undead's body to the pavement.

Will turned a slow circle, looking for the next unexpected zombie. The night sky crackled with thunder, and a moment later a flash of lightning lit up the the world. Will speed-walked out of the parking lot and into an overgrown area of vegetation. He knelt down and keyed the mic.

"Olandis, this is Will, where are you?"

There was a long pause. Thunder rumbled above. The rain soaked through his clothes. He was cold.

"I'm in the field house near the soccer fields."

A mile away. An eternity away. Will looked through the night. Nothing.

The radio crackled in his ear.

"I've got zombies all around me," Olandis whispered, his voice clear in Will's ear. "There's four or five of 'em out on the field near the gyros."

"Just stay put. Don't move. I'm on the way."

"What about the other guys?"

Will scanned through the darkness. George and Jeff were dead for sure, he'd watched them get torn to pieces in the shopping center parking lot. Hugh had run into the grocery store while the zombies were eating George and Jeff. Al and Greg were dead. When the runners had found them, they'd run the opposite direction from him and directly into a phalanx of slow walkers: the last image he had of them was Greg putting a round through a zombie skull while it bit Al's shoulder.

Frank was the only one he couldn't be mostly sure was dead. Frank had unloaded on a half-dozen undead with his Mossberg 500 before disappearing into the rain-darkened night, his shotgun booming every few seconds, the sounds getting weaker in the distance until silence. Will and Olandis had backed away from the mass of undead, Will working through the fifty-round clip, felling zombies with head shots while Olandis had cleared the way in the opposite direction with a Sig Sauer pistol. And then Will had had to change magazines, and in the seconds that took, Olandis was gone.

Will didn't blame Olandis for leaving him behind. It had been the smart thing to do when the horde had appeared. The stupid thing to do was what he and the rest of them had done, which was think they could fight so many off and salvage the operation. They were all supposed to run to the rally point if that had happened. It had happened, and only Olandis had done what they had decided in advance to do.

They were done as a group. They had all known they would never last, could never last. And, now, they hadn't lasted. It was weird to be on that end of the timeline of the story. The end. Only, for Will, it wasn't the end, not yet. It was the movie post-credit sequence or the beginning of the sequel or, maybe, some fan fiction where he was the spin-off character from Olandis' story. Or Frank's, if he had been the main character and Will had been some character the author had forgotten to kill off in the original story, leaving readers to wonder just what had happened to him and inspiring a thousand on-line discussion threads wondering what it could possibly mean to have had a minor character who simply "vanished" half-way through the story. Whatever happened to Will?

"They're all dead," Will whispered.

Will moved out from the trees and onto the street. It was overgrown with grass and saplings, the asphalt cracked into tiny pieces, the dirt migrating from below to reclaim its place in the natural world. This had been his neighborhood just a few years earlier, and it had been a vibrant community of shops and restaurants. He and his wife, Cora, often walked in from their nearby home for dinner and drinks. Now, the buildings were crumbling, the windows broken, the interiors littered with blown leaves and crumbling modernity.

"Shit," Will mouthed and dropped to the ground. Directly ahead of him, at the intersection of what had been Swissvale and West Hutchinson avenues, was a cluster of a half-dozen undead.

Lighting flickered and thunder boomed. Will was glad he'd seen the silhouettes first, or they'd certainly have seen him standing in the middle of the road. In the burst of light, he could tell the group was the "new" zombies. Wider mouths with sharper teeth, hands with longer fingers, and skin that was tough like a leather belt. They were still slow, but outrunning them was no mere matter of sprinting to safety like at the beginning of the pandemic. Now, outrunning them required endurance. He'd seen a handful of people who were run down by these versions because they had tired out.

All of this meant there was most likely a new runner or a toolie nearby. New runners made sense: if the slow walkers were evolving to move faster, then it only made sense that the ragers would evolve to run even faster, but the appearance of zombies that used tools had perplexed him. What they used the hammers, crowbars and other tools for was a mystery: he'd never seen the undead build anything.

The heavens opened up with a sudden burst of heavy rain, the drops beating down on his back. Rain is cold. He shivered for a moment before forcing his mind out of his body, concentrating on watching the undead in front of him. He began crawling backwards, moving toward the cracked-open storefronts that had once been bars and shops. He had to get out of the rain and regroup.

He crawled through the puddles and up onto what had been the sidewalk, which was now covered with splotches of wild grass, and up to the door of what had been Murphy's Tap Room. The door was ajar, and he pushed it open with the muzzle of his P-90 and dragged himself over the threshold. He pushed the door closed behind him and sat against the wall.

It had been his idea to come to this part of town. He'd convinced the others to come because he thought it might be safe to go back into the city and forage for supplies. As far as any of them knew, nobody had really been able to go through the city because, in the early days, it was choked with the undead. Everybody living had fled when it became apparent the city was overrun and the authorities were unable to do anything about it. He wasn't sure exactly why he had suddenly cared, but he had wanted to see if any pictures of his wife still existed in their home, and the shopping center was close by.

Will had fled to a small grass airstrip north of the city near the Kiskiminetas River where he and his fellow pilot buddies kept their gyrocopter aircraft. When Al, Greg and Frank all showed up within the week, they had taken it as a sign that they were meant to survive. They sat around the first few days retelling their harrowing journeys out of the city and mourning the loss of those that hadn't made it with them.

Al's wife Linda had gone out to get her parents the day before the zombies and never come back. Greg had been trapped in the PPG building for days before managing to sneak out of the city one night using a cardboard box for concealment. Frank had made his way to the Allegheny River and used a canoe to row upriver. Will had put a bullet in his zombie-wife's skull in the backyard of their home in Edgewood and barely managed to get on his Nashbar road bike and pedal his way to Route 28 ahead of the zombies.

The walkie clicked twice in his ear and Will realized he was shivering badly. He stood up and took a few steps into the main bar area. He stopped and let his eyes search through the gloom before clicking it on flashlight on the side rail of the P90s, the red lens dulling the brightness of the beam. They'd all found it interesting that the undead couldn't see the red beams, but they still used them with caution: the zombies kept changing, so you never knew what the next adaptation might be.

He played the beam through the room, looking for a lurking "waiter" zombie. He hated them. They could sit for days or weeks or maybe years, just waiting for the opportunity to bite somebody. Rich had been taken by a waiter zombie on a trip into Apollo a couple of months after they'd been living on the airstrip. That was also the day they met Olandis, then a twenty-two-year old with a thick Afro held fast by a dew rag. He kept his hair close-cropped, now.

"O, it's Will, I got your clicks, I'm still alive," Will said quietly, moving through the bar toward the back,

Click. Click.

Will sagged. Olandis was in trouble. "I'm gonna guess there are some zulus pretty close to where you are."

Click. Click.

"Just hang tight and stay quiet. I'm on the way, but there are new zulus everywhere here, so it's gonna take a little time to pick my way outta here and into the park. But I'm on the way."

Click. Click.

He'd found his wedding album in his home that morning and sat down and cried while looking through it in the master bedroom of his house. It had been weird walking into the house with Frank, guns at the ready. Inside, it was surprisingly well kept, albeit dusty. None of the windows had been broken, so Mother Nature hadn't wrought havoc inside. Memories of his life with Cora popped into his head with everything he saw, and he remembered the life they had talked about building, the kids they had anticipated having.

"The canned stuff is downstairs in the pantry, Frank," Will said. "I'm gonna head upstairs and look around a little."

Frank understood and just nodded. Frank's wife had been in Dallas on business and he had no idea what happened to her after the city shut down. He'd gotten a text after martial law had been declared saying she was okay. He'd texted back that he was going to come for her, but she never responded and his calls had all gone straight to voicemail. He still would say that she might still be alive and that one day he'd try to find her. But, then, everybody said that.

Will pulled a dozen photos of her and them out of the album and slipped them behind a spare magazine for his H&K .45 Tactical USP in a pocket of his Condor Deluxe Tactical Vest. He walked over to her dresser and pulled out the top drawer and stared at her clothes, the underwear and socks still in place. They were still where he put them when he last did laundry: Cora rarely did laundry and never put her clothes away. Indeed, there was a small stack of jeans and T-shirts covered with dust in the corner of the room. Will smiled.

He made his way down from the third floor to the second, pausing to look in the various rooms of their home, at the stuff they had owned. He wondered if he would ever move back into this house or if the new world order meant he'd be forced to continue living in an Army surplus canvas tent with Frank and Olandis. They joked that they were living the lifestyle of Trapper and Hawkeye in M*A*S*H, only without the still. Will's eyebrows shot up and he smiled and snapped his fingers at that thought.

He bounded down the stairs and through the living room to the hutch against the wall of the dining area, kneeling quickly and pulling a cabinet door open.

"Holy fuckin' hallelujah," Will said, reaching into the space and pulling out a bottle of MacAllen 12-year and a bottle of Balvenie Double Wood.

He heard Frank stepping quickly up the stairs and burst into the dining area.

"What's up? Everything okay?" Frank said quietly, but with utmost urgency.

Will turned and smiled broadly, holding up the two bottles.

Frank's face lit up. "No fuckin' way. Tell me that's why you really wanted to come here today. We're gonna get good and drunk on the good stuff tonight."

Will slipped his tactical backpack off and put the MacAllen into it and handed the other bottle to Frank, who put it into his pack. Frank looked around the room and then at his friend.

"Weird being back here, isn't it?"

Will nodded.

"You okay?"

Will shrugged. "Just one more thing I need to do."

Will walked past Frank and through the small kitchen, twisted the knob on the back door and pulled it open. The grass was a foot high in his small backyard, and branches from the tree next to the house littered the yard. He walked down the steps and stopped a couple of feet into the grass and looked down at the skeleton of his wife, her skull shattered above the right eye. He winced. He felt Frank's hand on his shoulder.

"You had no choice, bud," Frank said.

"I know ... but still."

For an instant, he remembered that last moment with her, the undead version of her in the back yard. He had known before going that he was going to have to put her down, but raising the pistol had been difficult, even as she lurched toward him, blood and mucus covering her chest, her skin a dull gray, her eyes filled with somnolent rage.

He pushed that thought out and remembered Cora on the day of their wedding, holding hands in front of the preacher as they stood on the gazebo, the entire world suddenly erased from his vision. He had stared at her eyes and watched them well with tears as she squeezed his hands, and he had been the kind of happy nobody knows they will be in such a situation, when all your dreams are coming true and you suddenly know it.

Then a deep bass rumble had broken his reverie and both he and Frank looked into the sky. Fast moving clouds were flooding the sky above them and the temperature was dropping quickly. The wind kicked up leaves from the grass in the back yard. The two men turned toward each other.

"So much for the weather," Frank said.

Will shined the red light on the back door of the bar. "Alarm will sound if door is opened" a small sticker said on the push-bar. Will hoped to god that was not the case. The electricity had been out in the city since shortly after martial law had collapsed. He turned flashlight off, shouldering the door open by inches and searching through the dark for the undead. He pushed the door open slowly, the wind instantly driving drizzle through the door and into his face.

He stepped into the alley and eased the door shut behind him. He turned left and stood stock still. The door made a small click as it settled into the frame. Will unsheathed his machete just as the two zombies in the alley turned around, stepping quickly to the side as they lurched toward him, trying to create some space between the two. He cut a hand off of one and circled as he listened to the incomprehensible babble from the monsters. The one less-a-hand growled and stutter-lunged at him and he chopped downward through its skull, lopping the top half off. The undead man dropped to the ground as Will pivoted for the other.

Too late.

The other zombie grabbed him from behind. It was strong. Stronger than he had imagined, and it dragged him quickly toward it. He tried to move, but now understood how so many could be taken so easily: they were far stronger undead than alive. He reversed his grip on the machete and swung it backward into the zombie's mid-section when a blast rang out and he felt shards of bone and a burst of fluid on the back of his neck. The zombie let go and slipped off him to the wet asphalt.

He scrambled for a moment and got into a crouch, pulling his blade from the dead zombie.

A figure stepped out from behind a nearby parked van.

"You okay?"

"Frank?"

"Shit, Will, you made it," Frank said.

"We gotta start running now, there's a half-dozen super zulus a half-block away on the other side of these buildings."

"Shit, let's go," Frank said.

And they ran. They picked their way around the silhouettes of trees, the occasional spider web slapping across Will's face as he led the way. There was no time to worry if the spider that had spun it had been on it when he ripped through it. His fear of spiders had been replaced by something much more deadly. They stopped after a while and each took a knee amid a copse of trees. Will was exhausted.

Click.

Will toggled his radio. "Olandis, man we're on the way. I just found Frank and we're in the woods maybe a mile from you. We might be there in fifteen minutes or it might take the rest of the night. Just stay cool."

Click. Click.

Will looked at Frank. "There are some of the super zulus around the aircraft. Olandis is already there, hiding in a building, but I think he's starting to panic."

Frank nodded. "Panic? I was hiding in that alley for hours waiting for a chance to move after those two Zs came down it and just stood there. When you came out that back door, I couldn't believe I had a chance. I'm glad it was you."

Will nodded. "Likewise. But you could have blown my head off at that range."

"I didn't know it was you until after I shot it," Frank said. "Anyway, you were seconds away from getting your head bitten off."

Will let out a tiny laugh. "I had the bastard right where I wanted it."

The rain changed from a downpour to a steady drizzle and both of them looked up through the canopy at the low clouds moving by. The wind slackened.

"I know this is going to sound crazy, but you don't have any water, do you?" Frank asked.

Will nodded and pulled the hose to his hydration pack from underneath his combat harness and offered it to Frank. Frank leaned in and took several long pulls before sitting back against the trunk of a tree.

"That fucking zulu that grabbed me tore my pack and everything off my back. Nearly dislocated my left shoulder before I slipped down a hill into a drainage ditch and was swept a hundred yards down it and into a metal screen covering a storm water drain," Frank said. "Went from terrified of being eaten alive to terrified I was going to drown."

Branches snapped, a sharp ripple of noise off to their left. Both of them rose onto a knee and pointed their weapons at the noise. If the paths through the park still existed, they were long-since overgrown, and in their mad dash through the park, Will had made sure to avoid them, but someone or something was on one. Now, silence.

Will turned to Frank and shook his head in disbelief before making a couple of hand gestures indicating they begin slowly moving away from the sound.They crept through the underbrush, eyes out, ears attuned for any sound not created by wind or rain. They paused every ten yards or so for a listening break, each taking a knee for a minute and searching through the darkness for some evidence of the undead walking near them.

The progress was slow. Will was navigating off of a changed landscape, no longer the one he had taken weekly mountain bike rides through. Those paths were long gone, and new trees and bushes had sprung up everywhere in the absence of the county parks maintenance teams' pruning. Nature had taken back the park and exposed all that human activity as nothing more than a temporary setback to Mother Nature's dream of ruling the planet.

And then the drizzle stopped and moonlight poured down through the forest. Both men dropped instinctively to the ground and disappeared into the flora. Will looked up and saw the near-full moon and more stars than he'd ever seen before from inside the city limits of Pittsburgh. Without the light scattered from the streetlights, the night sky was a brilliant affair. He looked at his Luminox Navy SEALS watch: the sun would be up soon.

Frank tapped him on the shoulder and pointed forward. Will looked. Fifty yards in front of them, standing at the edge of the woods were a dozen of the new zombies standing in a line inside the trees, watching the overgrown field Will and his friends had landed their aircraft in that morning. Beyond them, Will counted four more zombies wandering not-quite-aimlessly among the aircraft.

"Motherfucker," Will said under-his-breath.

Frank nodded.

Will keyed his walkie's microphone, "O, you still there?"

Click. Click.

"We're here at the edge of the field, maybe two hundred yards to the east in the woods, so hold on a little longer."

Click. Click.

"Give us a couple of minutes to figure something out," Will said and turned to Frank.

Click. Click.

Frank slung his shotgun over his back and pulled his Smith & Wesson .40 pistol from its holster. "I say we creep in as close as we get, and I shoot 'em in from the right side and you take 'em from the left."

Will nodded. "Yeah, but then we've got the other four on the field. And if there's a dozen of them waiting here, how do we know there's not a dozen on the other side of the field?"

"They ain't that smart," Frank said.

"They know we're coming, so they're smart enough."

"We can't kill that many with blades, Will, there's too many."

Will looked at the problem. Twelve headshots from this range - or any range - was impossible in the woods. Maybe if he had a silencer, but he didn't, and his many attempts to try to build one had all failed. And even if that could've worked, they'd be walking into an open field in broad daylight with some super Zs right in front of them.

Will began feeling the pockets on his combat vest and smiled when he touched the pocket with the two M67 fragmentation grenades. He clicked his walkie.

"O, are you still armed?"

Click. Click.

"What are you thinking?" Frank asked.

Will pulled the grenades out and then produced a small spool of kite string. "We're gonna build a little sound diversion back here to divert their attention and make them come this way when we run for the gyros."

"O, when the sun comes up, we're going to create a diversion on our side of the field. You wait until you see us come into the field running for the aircraft, when you see that, come out and look in every other direction but where we're coming from and shoot anything coming," Will said into his walkie. "You copy?"

Click. Click.

After Will explained the plan, Frank looked at him in disbelief.

"I ... you wanna ... I mean, that's," Frank said, turning and looking at the super-zombies a half-football field away. "I don't think we're as bad shots as you think we are."

"Maybe not, but we start the kind of shooting you want to do, we're going to be the center of the zombie universe. If there's any on the other side of the field, or if some of them from Regent Square followed us into the woods last night looking for us, then we're in a world of hurt real quick if anything goes wrong.

"And something always goes wrong. We just need them all looking somewhere else for the couple of minutes it's going to take to get to the aircraft and start them up," Will said.

Twenty minutes later, Will and Frank were picking their way through the waist-high grass on the southern side of what had been a field used for soccer and dog walking. The sun was poking up from the east, the sky easing from black to blue, and despite the beauty of the park, Will was filled with tension. He looked at his watch. Two more minutes.

"I only wish we could be there to watch and see if it actually fuckin' works," Frank said, looking toward the tree line to the east.

Will nodded. "Either way, we're going to know if it worked pretty soon."

Will turned his P90 over in his hands and checked the magazine, confirming it was fully loaded. He glanced at his watch and raised the weapon, sighting across the field at one of the zombies moving among the aircraft. Frank pulled out his Smith & Wesson and sighted on the closest undead walker, forty yards away.

There was an explosion in the woods a hundred yards to their left, and Will squeezed the trigger a half-instant later, putting a round into the zombie's ear and finishing its undead existence. He turned to his left and quickly acquired the next zombie when its head popped open and Olandis suddenly appeared from the underbrush in the field. A couple of seconds went by and a second explosion erupted in the woods. Will swung the rifle through the field and saw no more targets.

"You got 'em both?" Will asked.

Frank shook his head. "Fuck no, the other one is behind Greg's airplane not moving. No shot on it from here."

"Fuck. Time to run," Will said. "Watch the tree lines."

They got up and sprinted into the field, Will pointing to Olandis to watch in the direction of Greg's parked aircraft. Olandis turned just as the waiting undead monster started skip-hopping right at him. Olandis dropped to a knee, raised his Winchester and put a round through the creature's neck, causing it to pause for a moment to regain its balance. Olandis pulled the bolt back and slammed it forward, but Will had the creature in the the sights of his P90 and put two rounds through the back of its skull. It collapsed in a heap.

"Go! Go! Go!" Will yelled as he ran for his aircraft and began spinning the rotor blade madly.

He hopped in and sparked the engine to life, throttled the engine up, and began rolling forward, gaining momentum, the blades beginning to spin and generate lift. He looked behind him and saw Frank rolling along with Olandis in the back seat of his two-seater. Behind them, he saw more than a dozen super-zombies streaming out of the woods, some of them in full-spittle sprints.

And then Will was in the air, adjusting the controls and gaining altitude above Beechwood Boulevard, turning quickly to watch as Frank pulled into the air with ease, the nearest undead twenty yards behind him. Will stuck his hand into the air and gave Frank the "thumbs up" before motioning for him to take trail and follow him. Will climbed to a thousand feet and turned the aircraft to the north, cutting across the city and turning to the right to follow the Allegheny River upstream, adjusting his altitude down to just a hundred feet above the river: he didn't want the undead to see him at altitude and, maybe, figure out what direction he was heading in. And, for whatever reason, the undead avoided water. He figured they couldn't swim.

Twenty minutes later, Will rolled to a stop on the little make-shift grass strip a mile outside of Leechburg. He drove the aircraft to the parking area and shut it down. He leaned forward in the cockpit and rested his head against the instrument panel, working on controlling his breath. Greg was gone. Al was gone. George was gone. Jeff was gone.

All so he could get some snapshots of a wife he'd shot dead years earlier.

He leaned back in the cockpit and began weeping, tears streaming down his face, his nose filling with mucus. Everyone died. Everyone. The world was lost. He pulled the photos of his wife out of the pocket on his vest and stared at them, looking at the blonde-haired, blue-eyed woman he'd know for a total of four years. He'd known Greg and Al for ten, George and Jeff for fourteen. And he'd risked all their lives for a handful of pictures of her and the off-chance that the Giant Eagle supermarket hadn't been raided by whoever was surviving in the neighborhoods near the shopping center.

He had now failed nearly everyone he had ever loved.

Out of the corner of his eye, he could see Frank park his aircraft and both he and Olandis walk away toward their encampment. Will calmed and sat still, looking through the photographs, staring at one he had taken of Cora in the spare bedroom one day, her hair falling across her shoulders, an errant strand caught in the hinge of her glasses and laying on her cheek. She was smiling. The most genuine smile of any of the hundreds of photographs he'd taken of her. She had hated being photographed and most of her smiles looked faked, at best. In this one, she looked happy.

He put the pictures back in his pocket and looked up into the morning sky. He never tired of the blue of the sky, never was less-than-awed by the way the landscape looked from altitude. The zombies may have come to rule the planet, but they hadn't taken away its beauty. A gust of breeze coursed over him and he enjoyed the sensation. He climbed out of the aircraft and looked around at the world, listened to the trills of birds as they awoke, felt the softness of the grass under his feet.

He walked across the field to the tents in the tree line and pushed through the flap. Frank and Olandis were sitting on the edge of their cots, whatever conversation they had been having suspended by his entrance. Both were quiet as Will stripped out of his gear and dropped it on the ground by his cot. He was exhausted. Sleep pushed in on him, overwhelming all of the emotions he knew he would have to deal with later.

Later.

The world still hadn't ended.

WHAT HRISTO GRUEV SAW

Devin, Bulgaria - Day (-) 8

The shed behind the house collapsed in a loud clash of splintering wood and clanging garden tools. The four walls fell away from each other and the roof spit up chunks of shattered wood and tar shingles. Everyone in town had heard the noise, and lights flipped on throughout the town. Hristo got out of bed and looked through the window into the backyard and saw nothing. He looked over his shoulder at his wife, who was sitting up in bed, and shrugged.

"I'll check it out."

He stood playing the beam from his flashlight across the wreckage, his shotgun held idly in his left hand. He shook his head in disbelief: the shed was little more than a year old. What the hell had just happened?

Elena walked up behind him and put her hand on the back of his left shoulder, patting him ever-so-gently. Hristo turned and rolled his eyes. Elena smiled.

"What happened?" Elena asked.

"I don't know," he said, handing his wife his shotgun and stepping onto one of the fallen walls, moving the beam back-and-forth through the rubble. "Maybe an airliner dropped its toilet blue ice and it hit the shed?"

"Don't touch anything then," Elena said. "You don't want to get that filth all over you."

"I don't see any filth, so it must have been something else."

"Like what?"

"Maybe a micro-downburst?"

He walked away from the ruined structure and took the weapon out of his wife's hands and nodded toward the house. "Did it wake the kids?"

"Just for a minute and I told them to go back to bed."

"Good. Let's do the same. I'll check it out in the morning before I go to work."

The next morning, Hristo Gruev walked into his back yard with a cup of coffee and looked on the ruination in the light of day. His first thought was that maybe it could be rebuilt from the existing pieces, but as he looked closer, most of the walls had suffered severe cracking and most of the studs were broken. On the plus side, most of the tools and equipment seemed undamaged.

And then he saw it: a small, fist-sized rock in a divot on the dirt floor. He crouched down and looked at it. It was a deep gray color with hundreds of pockmarks and small pimples, shaped almost like a seed attached to a wing, like a Maple tree seed. He looked up into the sky and laughed: his shed had been destroyed by a meteorite. He wondered if it was worth money and picked it up, amazed at the weight of the thing in the ball portion. He guessed maybe two or three kilos in all, a solid piece of rock or metal. Hristo finished his coffee and went back into the house.

"Well, I'm off to work, honey," Hristo said, putting the meteorite down on a bookshelf in the living room. "We were hit by a meteorite, I think. It would be a a lot cooler if it hadn't destroyed the shed, though."

At work, he spent time online researching meteors, meteoroids, and meteorites, the last of which apparently impacted the planet hundreds of times a year, mostly without anyone noticing. During this research, he came across numerous sites detailing the asteroid Apophis, which apparently passed close to the Earth on a regular basis and had the potential to devastate a large area of the planet if it struck. He was surprised to find out that scientists across the globe had feared it would strike in 2004 and would be in position to hit again by 2036.

He had had no idea the Earth was in such peril from the universe.

He swiveled his chair and turned to Abel, who was staring at a chart on his computer screen and puffing furiously on an eCig.

"Have you ever heard of an asteroid named Apophis?" Hristo asked.

Abel paused and shook his head. "I didn't know asteroids had names. I thought they had numbers or letters or some combination of the two."

Hristo glanced at his monitor. "Well, sure, it's also known as 99942."

Abel swung his chair quickly around and dropped his eCig into his lap, exhaled a cloud of water vapor, and brightened. "Nine-nine-nine-four-two? Of course I've heard of it! Everyone is talking about it."

"Jackass."

Abel smiled. "Why should I know about it?"

"Apparently the thing comes close enough to the Earth every couple of decades that scientists are worried it could hit the planet."

"Can it destroy the planet?"

"No, but it can kill a significant part of it."

"Like what? Tunguska?"

"Bigger than that."

"But not like the one that killed the dinosaurs?"

"No, a lot smaller than that."

Abel shrugged. "Well, unless the Americans are going to do something about it, there's no real point in worrying about it. It's a rock in outer space."

"I'm not worried, it's just that a meteorite struck the shed in my house last night," Hristo said. "Knocked the damn thing down. I only built it just last year."

Abel laughed. "A meteorite hit your shed last night?"

Hristo nodded.

"Seriously?"

"Yeah, seriously."

"And it destroyed your shed?"

"Yup."

Abel drummed his fingers on his lap, put his eCig in his mouth and puffed a few clouds of vapor. He shrugged. "Are you supposed to report it to the authorities?"

"Probably only if it were made out of gold so they could tax it."

Abel laughed.

"But this one is made out of something else. Iron or rock or something, I don't know," Hristo said.

"I don't know what to tell you, but I've got to get back to this report."

After dinner, Hristo took the meteorite from the shelf in the living room and into the home office. He set it down on the desk, examining it with a magnifying glass he'd found in a science kit his older son had gotten for his most recent birthday. He couldn't figure anything out about it and wasn't sure if there was anything for him to discover. It looked like a tree seed made out of a weird kind of rock.

There was a light knock on the door jamb and Hristo looked up to see his son Bogdan.

"When do we start packing? I feel like I should start now so I don't forget anything," Bogdan said.

Hristo smiled.

"You're not going to forget anything. Your Mom has a detailed list of everything everybody needs to take. She's been working on it for the last two months, so I'm pretty sure it's more-than-complete," he said. "We've still got a couple of days to go before we worry about that, anyway. But you might want to start thinking about what you're going to take on the plane to keep you busy. It's a long flight to Los Angeles."

"We'll be able to get off the plane, won't we?"

Hristo nodded. "I think there are short layovers in Italy and New York City, but we won't be able to see anything but the inside of the airport in either of them, so you'll need something to read or a video game to play."

"I can't believe you're taking us to America. I don't think I'll believe it until I actually see Uncle Gavril and Aunt Sara."

Hristo laughed. "Really, that's first on your mind, not the whole Disneyland trip?"

Bogdan screwed up his face for a moment in embarrassment: caught. "Well, sure, Dad, but I think Branimir is more excited about that. I just really want to see if America looks like it does in the movies, if everything is really more modern than everything here."

Hristo rolled his eyes. "There's plenty of old stuff there, too, Bogdan. It's been lived in for hundreds of years."

"Can I look at the meteorite?"

Hristo nodded and handed the magnifying glass to Bogdan. After a minute, his son put it down and shrugged. "I thought it would be a lot cooler than this, since it came from outer space."

"Yeah, well, it's just a rock like any other rock. Apparently, the galaxy is full of them."

Hristo tossed the meteorite up into the air as hard as he could and watched as it fell back to earth, making one quick spin around before landing with a thud in the grass. He had no idea how much force a falling object had on impact. He had searched online and found numerous sites with calculators to determine the kinetic energy released by a falling object, but not being a science or math person, he had been unable to figure out why the meteorite had only destroyed his shed and not the entire town. It didn't seem heavy enough based on his throwing it up, but he could only throw it up twenty feet, and it had fallen from outer space.

He threw it up again. It landed with another thud, but for a moment he thought he saw a brief flash of yellow - dust? powder? light? - when it landed on the ground next to him. He picked it up and looked at it, noticing a tiny sand-crystal-sized spot of yellow on its surface. He brought it close to his face and looked at it and then sneezed so forcefully he dropped the meteorite. He sneezed again and stood up. And sneezed again.

Hristo shook his head and took several deep breaths. He was lightheaded. The inside of his sinuses tickled intensely, and the back of his throat quickly followed suit. He stood in the back yard and rubbed his tongue against the back of his mouth, trying to scratch the itch to no avail. His eyes watered. Hayfever? He'd never experienced it. He sneezed several more times in rapid succession, deep, full-body explosions that weakened him and made his eyesight wonky.

After a minute he stopped sneezing, but the itching in his nose and throat persisted. He picked up the meteorite and put it on a table on the back patio, thought better of it, and put it back where he had originally found it, in the splintered shed.

Inside the house, he searched through the medicine chest in the bathroom looking for antihistamine tablets.

None of them were allergic to anything, so he knew it was a long-shot to find anything.

"Honey, do we have any allergy medicines in the house?"

Elena appeared in the doorframe. "What for?"

Hristo turned to look at her, "I've got some sort of thing going on in my head. Sneezing, itchy throat, watery eyes. I think it's hayfever."

"It's December, people get hay fever in the spring and summer," Elena said, closing the distance between them and looking at his blue eyes. "Your eyes are completely bloodshot."

"They feel weird. Kind of watery with a little itchy, too."

"I've got drops," Elena said. "Did you get dust or something blown in your face."

Hristo nodded lamely. "I guess. I was in the backyard near the shed."

He spent the next two hours on the couch in the living room with his boys, watching them argue-cooperate their way through a video game, sometimes having to mediate their disagreements, and sometimes having to tell them how to solve the level. He couldn't remember if he and his brother had been like that as kids, switching from best friends to bitter enemies over and over again during the course of a day. Gavril's three kids were the same way. Hristo's father said that's exactly how Hristo and Gavril had been as kids. Hristo just assumed that was how kids were, and it was the most unsatsifying aspect of being a parent: you couldn't train your children to always be on the same side.

How true was that? Gavril had moved to America over the objections of their father after writing some software that had gained notice, and he had done well, married an American girl, and had - as he called them - American kids. The last twelve Christmases had been spent without Gavril; this one would be spent without their dad: their dad didn't want to go to Los Angeles for Christmas, he wanted Gavril and his family to come back home so Gavril's kids could see their heritage, their homeland. So while everyone was planning on twelve days in sunny southern California, their father was going to stay home and endure the cold. Not even Disneyland swayed him.

Hristo woke up just before noon the next day, thirteen hours of sleep under his belt, and still he felt dead tired. But his body couldn't take laying down any longer, so he had risen from the bed, showered and made his way to the kitchen. His head hurt, but not like a headache, and he felt a vague sense of nausea, but not enough to curb his desire to eat something.

"You look pale, honey, do you feel okay?" Elena said as he entered the kitchen.

He shook his head. "I feel weird."

"Maybe you should lay down and take it easy."

He shrugged. "I've been laying down since we went to bed. I'm tired of that. I feel like doing something."

"Maybe you could fix the shed," Elena said and smiled.

"That can wait. I need some bacon or sausage or something meaty. I'm starving."

The week had not gone well for Hristo. He had fluctuated between feeling better than he'd ever felt, to suddenly ill. At night, he dreamed of hunting deer and eating their raw meat. He found himself in the backyard one night, clad only in his pajamas, stumbling around as if he were drunk. He had no idea how he had gotten there or how much longer he would have lived exposed to the frigid night. He hadn't felt cold, though.

Christmas day had been awkward: he'd spent the entire day eating meat and then barfed it all out before bedtime. Afterward, he sat on the floor of the bathroom and felt dizzy, the world spinning around him as if he were epically drunk. He felt bone tired, as if he could sleep for days.

"You should see the doctor," Elena said.

"I'm fine. It's a stomach thing."

"Hristo, you've been having symptoms of something all week."

"They come and go, though, so it's not a something they can do anything about," Hristo said, wiping sweat from his forehead onto the palm of his hand.

"I was looking online, maybe you were poisoned?"

Hristo smiled. "Poisoned? Who would poison me? You make all the food I eat, so if you were poisoning me, I don't think you'd tell me to go to the doctor to find out if someone was poisoning me."

When they boarded the plane for America on Wednesday, Hristo felt fine. He'd awoken from a series of nightmares and eaten nearly a pound of breakfast sausages and several fried eggs, and felt better. But after the plane had been in the air, he'd started to feel wrong. There had been a layover in Rome and he'd barfed the entire breakfast up in a stall in the terminal bathroom, and had been startled to see blood in his vomit. What was wrong with him?

During the trip over the Atlantic, he'd slept fitfully, sweating profusely and dreaming of hunting creatures he'd never seen before. He could almost taste the brains of the creatures he hunted.

Brains? He'd never eaten a brain of anything in his entire life.

"Hristo, wake up, we're in America," Elena said, jostling him awake.

"What?"

"We're in America. We've got to change planes. Wake up."

"I need water."

"After we get off the plane. Come on."

He took her hand and the look on her face morphed into sudden concern. She put her hand on his forehead. "You're burning up."

She bought a bottle of aspirin in a convenience store in the airport and made him take two with some water, telling him it would help to break the fever. He could feel the water and pills as they entered his stomach, a weird rush of cold that turned his stomach and made him feel every square-centimeter of its interior surface, a sensation he'd never had before. His first thought was that he wasn't going to be able to keep the water and pills down because nausea quickly settled in, twisting his stomach. He could feel sweat bead up on his face on his upper lip and chin, could feel droplets of it in his hair as they moved down under the force of gravity.

He looked over at his sons in the waiting area of the gate, each playing on PlayStation Vita handheld gaming consoles, the centerpiece present for each this past Christmas. This past year had been the most successful of his career as a software engineer, and he'd been glad that he'd taken the chance and jumped to the start-up firm in Sofia rather than remaining with the information technology division of the hospital. The next year would be even better and the future looked bright. This trip to California to visit his brother was sort of an advance on his future earnings and a carrot on a stick to lure him to America where he might find a better software company, yet.

For the first time in his life, he felt that he was finally in control of his destiny.

He didn't realize he had fallen asleep on a chair in the waiting area until Elena woke him. "It's time to get back on the plane, honey."

Hristo nodded. He felt awful. Elena touched his forehead.

"Your fever's come down. You actually feel colder than you should."

"I feel worse than I should. We're on vacation and I'm coming down with a bug. I have a feeling I'm going to find out how good this world renowned American medical system is," he said and smiled.

Shortly after the non-stop flight to Los Angeles had taken to the air, things changed dramatically for Hristo. He dozed fitfully, his body a furnace again, the sweat streaming off of him. He kept losing his color vision. He thought he could see sounds. And he was sure his bones were vibrating inside his body. He looked around the plane and everyone looked the same to him for long periods: he could see differences in size and sex, but they all appeared in his mind as generic mannequins. Something made him wonder about how he would identify the weak in the herd.

"Are you alright?" Elena asked, leaning in close to him and grasping his forearm with both her hands, her face a mixture of concern and panic.

He shook his head, slowly. "I have to go to the restroom."

He stood up and paused, the interior of the plane losing its tubular shape, dizziness set in quickly and he swooned before suddenly vomiting a stream of blood and mucus over the passengers near him. He turned to make his way out of his seat, stumbled, reeled, took a step, grabbed the upright seat back and felt the fabric beneath his fingertips. He heard screams. He saw no colors. He gulped air.

"Hristo!"

A female voice.

The world tilted and spun around him and he felt hands on his body, pulling him back. Inside his body, he could feel every cell twitching, changing from ones to zeros. His teeth hurt. He couldn't keep his head up, sleep bore down on him and crushed him into an atom and exploded. For a moment, he saw Elena coming after him down a path through a sea of chairs, her face pale with emotion. He smiled at her before shuddering violently and going slack in the arms of those who had grabbed him.

Then he heard the strangest thing he'd ever heard.

"He's dead. Note the time of death on his chart and notify his next of kin."

And then he fell asleep.

THE FINAL SOLUTION

Orth an der Donau, Austria - Day 1403

One day, I hope to sit street-side in a cafe in Vienna and watch the crowds move by, drinking wine with friends or having Sunday morning coffee with my husband. If I ever have friends again. Or get married. Two big ifs. But at least they are "ifs" again. For years, they were just "what ifs" that we used to chat about in the off-hours from the laboratories. What if we found a cure? What would the world turn back into? Would the previously infected remember their lives as zombies?

But we hadn't found a cure. What was done to them could not be undone. They were no longer human. A DNA-altering retrovirus of unknown origin had genetically changed them, and over the years had continued to modify them into what they now were: a new species of biped. It had taken millions of years and a dozen or more mutations to form homo sapiens, it had taken only a few months to transform most of us into some base unit of them, and then a few more years for the new traits to appear. And nobody thought we had yet seen the endpoint of the species.

"What we've developed is not a cure," Gunter said at the staff meeting. "It's not going to undo the genetic modifications that have occurred in the infected individuals. What it will do is kill them. And, in the process, convey an immunity to infection to any surviving people so that we don't have to worry about a re-infection in the future.

"We've managed to aerosolize it as a delivery system and we know from extensive testing that the undead will transmit it to each other by being in close proximity. It works like a virus, so once we get it into a population, it will spread of its own accord, so we don't have worry about dosing individuals.

"On the plus side, everyone in this facility is now carrying the anti-virus in them, so none of us can be turned should we get bitten. They can still eat us, however," Gunter said with a quick smile. "On the downside, we have no means of delivering the virus to the infected population, although what's left of the army command claims to be able to modify artillery shells for that purpose. But we have to get it to them."

The room stirred with the first half of that realization.

"You infected us without telling us?" Adolf asked.

"Not intentionally. The seals on the exam rooms haven't been maintained in years. We just assumed they worked. They didn't, and we kept it quiet to see what happened to avoid a panic."

"Just like the Americans did when this broke out," Adolf said, shaking his head.

Gunter ignored him. "The only problem is that we have no means of delivering it anywhere but here in Austria, which means it will take months, maybe years to travel the globe and spread throughout the infected population. We'll have zombies somewhere on the globe for as long as their lifespans are.

"And if they mutate into the ability to sexually reproduce, we may have to deal with them for a decade or more. Maybe forever. But one thing is for sure, this anti-virus will kill them."

"At least in their present state. Who knows what another mutation might bring?" Adolf said.

Adolf had wanted to cure the infected. Instead, his discovery of the virus' effect on the human genome had led to another lab working on a shut-off switch, an anti-virus that could be inserted into the undead which would kill them. Or, as I liked to think of it, resurrect them back to death. It had taken Adolf a while to accept that his discovery could save humanity. Millions, probably billions, of beings that had once been humans would be consigned to death because of his work.

When word of the plague hitting Paris and Berlin had reached us, the government had immediately shut down the borders. That hadn't saved Vienna or Innsbruck or most of the other cities of the country, but the 3rd Mechanized Infantry Brigade had deployed around Orth and managed to keep the zombies out.

Until today.

Which is why I'm running for my life down Rudolf Zoempfenning Way right now. A hundred meters behind me are a half-dozen of the super-ragers, the latest version of the running zombies. Versions: I still can't believe they specialize.

Anyway, earlier today a super-horde from Vienna streamed across the Danube and down Highway 3. The super-horde was so big and destructive that a wave of human survivors came into Orth a half-hour ahead of the zombies, giving the army enough warning to man the positions and light the kerosene moat between Orth and our biomedical facility. I was on the roof with Gunter watching the snipers pick off the sonars - the zombies who step out of the mob and figure out where to go and who to attack - when a stream of super-ragers poured out of the woods near the north parking lot. The company of soldiers guarding that area was quickly overrun and someone set off the line of mines meant as a last-ditch defensive measure.

But there were still too many of the fast movers and the other army units began falling back.

"Shit, they're going to get into the building," Gunter shouted, turning and running for the door to the stairwell. "We need to get inside and get the anti-virus before the undead break in and cut us off."

We ran through the facility to the lab. Outside, machine-gun fire filled the air. A siren pierced the night followed by an explosion: every man for himself.

"Come on, Heike, we've got to do this," Gunter said as we bounded out of the stairwell into the basement labs. He tore down the hall ahead of me and burst through the doors to the main laboratory. It was a couple of seconds before I caught up, but inside the lab Gunter was frantically working the combination to the storage refrigerator. Automatic gunfire filled the night. So much for head shots.

Adolf ran into the lab and skidded to a stop just short of Gunter. "Give me some, I'm going to try spraying it from the roof."

"It doesn't work that quickly," Gunter said, stuffing vials into a small canvas bag and handing it to me. "You need to run. We all do. We need to get somewhere else, where we can find someone who can deliver this appropriately."

Adolf laughed. "Appropriately? What, like an airplane with a crop duster? We don't have time for that."

Adolf grabbed a few vials and looked at us. "Maybe they won't make it onto the roof?"

He shrugged and took off, brushing past Sergeant Herman Werksman as he came into the room smelling of gun smoke. He looked around and immediately knew that we were ahead of the curve.

"Good," Werksman said. "The colonel wants me to take a platoon and get the two of you to the river. There are a pair of police patrol boats tethered there for just this situation."

"Just this situation? You guys have never said anything about this before," Gunter said.

Werksman shrugged. "The colonel never thought you guys would come up with a cure."

"It's not a cure," I said.

Werksman shrugged. "Well, a solution, then."

He turned and poked his head through the door, said something to whoever was on the other side, then turned his attention back to us. "You've got sixty seconds to get your stuff and follow me."

Gunter nodded at Werksman and handed me a nylon shoulder bag. "This should be enough."

Four loud explosions sounded outside, the sound of the town being demolished by the buried charges the army had put in it last year as a means of both distracting and destroying any zombie horde that might come through the town. The town was lost, then. I didn't think the zombies would be distracted by it, though: they were already everywhere.

"Let's go!" Werksman shouted from the hallway.

I smiled at Gunter. "Well, it's a little over a kilometer to the river. A couple of minutes of running and we're there."

He smiled weakly. "I was never much of a runner."

"Now's your chance to shine," I said. "Let's go."

We dashed out into the night and into a perimeter of two dozen soldiers, most armed with Remington 870 shotguns and Steyr AUG machine guns. A pair of spotlights played across the ground, illuminating pockets of zombies for the snipers on the roof. I looked up to see if Adolf was up there but couldn't pick him out, just the full moon above the facility looking down on us without concern.

"You two, let's move it," Werksman said to us before turning his attention to his men "Platoon, begin falling back, five meters and pause!"

The perimeter of men all moved en masse, the three of us in the center, the soldiers around us all firing their weapons as the zombies pressed in on us.

"The undead can't know what we've got with us, can they?" I asked.

"Impossible," Gunter said and shook his head.

He paused. "But you have to admit, it is one of the most unfortunate coincidences imaginable."

We had just made it to the park access trail through the Danube-Auen National Park when the firing from the soldiers ratcheted up intensity. We had made it maybe a hundred meters south. Already, I could see soldiers using their weapons with bayonets. They were being overwhelmed.

Werksman turned to us, his voice calm, resigned to the situation. "You two should run, we're going to stand here and hold them off. Run. Just run as fast as you can. The boats are at the ferry station. There's a squad there waiting for you. Go. Run."

With that he turned and began taking shots at zombies. Gunter looked at me, his eyes hollow, the emotion drained from his face. "I'm going to run down the trail into the forest and maybe try to make it to Eckartsau where I can try to find a way to get in contact with someone in charge of something. You run for the river. The soldiers there will be in contact with someone else in the Army, so you should be fine once you get there."

"Gunter, we should stay together. It's dark in the forest. The run isn't that long. A kilometer or so, maybe."

Gunter's eyes widened for a moment as he looked over my shoulder. I turned and saw Werksman swing his rifle butt at a rage-runner and then draw his service pistol out and shoot it in the head. The sound of gunfire was becoming sporadic and the murmuring of the undead was getting louder.

I turned and saw that Gunter was already running into the forest, took one last look behind me at what must surely have been the last defense of civilization, and sprinted down the road toward the river. A kilometer or so. Easy. I used to run five or six of them at a time, several times a week before the undead laid claim to the world. I looked back over my shoulder and saw a half-dozen super-ragers twenty meters away and coming toward me, foam dribbling from their mouths, teeth bared.

And then I ran. Faster than I have ever run. All I ever wanted was a normal life, to fall in love and have a family. I never wanted to be one of the last few hopes for mankind's survival. Maybe Gunter will make it to the next town? Maybe Adolf will save the world from atop the biomedical facility?

But right now, the only thing I really want to see, the only thing that matters, is the moon's reflection on the Danube.

ABOUT THE AUTHOR

William Young can fly helicopters and airplanes, drive automobiles, steer boats, rollerblade, water ski, snowboard, and ride a bicycle. He was a newspaper reporter for more than a decade at five different newspapers. He has also worked as a golf caddy, flipped burgers at a fast food chain, stocked grocery store shelves, sold ski equipment, worked at a funeral home, unloaded trucks for a department store and worked as a uniformed security guard. He lives in Pennsylvania in a small post-industrial town along the Schuylkill River with his wife, three children and their cat.